Michael wo **costs. He just hoped she wouldn't shoot him for what he was about to do...**

Michael placed himself between Annie and the other police officers. "Annie is seeing me. She's my fiancée."

Annie gasped and jabbed him in the back.

"Really? When's the wedding?" another officer asked.

"Maybe the fall." Michael turned Annie's flushed face to his. "Maybe Christmastime."

Annie clenched her jaw. "If you think I'm going to stand here and—"

Michael silenced her with a kiss.

Though only intended to keep her quiet, his kiss became real when Annie's initial struggle calmed. Her arms encircled and embraced him. Her lips were sweet and soft. Her supple curves molded to him, and the fire of her anger took on a passion of its own.

Reluctantly, he broke away.

"Guess that settles it," the police chief said. "If you two aren't engaged, you should be. Congratulations."

Annie's blue eyes were dazed. Her full lips parted, but no words came out.

Dear Harlequin Intrigue Reader,

Harlequin Intrigue has such an amazing selection this month, you won't be able to choose—so indulge and buy all four titles!

We're proud to present an exciting new multi-author miniseries, TEXAS CONFIDENTIAL. By day they're cowboys; by night they're specialized government operatives. Men bound by love, loyalty and the law—they've vowed to keep their missions and identities confidential…. Amanda Stevens kicks off the series with *The Bodyguard's Assignment* (#581).

Ruth Glick writing as Rebecca York has added another outstanding 43 LIGHT STREET story to her credits with *Amanda's Child* (#582). When sexy Matt Forester kidnapped Amanda Barnwell from her Wyoming ranch, he swore he was only protecting her. But with her unborn baby's life at stake, could Amanda trust her alluring captor?

We're thrilled to bring you *Safe By His Side* (#583) by brand-new author Debra Webb. This SECRET IDENTITY story is her first ever Intrigue and we're sure you'll love it and her as much as we do. Debra has created The Colby Agency—for the most *private* of investigations—and agent Jack Raine—a man to die for!

In *Undercover Protector* (#584) by Cassie Miles, policewoman Annie Callahan's engagement to Michael Slade wasn't going to lead to the altar. Michael's job was to protect Annie from a deadly stalker. But nothing would protect Michael from heartbreak if he failed….

Next month, join us as TEXAS CONFIDENTIAL continues and a new series, THE SUTTON BABIES by Susan Kearney, begins…and that's just for starters!

Sincerely,

Denise O'Sullivan
Associate Senior Editor
Harlequin Intrigue

UNDERCOVER PROTECTOR
CASSIE MILES

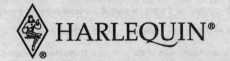

HARLEQUIN®

TORONTO • NEW YORK • LONDON
AMSTERDAM • PARIS • SYDNEY • HAMBURG
STOCKHOLM • ATHENS • TOKYO • MILAN • MADRID
PRAGUE • WARSAW • BUDAPEST • AUCKLAND

ISBN 0-373-22584-9

UNDERCOVER PROTECTOR

ABOUT THE AUTHOR

Award-winning author Cassie Miles has written thirty-five novels of romance and suspense. She grew up in southern Illinois and Los Angeles, California, and spent enough time in Chicago to become a lifelong Cubs fan before making her permanent home in Colorado, where she raised two daughters. Before she started writing full-time, she held many positions, including personnel secretary, kiddy photographer, waitress, shipping clerk and reporter for a mountain newspaper. Her favorite things are long walks on rocky beaches or in the mountains, reading, Impressionist art, slot machines, sailboats, Elvis and falling in love the second time around.

Books by Cassie Miles

HARLEQUIN INTRIGUE
122—HIDE AND SEEK
150—HANDLE WITH CARE
237—HEARTBREAK HOTEL
269—ARE YOU LONESOME
    TONIGHT?
285—DON'T BE CRUEL
320—MYSTERIOUS VOWS
332—THE SUSPECT GROOM
363—THE IMPOSTOR
381—RULE BREAKER
391—GUARDED MOMENTS
402—A NEW YEAR'S CONVICTION
443—A REAL ANGEL
449—FORGET ME NOT
521—FATHER, LOVER, BODYGUARD
529—THE SAFE HOSTAGE
584—UNDERCOVER PROTECTOR

HARLEQUIN TEMPTATION
61—ACTS OF MAGIC
104—IT'S ONLY NATURAL
170—SEEMS LIKE OLD TIMES
235—MONKEY BUSINESS
305—UNDER LOCK AND KEY
394—A RISKY PROPOSITION

HARLEQUIN AMERICAN ROMANCE
567—BUFFALO McCLOUD
574—BORROWED TIME

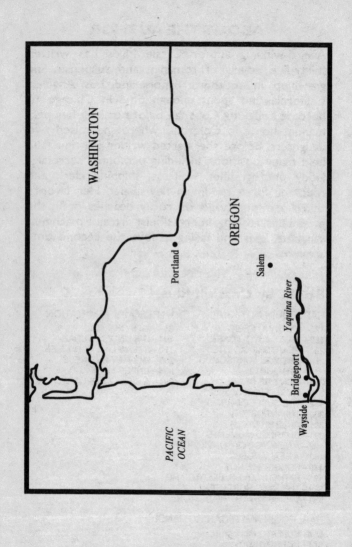

CAST OF CHARACTERS

Annie Callahan—The cool policewoman devoted her life to protecting others—and forgot to protect herself.

Michael Slade—Bridgeport's infamous bad boy is back in town, more protective—and secretive—than ever.

Lionel Callahan—Has Annie's grandfather known where to find Michael all this time?

Drew Bateman—Eleven years in prison gave him time to plot the ultimate revenge.

Derek Engstrom—The Bridgeport police chief has more to solve than local crimes.

Jake Stillwell—The richest man in town is going broke—what might he do to save himself?

Bobby Janowski—The former bully is now a cop, with the law standing behind him.

Marie Cartier—She touched many lives in Bridgeport before her untimely death.

To Jerry and Jean, Oregonians.

Prologue

The gusting spring rain shimmered in her headlights and reflected off the slick asphalt in the parking lot outside the gray three-story apartment building where Annie Callahan lived. She swerved into the only available space, at the far end, then cut the engine and turned off the lights. The wet heavy darkness descended like the final curtain of a very long play.

But there would be no applause. Annie's only performance was everyday common-sense living. She peered through the windshield, wishing there had been a closer parking space. She'd be drenched before she reached the front vestibule.

"Might as well get it over with." She shoved open the car door and stepped outside. Long strands of blond hair escaped her ponytail and were plastered to her cheeks by the wind. Shivering, she splashed through little puddles on her way to the trunk. It had been a long day.

After she'd completed her regular eight-hour shift on the Salem police force, she'd visited her grandpa at the hospital, where he was recovering from a stroke. In just a few days Grandpa Callahan would be Annie's full-time job. She'd taken a month's leave of absence so she could move back home to Bridgeport and take care of him. He was the only family she had left.

Faraway lightning cracked the black skies as she popped the trunk and grabbed a paper sack of toiletries, which she balanced on her hip next to the holster on her police utility belt. There hadn't been time to change out of her uniform. The sopping wet navy blue fabric clung to her arms and legs. If her captain could see her now, she'd get a serious reprimand. *Where's your slicker, Callahan?* She'd forgotten it. This morning had been cloudless and sunny, and she hadn't been thinking about rainwear. Just because this was Oregon didn't mean it had to rain every single day. *No excuses, Callahan. You're a cop. You're supposed to be prepared for anything.*

Muttering to herself, she slammed the trunk and turned.

A dark solid form loomed in front of her. The rain splattered on his black poncho and dripped off the bill of his baseball cap. The streetlights outlined his powerful shoulders. He was at least as tall as Annie, and her height in shoes was six feet.

When he took a step in her direction, her instincts warned her that his intentions might not be friendly. She would've felt a whole lot safer if she could reach her gun, but the shopping bag was in the way and her piece was holstered. Warning herself not to overreact, she asked, "Can I help you?"

"You're late tonight, Annie." He knew her. He'd been waiting for her. His ominous whisper confirmed her sense of danger. "Very late."

His arm raised. He'd been hiding a baseball bat under the poncho. He gripped the handle with both hands as if he was stepping up to the plate. "This is nothing personal."

Her self-defense training at the police academy should have prepared her to face him, but she'd been caught unawares. She'd never expected to be accosted in her own parking lot. That kind of thing happened to other women.

Annie wasn't a victim. She was a cop. "Hey!" she shouted at him. "Back off!"

The tip of his bat quivered. He lifted his chin and she saw the face under the cap. His features were distorted by a nylon stocking pulled over his head.

He took a swing. She dodged. The bat slammed against the left rear fender of her car with a sharp metallic crunch.

She dropped the sack. Plastic bottles of shampoo, conditioner and lotion bounced and scattered across the asphalt. Annie went for her gun.

Before she could aim, the assailant struck again. His bat connected with her right forearm. Pain flashed through her like the strike of a lightning bolt. She dropped the Glock automatic and protectively pulled her injured arm close to her torso. *This shouldn't be happening. She was supposed to be prepared for anything.*

Again he raised the bat and she whirled away from him. She wanted to fight back, but she couldn't get close enough to grapple with him. She was injured, unarmed, helpless. Her only defense was to run. She hurled herself into the downpour.

The hardwood bat swished past her shoulder, missing her by centimeters.

She looked back and saw him take another one-handed swat.

The bat struck a glancing blow to her skull and at the same time she heard a shout. "What's going on over there?"

"Help me!" Her scream intensified the pain inside her head. Oh God, it hurt. She couldn't think. Her brain was numb. The lights in the parking lot blurred in the rain, the endless rain. Stunned, she dropped to her knees.

The assailant was right on top of her, but he didn't touch her again. He was running, fleeing the scene.

The cop in her wanted to apprehend him, but she

couldn't move. She fell forward onto the wet asphalt. A chill sank into her body. The rain tugged like damp tendrils of seaweed in an undertow, pulling her down into a fathomless dark.

Almost unconscious, she felt someone holding her, cradling her. "It's okay," he said. "I've got a cell phone. I called an ambulance."

There was something reassuring and familiar about his voice. She wanted to look up and see the face of her rescuer, but her eyelids wouldn't open.

Gently he murmured, "You're going to be all right."

The night washed over her in dark waves. She *had* to be all right. If she died, who would take care of her grandpa?

"G'night," she said. And sank into unconsciousness.

Chapter One

"I know you. You're Lionel Callahan's granddaughter." The checkout clerk at the Bridgeport Mini-Mart peeped over her half glasses. "It's Annie, right?"

"That's right." Though she recognized the round face and tiny pug nose of the gray-haired woman, Annie had to read the name tag pinned above the breast pocket of the orange smock. "Edna."

"So, Annie. How long have you been back in town?"

"A couple of days."

"What did you do to your arm?"

Annie glanced down at the adjustable cast. She'd been lucky to escape from the parking-lot assault with only a hairline fracture and a mild concussion. The bruising was worse than the break.

"It's nothing," she said. News traveled quickly in a small town like Bridgeport, and Annie preferred not to spread this story. It was more than a little embarrassing for a cop to get mugged. "Could you sack my groceries in this canvas pouch? Then I can carry the handle over my left arm."

"Sure thing," Edna said. "And how's Lionel doing?"

"As well as can be expected after a stroke."

She wasn't happy with her grandpa's progress. Though he seemed to be resting comfortably, his attitude bordered on depression. He wouldn't talk on the telephone, wouldn't get out of bed and refused to see visitors because he didn't want people to see him at less than one hundred percent.

Her grandpa had always been an important man in this town. He was the former high-school football coach, and he'd served for two decades as the municipal judge—an elected part-time position for handling minor violations, like breaking curfew or failure to pay parking tickets. Everybody in Bridgeport respected Lionel Callahan, and he didn't want his status to change.

"Poor Lionel," Edna said as she slipped a bag of Hershey's Kisses into the pouch. "I'll drop by tomorrow with some of my special homemade chicken soup."

"That's not really necessary," Annie said. The freezer was already crammed full of casseroles from friends and well-wishers. They had enough frozen pasta to feed Italy.

"Tell me, Annie." Edna's button nose twitched, sniffing out fresh gossip. "Are you married yet?"

"Not yet." Annie forced a smile.

"A career woman, huh? I heard you were a policewoman. Ever kill anybody?"

"No." Other people seemed to think her life was one big action-adventure movie.

"But I'll bet you've shot somebody."

"No again." Annie shoved a loaf of bread on top of her other groceries, slung the canvas pouch over her shoulder and headed for the door. "See you around, Edna."

At the corner she turned. It was four blocks from the mini-mart back to her grandpa's house on Myrtlewood Lane.

Had she ever killed anybody? What a question! Her job was mostly paperwork and common sense. She seldom unholstered her gun and had never purposefully intended to shoot another human being—with the notable exception of the man who'd assaulted her in the parking lot four days ago. If she'd reached her gun in time, she would have fired. That incident, however, was more about self-preservation than policework. Or was it?

For a couple of weeks she'd been on the receiving end of some very strange harassment. Some unknown person had been leaving cheap porcelain figurines where she'd be sure to find them. It started with a skunk on her desk at work. Then there was a ballet dancer on the hood of her car. In the hall outside her apartment she'd found a chipmunk with a chipped ear.

These odd gifts, unaccompanied by a note or any type of explanation, didn't make sense. At the time she hadn't thought they were meant as threats.

She rounded the corner onto Myrtlewood Lane, enjoying the comfort of wearing khaki walking shorts and a red T-shirt, instead of a police uniform with a utility belt that weighed thirteen pounds. Her long straight blond hair was free from the regulation ponytail or bun that went with her uniform. In spite of the slight residual headache from her concussion, she felt good.

Here at home, the air always smelled fresher. The red-and-gold sky before dusk shone with more brilliance. Her ears resonated with normally unheard sounds, like the whirr of a hummingbird's wings.

Though Bridgeport lay only fifteen miles from the coast on the Yaquina River, it was nothing like the bustling touristy seaside towns. Instead, the profound stillness—so different from the city—gave an illusion of security, as if they were sheltered by the old-growth forests that Bridgeport, being a logging town, had done its best to destroy.

The screech of brakes interrupted her reverie, and she watched a dusty beat-up black pickup park at the curb. The guy who climbed out from behind the steering wheel stared directly at her. Was he somebody she knew? Or was he a threat?

Warily Annie halted as he came toward her. He wore work boots, worn jeans and a faded flannel shirt with the sleeves cut off and frayed—a typical logger outfit. He was solidly built, probably six feet tall and two hundred pounds. "You're Annie."

"That's right." She couldn't place him, and hoped this was an innocent encounter. Forcing a smile, she said, "I'm sorry. I don't remember your name."

"On account of we never met." Up close there was no other word for him but ugly. Limp strands of yellow hair dangled across his narrow forehead. His mouth twitched. The scent of fruit-flavored chewing gum mingled with the acrid smell of his sweat. "Ain't this a pretty sunset. I always missed the sunsets when I was in prison."

Prison? A shudder went through her. This meeting felt horribly familiar to the one in the parking lot. He'd come out of nowhere. She was carrying groceries. "Wh-who are you?"

"You're a cop, right?"

She nodded, not wanting to speak because he'd hear the tremble in her voice. What was the matter with her? She wasn't usually so easily spooked.

"Some ex-cons don't cotton to lady cops. But me?" He thumped his chest and chewed his gum faster. "I like a woman in uniform."

Was he the assailant? Had he followed her to Bridgeport? She tried to picture him in a black poncho and baseball cap. Her mind flashed back to that chilly rainy night. She saw the baseball bat. Her arm twitched with remembered agony. Icy fear crept up and ambushed her.

Her ears drummed with the remembered sounds of pelting rain and thunder. Darkness danced behind her eyelids. She wanted to run. Her grandpa's house was less than fifty yards away. But her muscles froze, and she was unable to move.

"The name is Drew Bateman," he said.

She blurted, "What do you want?"

"I'm just hanging around." He stared so hard that his head came forward like a snake. "But I ain't going away. Every time you look around, I'll be there. Tell your grandpa."

Was he threatening her grandpa? Oh, God. She had to pull herself together. For Lionel's sake, she had to be strong.

Bateman continued, "Me and Lionel go way back. Every time I came up for parole, they checked with Lionel Callahan, the municipal judge. He never once spoke up for me."

Her eyes darted. There was no one else on the street. It was dinner hour. Everyone must be inside around the table, saying grace, unaware of the danger. If she screamed—

"Your grandpa kept me in jail."

He took a step toward her. She'd been caught unprepared. Again. Helpless. Again. "Stay away from me."

"I won't touch you. I'm no fool. I won't get busted for assault and go back to jail like your grandpa wants."

"Leave him out of this!"

She heard the door slam and glanced toward the sound. From her grandpa's house, a dark handsome man emerged. Even before he was near enough for her to clearly see his features, she recognized his stride. She would never forget the way he moved.

His thick black hair glistened in the last glow of sunlight. His dark tan contrasted the white of his button-down shirt with the sleeves rolled up to reveal muscular forearms.

"Michael." His name choked in her throat. She was blinded by a brilliant flash of memory. He was her first love, her deepest love. *Michael*. She never thought she'd see him again. Against her will, a smile cut through her fear. He was still strong and unbelievably handsome. *Michael Slade.* Eleven years ago he had broken her heart.

He approached quickly. His jaw was set, hard as stone. His dark eyes stared past her at Bateman. Hatred simmered between the two men. A harsh tension charged the atmosphere with the impending danger of a lit fuse.

Michael said, "Move along, Bateman."

"I got a right to be here. It's a public sidewalk. I'm not breaking any laws."

"You're loitering."

Michael hadn't even looked at Annie, hadn't acknowledged her presence in any way. His behavior seemed rude. He could've patted her shoulder or at least given her a nod. It was as if she didn't even exist. Anger cut sharply through Annie's fear. *Damn you, Michael Slade.*

"Loitering is bull," Bateman said, snapping his chewing gum. "You ain't got nothing on me."

"You were harassing this lady."

This lady? Was that her only significance to him? After all these years, after the way he'd left her without a word, she deserved name recognition at the very least. "This lady can take care of herself."

"I'm not talking to you, Annie."

"Obviously."

"I'll handle this."

A moment ago she'd been frightened, ready to scream and run away. Now, Michael, whom she hadn't seen or heard from in years, had come to her rescue and she was absolutely furious. Irrational? Maybe, but Annie didn't care. Stiffly she said, "When I need your help, Michael Slade, I'll ask for it."

Bateman hooted. "She doesn't like you."

"You shut up," Michael snarled.

"Make me. If you throw the first punch, I can fight back. It's self-defense. Annie is a witness."

"Not for long," she said. "Much as I'd love to stick around and watch this spitting contest, I've got things to do."

She pushed past Michael and proceeded down the sidewalk toward her grandpa's house. Though she wasn't scared anymore, this emotional roller-coaster ride unnerved her. Slightly disoriented and dizzy, she had to concentrate on placing one foot in front of the other.

At the wide veranda that wrapped around her grandpa's two-story wood-frame house, she climbed the three steps, went inside and slammed the screen door behind her. Why was Michael here? Her grandpa must have invited him.

But Michael had vanished without a trace. If her grandpa had known how to contact Michael, why hadn't he told Annie? She didn't like secrets, and she hated lies.

"Lionel," she yelled as she passed the old oak staircase leading up to her grandpa's bedroom, "you've got some explaining to do."

Down the hall in the kitchen she dropped the canvas pouch on the table. Bracing herself against the countertop, she exhaled in a whoosh. The terrifying flashback had been erased from her mind, but she was still trembling. The pent-up fury of eleven years shivered through her. How could Michael ignore her? How could he be so indifferent?

He was the first man she'd ever loved and the last person she ever wanted to see again. Raising her left palm to her face, she felt the hot flush of her cheek.

Even after all these years, he had the power to spark her emotions. He had faded safely into her past, an unsolved mystery who she would never see again except in dreams. Now, he was here in the flesh. His unexpected return was nearly as puzzling as his disappearance. Eleven long years ago, she'd trusted him with her first fragile love, and he'd betrayed her. *Oh, Michael, why did you leave me?*

She glanced toward the hallway leading to the front door,

pulling herself back to the present. Why hadn't he yet returned to the house? Her policewoman's instincts kicked in. She really hoped he hadn't been fool enough to get into a fistfight with Bateman. Though she didn't want to care about Michael, she'd hate herself if he got hurt and she did nothing to stop it.

Her gun was all the way upstairs in her bedroom, and her injured arm was too weak to aim and fire, but Bateman didn't know that. Just showing her Glock automatic ought to be enough to chase him away.

She dashed down the hallway toward the staircase. Before ascending, she looked out and saw Michael step onto the veranda. Equal parts of anger and relief flooded through her.

He grinned at her through the screen door. "May I come in?"

Though she wouldn't have thought it possible, he was even handsomer now than when he was a teenager. The years had chiseled away any hint of youthful softness, leaving well-honed strong masculine features. He looked hard, dangerous and amazingly sexy. "Give me one good reason why I should open this door."

"Because I want to talk to you."

If she invited him inside, the old wounds would rip open, exposing her heart to more devastating hurt. "We have nothing to say."

"Fine." He gave a quick nod. "I'll wait out here until you've spoken to Lionel."

"What does he have to do with this?"

"Ask him."

"Damn it, I'm asking you." She had a million questions for him. *Why did you leave me? Why did you shred my heart like a paper valentine?* Unprepared to talk about his long ago betrayal and her pain, Annie decided to leave the past untouched. It was ages ago, and she didn't know the man Michael had become. "Why are you here? Did Lionel invite you?"

"May I come in?" he repeated.

"Why should I trust you? You might be as dangerous as that creep out on the street."

"Will you open the door?"

"Fine." She shoved open the screen door. Immediately she realized that she'd used too much force. The door was going to smash into Michael and probably break his perfect straight nose. She made a frantic grab for the handle.

Michael stepped aside as the door hurtled past. He caught the edge and entered the foyer.

Suddenly they were standing less than a foot apart—near enough to touch. When she looked up into his coffee-brown eyes, she catapulted back in time, remembering his caresses, his strength, his warmth. He was the first man she'd ever *really* kissed. That long hot tantalizing kiss had transformed her from a sixteen-year-old tomboy into a woman. The memory of sweetly awakening passion spun through her like a cyclone, lifting her off the ground into clear blue skies.

Michael cleared his throat. "How have you been?"

"Fine." She thudded back to earth. Both feet on the ground, she hardened herself, sealed off her emotions. She wouldn't give him the satisfaction of knowing how much he affected her. He'd get nothing else from her. *Nothing.* Coldly, she asked, "And you? Are you well?"

"I'm okay."

"How nice."

"I guess so." Michael's smile felt rigid as a death mask. He hated the stiff formality of their conversation. "It's good to see you again, Annie."

"I'm surprised you even recognize me."

He could never forget her. His gaze lingered on her. She was the most naturally beautiful woman he'd ever known.

Her lips were full and pink, untouched by lipstick. Light freckles sprinkled across the bridge of her nose. She didn't need makeup to highlight blue eyes that shone with honesty and, at the moment, hostility.

He'd always thought she was incredible. In all the years they'd been apart, he'd never stopped wondering about Annie, about the budding love he'd sacrificed. Regret burned within him. He still carried a battered photo of a sixteen-year-old Annie in his wallet. "I've missed you."

"You're the one who disappeared." Briskly she walked away from him, heading into the front parlor, where she turned on a brass table lamp. Apparently, she wasn't going to bring up the past.

Following her, he was amazed by how little the room had changed. The claw-foot brown velvet sofa was in the same place. The same framed photographs hung on the wall. The only difference was an air of neglect. The walls needed a fresh coat of paint, and the hardwood floors could use a buffing. When Annie yanked the drapes closed, a cloud of dust escaped.

"The old place is looking a little…"

"Shabby?" she snapped. "You'll have to pardon the mess. I wasn't expecting company."

"I didn't mean to insult you."

On the opposite side of the room, she turned to face him. "You're right, Michael. Lionel hasn't been keeping up with repairs. But I'm going to be here for a month, and I'll get everything shipshape again."

He wanted to help. He'd always liked this pleasant old house on Myrtlewood Lane. For the first seventeen years of his life he'd ached to live in an orderly neighborhood like this one—a safe haven where nobody drank too much or yelled all the time.

"It's been eleven years," Annie said as she came toward him. "I believe this is the first time you've come home."

"Bridgeport was never my home. I just lived here."

She stopped a few feet away from him. Her eyes narrowed as she demanded. "Who is Drew Bateman? What does he have to do with my grandpa?"

"What did he say to you?"

"Don't answer my question with another question. You knew him right away. Who is he?"

"Somebody who used to live around here."

"A logger?"

"I don't think he ever worked at the mills." Bateman had probably never worked at all. His profession was criminal.

Curtly she nodded encouragement. "What's with the chewing gum?"

"He has a bit of a sweet tooth."

"That's good to know." In spite of her visible anger, she eased into an interrogation mode. Like a good cop she used the slight information she'd garnered to push him toward more revelations. "And why was Bateman in prison?"

"Aggravated assault on a police officer. He shot a cop." Though Michael didn't want to scare her, she needed to understand that Bateman was a serious criminal, not just a small-town bully. "Annie, I think Lionel should be a part of this conversation."

"No." She shook her head. "I don't want to upset him."

"He has a right to know."

When Michael had arrived at the house half an hour ago, he'd been shocked by Lionel's frail emaciated appearance—so different from the gruff invulnerable man who'd coached him in football and taught him the meaning of honor that went deeper than sportsmanship. It hadn't taken long for Michael to realize that Lionel's willpower and dignity were still there, stronger than ever. A lesser man would've given up and died. Lionel was alert enough to know he needed help, wise enough to call on Michael.

Michael turned to Annie and said, "You can't treat your grandpa like a helpless invalid."

"Excuse me." Her voice turned hard and brittle. "You know nothing about what's gone on here. You've been gone for eleven years, Michael. Why now? Why are you here?"

"Because your grandpa needs me."

"Are you telling me what Lionel needs? Are you suggesting that you know how to take care of my grandpa?"

"I guess I am." Giving orders came naturally to him, and he wasn't accustomed to dealing with women. He probably needed to be more careful about how he phrased things. "Let's go see Lionel."

"Just a minute." She dug in her heels. Though she wanted to resist anything Michael suggested, Annie knew he was right about her grandpa. She had to protect him without smothering him. Still, she didn't want him to worry. He needed to concentrate on getting better. "Lionel has been hurt enough."

"He's still a man."

"Don't I know that," she said. "An ornery old buzzard, if you ask me. When he was in the hospital, he refused to take his medicine. And he bribed one of the orderlies to bring him one of those big stinky cigars he loves so much."

Actually it had done her heart good to walk into his sterile white hospital room and see Lionel with a naughty grin on his face, puffing away like a chimney. "He's a man, all right. Grumpy. Inconsiderate. Stubborn."

"That's exactly what he needs to make him well." Michael gestured toward the staircase. "Shall we go upstairs?"

"I suppose. If that's the only way I'll get straight answers." She crossed the foyer and automatically reached for the railing with her right hand. When she bumped the splint, she winced.

"Looks like you've been hurt, too," he said.

"I got mugged."

"I know. A mild concussion and hairline fracture."

She figured Lionel had told him. "It could've been a lot worse. I was lucky that a good Samaritan stopped to help me."

"Lucky? I don't think so. This so-called Samaritan didn't come fast enough."

"He saved my life. And I never had a chance to thank him. He took off when the paramedics arrived."

She didn't expect him to understand, didn't expect anything from Michael Slade but lies and a tendency to run away when the going got tough. Turning her back on him, she hiked up the stairs and crossed the upstairs landing to her grandpa's bedroom.

In the doorway she stopped in her tracks and stared. Then she beamed a wide grin, delighted by what she saw. Lionel was out of bed. He was sitting in the easy chair by the bay window. Though the weakened left side of his body slumped, he looked like his old self. "Grandpa, how did you—"

"Mikey helped me get over here. You two want to tell me what the hell was going on outside?"

Her anger was completely disarmed. Having Michael pay a visit might be sheer agony for her, but his presence seemed to have had a positive effect on her grandpa. It had gotten him moving. "Grandpa, what is Michael doing here?"

"First things first," Lionel said. "Who was that guy on the street?"

"Drew Bateman," she said.

Lionel exchanged a meaningful glance with Michael. "I haven't heard that name in a while."

"He's an ex-convict," Annie said, "and he seems to blame you for keeping him in jail."

"Well, he's right about that. If it was up to me, I'd lock him up and throw away the key."

"I didn't recognize him." And she surely would've remembered somebody so ugly. "Is he from Bridgeport?"

"He's from Wayside, over on the coast."

"Why does he blame you?"

"I helped get him convicted."

That didn't make sense. As municipal judge, her grandpa hadn't dealt with felony crime. A serious criminal like Bateman wouldn't have been arraigned in Lionel's makeshift courtroom at the back of the police station. So how was he involved with a case that included aggravated assault on a cop? She drew the obvious conclusion. "You were a witness at his trial. You testified against him."

"That's right." He held out his right hand toward her. "Come here, honey."

She went to him and perched on the arm of his chair, gazing fondly at him. Though his cheeks were sunken and his body ravaged from the stroke, she still saw him as the strong kind man who'd taken her in and raised her after her parents were killed in a boating accident. She'd been only ten years old. If it hadn't been for Lionel, Annie didn't know what would have become of her. He'd been her solace and her inspiration. Everything she was she owed to him.

He gently patted her arm. "Did he scare you, Annie?"

"Grandpa, I'm a cop."

"That's not what I asked."

She wouldn't tell him about the flashback of rain and fear. Annie didn't understand the sudden panic attack herself, and she surely didn't want to worry her grandpa. "I'm all right."

"Did he threaten you?"

''He did the opposite. He said he wouldn't touch me because that might get him arrested. At the same time he promised to always be around, watching.''

''I'm sorry, Annie. Bateman is my problem.''

Once upon a time she would've left all the worry to him. She'd believed her grandpa could do anything. He could chase away the monsters under the bed and keep her safe. But it was her turn now. She was the caretaker.

''Bateman is *our* problem.'' She lifted his hand to her lips and planted a little kiss on the knuckles. ''Tomorrow morning I'll stop by the police station and take out a restraining order. Is Derek Engstrom still running things?''

''For the past six years,'' he said. ''You're a good kid, Annie.''

''So are you.''

''By the way,'' her grandpa said, ''Michael is going to be staying with us for a couple of days.''

''What?'' She bounced to her feet.

''Or maybe a week,'' her grandpa said.

A week? She couldn't stand to have Michael here for a week. It would be too strange. Though she didn't want to push Lionel or dampen his positive mood, Annie had to be direct. ''Since you've mentioned Michael, I'd like very much to know how you happened to get in touch with him.''

''Well, that's an easy question. We talked on the telephone.''

''Just like that? After all these years?''

''I've kept track of Michael,'' her grandpa admitted.

If Annie had heard those words eleven years ago, possibly even eight or seven years ago, she would have been devastated. Michael had meant so much to her. He was the only person, other than Lionel, she'd trusted after the death of her parents. When Michael had abandoned her without a word, she'd lost her first true love and her best friend.

But she'd made her peace with the past and had moved on with her life. If her grandpa and Michael had been pen-pals, and kept it from her, she wouldn't let it matter. But she still didn't want him staying at the house, raking up old memories. "Grandpa, this isn't a real convenient time for Michael to visit."

"You misunderstand, Annie. He's not here for a visit. Michael came here to help take care of me. Just until I get rid of this dang clumsy walker and can stand on my own two feet."

She glanced at Michael, who stood with infuriating calm, observing their conversation. Annie tried to equal his cool detachment. She knew nothing about him. They'd been apart far longer than they'd been together. "Are you some kind of medical professional?"

"No," he said.

"Not a doctor or a male nurse?"

"No."

She turned back to Lionel. "We don't need Michael. You have a physical therapist coming by three times a week, and I'm here. Grandpa, that's why I took a leave of absence. To help you."

"Well, honey, I'm just not comfortable with you doing some things for me. It needs to be another man. I got to have help getting dressed. Getting in and out of the bath-tub."

"I can do those things," she protested. "My arm is going to be healed in no time, and I'm plenty strong."

"That's not the point, Annie."

It sure as heck was! "We don't need—"

"I *want* Michael to stay."

Too agitated to stand still, she crossed the room to his rumpled bed and began pulling the covers together. "If you really need a man to help, we can hire somebody. Maybe one of the football players from the high school."

"No," Lionel said firmly. "That's not who I am in this town. I can't have folks thinking of me as a helpless old codger. I got plans for the future, and they don't include being tended to by some teenager I don't even know."

"I won't get in the way," Michael said smoothly. "Lionel says you have a guest bedroom downstairs."

Viciously she plumped the pillows on his bed. Their plans were made. She had no choice but to accept Michael's presence, but she didn't have to like it.

The telephone on the bedside table rang, and Annie snatched up the receiver. "Hello?"

"Hi, Annie. I heard you were back in town. This is Jake Stillwell. Remember me?"

"Of course I do." She could hardly forget Jake Stillwell. Not only was he blond and good-looking, but he was the only son of the richest family in Bridgeport, the owners of the last remaining lumber mill.

"I'd like to get together while you're in town. Maybe tomorrow night?"

But he was married to Candace Grabow, the most popular girl in school and the bounciest cheerleader in the history of the Bridgeport Badgers. And, Annie remembered belatedly, Candace was the daughter of Edna who ran the local minimart. "You're married, Jake."

"Divorced," he said. "How about it, Annie? We can have dinner. I know a nice little place on the coast."

"Sounds lovely, but I'll have to take a rain check. Until my grandpa is settled in, I don't want to be away from the house for too long."

"I understand," he said. "Give me a call when you're ready to go out."

"Sure thing."

She hung up the receiver. Both Lionel and Michael stared at her with wary eyes.

"Jake," Michael said disgustedly. "Was that Jake Still-well?"

"It's none of your business."

"You can't go out with him, Annie."

She gaped, unable to comprehend his colossal arrogance. "Are you presuming to tell me what I can and cannot do?"

"All I'm saying is that you shouldn't date any of the guys in town until we know what's going on with Bateman."

"Get real! There's no way scum like Bateman is somehow involved with the Stillwell family."

"We don't know," Michael said. "You were attacked four days ago in Salem. Was it Bateman?"

That thought had been gradually forming in the back of her mind. Her confrontation with Bateman on the street had been very similar to the mugging. It felt the same. But the shapeless poncho had disguised her assailant's girth, and his face was distorted by the nylon stocking. "I can't make a positive identification."

"Could it have been someone else?"

"Yes," she conceded. "But it seems unlikely, especially since Bateman has a history of attacking police officers."

Lionel said, "Bateman might be working with somebody else. A long time ago, when he was arrested, he was part of a gang. Michael is right. Until we know what's going on, you should be very careful about who you spend time with."

Once again the two of them had united against her with an outrageous plan. She glanced between them. "Well, boys, if Bateman is part of some sort of conspiracy, I suggest you leave the detective work to me. After all, I am a trained policewoman. You, Lionel, are a retired football coach, and you…" She focused on Michael. "I don't know what you are."

"I captain a charter vessel based in Seattle."

"So, you're *not* a professional detective." She made a slashing motion with her good hand. "End of story. If anybody is going to be investigating around here, it's me."

"You and Mikey could work together," Lionel said. "Like partners."

"I don't think so." She turned on her heel and headed toward the door. "I'll be in my bedroom."

"What about dinner?" Lionel asked.

"Michael wants to be your little helper. Let him cook."

Head held high, she crossed the upstairs landing to her bedroom, closed the door and fell backward across the hand-stitched blue-and-white quilt. She stared up at the ceiling. Less than an hour ago she'd seen Bridgeport as a peaceful sanctuary with sheltering forests and hummingbirds sipping nectar. Now it was chaos. Her inner turmoil twirled like a kaleidoscope centered on the flower-patterned light fixture.

She closed her eyes, settled down and almost immediately realized she was hungry. Unfortunately, after her high-handed exit, she didn't feel ready for another encounter. She'd wait to eat until after Lionel and Michael had gone to bed.

She checked her wristwatch. It was only half-past seven. How late would they stay up?

After taking a shower, washing her hair, adjusting the splintlike cast on her arm and dressing for bed in a satin pastel nightgown, which was—as she readily admitted—an overly feminine reaction to her daytime uniform, she could still hear the rumble of male voices from the bedroom across the hall. There was also laughter. Her grandpa and Michael were sharing a joke. No matter what else she thought about Michael Slade, he was good for Lionel.

There had always been a bond between the two males. Annie remembered teen-aged Michael, tall and lithe, with his untrimmed black hair flopping across his forehead and his eyes squinted in concentration as he ran patterns across the backyard while her grandpa threw spiral football passes. Though Michael had a reputation as a tough kid, he'd followed all of her grandpa's team rules and restrictions. Except for one. *Keep away from my granddaughter.* Lionel had warned all the guys on the team. Only Michael had disobeyed.

Their stolen moments together were poignant and sweet. She'd been touched that he would risk his position on the team in order to spend time with her.

Was he still a rebel? He was certainly more solidly built, more manly. His appearance impressed her. And he seemed to have done well for himself, becoming the captain of a charter vessel in Seattle.

But she didn't like his arrogance. Ordering her not to date anybody in town? Ridiculous! If Michael thought he could swagger in here like the prodigal hero and expect her to salute, he had another think coming.

His suggestion that Bateman wasn't acting alone was fairly ludicrous. Unless…

The man who attacked her in the parking lot had said it was "nothing personal." Bateman might have hired him. Newly released from prison, he had the necessary criminal contacts to locate a hitman.

But why would Michael leap to that conclusion? Maybe it was because he knew more than he was telling. The more Annie thought about it, the more certain she was that Michael had inside information about Bateman. But what? And why?

She slipped between the sheets and turned off the light. The clock beside the bed read nine-thirty-three. It was past time for Lionel to be asleep.

In the dark she listened. The voices from across the hall went quiet. She'd give it a few more minutes, then sneak downstairs for a snack.

As she eased one toe out of the bed, her door opened a crack. "Michael?"

"I didn't mean to wake you. I was checking to make sure you were all right before I went to sleep. Do you need anything?"

The sound of his deep voice was pleasantly reassuring. She lay back on the pillows. "I'm fine."

"It's been a long day," he said. "We'll talk tomorrow."

His voice...

"Good night, Annie."

"G'night."

The bedroom door swung closed with a click.

Her mind was racing toward a conclusion, but she didn't know what it was. All thought of food vanished as she concentrated with all her might, reaching for an answer that was just beyond her grasp. What was it?

Moments passed as she searched the corners of her mind. What had he said?

Annie bolted upright on the bed. *His voice!* She'd heard his voice in the rainy darkness four days ago.

Michael had been the good Samaritan.

Chapter Two

Michael descended the staircase, thoughts of Annie lingering in his mind. He tried to match his memory of a sweet, spunky sixteen year old to the reality of a competent, strong woman. Though now a cop, her gentleness and vulnerability were still there. And she was still beautiful, naturally lovely.

He turned out the lights as he went through the house to the guest bedroom at the rear. When he'd left Bridgeport, he never expected to see Annie again, never hoped she would forgive him for abandoning her. And now? He wondered if she would ever be able to trust him again.

In the guest room, he tossed his suitcase onto the bed and opened it. His hanging clothes were already in the closet. From the moment he'd arrived, there'd been no question about whether or not he would stay. Annie and Lionel were in danger, and it was Michael's fault. He would not leave them here unprotected.

He stretched, yawned and unbuttoned his white shirt as the stillness of a Bridgeport night settled around him. The deceptive quiet masked dark motives and old hatreds.

Michael heard a sudden crash.

Unlike the clean snap of gunfire, the noise resonated with a faint tinkling aftermath. A smashed window. A break-in.

Automatically he responded to the threat. From his open

suitcase, he grabbed his Smith and Wesson automatic and snapped the 10-mm clip into the magazine. He turned off the overhead light in the guest bedroom and slipped into the unlit kitchen.

Above the half curtains, moonlight spilled across the countertops, the table and tile floor. With eyes unaccustomed to the dark, Michael scanned. He expected to find an intruder, and he hoped it was Bateman. Caught redhanded, Drew Bateman would be sent back to jail where he belonged.

There was nothing unusual in the kitchen. No movement except for the shifting shadows of wind-tossed tree branches outside the windows.

He moved on, swiftly and silently. This house was a security man's nightmare. There were too many windows, some of them open to the fresh spring air with nothing but a mesh screen protecting the people inside. The door locks were a joke. There weren't even dead bolts. Tomorrow he'd get this place wired with burglar alarms and sensors. He couldn't have Annie and her grandfather living in a fishbowl.

Bracing his gun in both hands, Michael listened for betraying noises. A cough. A creaking floorboard.

From overhead, on the second floor, he heard the alarming shuffle of someone moving around. Damn it! The crash had come from the front of the house. Most likely the intruder would go upstairs first—to the bedrooms where Annie and her grandpa slept.

If he'd failed her again… Michael hurried toward the staircase. Flattened against a wall in the hallway, he saw the front entry. Two etched-glass windows, twelve inches wide and three feet tall, bordered the carved oak door, which was still closed and apparently locked. The window on the right side of the door, nearest the handle, had been broken. Porchlight shone through the jagged shards still clinging to the frame. On the floor lay a good chunk of brick and more shattered glinting glass.

"Annie!" he called out. "Annie, are you all right?"

He waited. Seconds dragged into an eternity of apprehension as he imagined Bateman standing over her, threatening her, touching her with his filthy hands. Michael prepared himself to charge up the stairs.

Finally he heard her clear voice from the landing. "We're okay."

Thank God! "Stay up there."

She peeked over the railing. A small cry escaped her. "They broke Grandma's roses."

"What?"

"Those decorative windows were one of my grandma's last projects. Grandpa is going to be really furious when he finds out that—"

"Annie! Listen to me! Go into Lionel's room and lock the door."

"I'm the professional here," she responded. "We need to secure the first floor and the basement, and two sets of eyes are better than one. You need backup."

She was correct of course. But her security intelligence bothered him. He didn't like to think of sweet beautiful Annie in danger. Being careful not to silhouette himself in front of the two windows flanking the front door, Michael ducked down and approached the front-porch light switch. From a crouched position he looked up the staircase.

Annie stepped down from the second-floor landing. Her sleeveless pink satin gown fell past her knees, outlining every graceful curve of her long lean body. Her sleek blond hair splayed out on her shoulders. In her left hand she held a black police-issue nightstick. In her right hand—in spite of the splint—she aimed a can of pepper spray.

The incongruous combination of sexy, slithering satin

and dangerous weapons was appropriate for her. She was half "Come hither," half "Touch me and I'll kill you."

"What are you waiting for?" she whispered. "Turn off the light."

He flipped the switch, and shadows consumed the foyer.

In her white running shoes, she darted across the glass-strewn floor and crouched beside him. "There's nobody upstairs, and Grandpa is still snoring. His nighttime medication is heavy-duty stuff."

He gave a brief nod.

"I guess we should assume this isn't an act of random vandalism. It was Bateman. But why?"

"He wanted to get inside," Michael said. "After he broke the window, he could reach inside and open the door."

"But there are a lot more subtle ways to break into this house. We're not exactly Fort Knox." She looked up at the shattered window and frowned. "I don't understand this. He didn't have to ruin Grandma's roses."

"Maybe he did it to lure us to the front of the house," Michael said.

"For what purpose?"

"A sniper. That's why I'm crawling around on the floor. I don't want to stand up and be a target."

"Or a distraction," she said. "He might have broken the front window as a distraction so he could come in through the back. Or through the root cellar."

"Or he might have just wanted to scare you."

"Well, that didn't work. I'm a whole lot more fired up than frightened. What a creep! I'll never find another window to match the one that's broken."

"We should secure the downstairs," he said.

"Right." She glanced at his Smith and Wesson. "Is that standard equipment for captains on fishing vessels?"

"It's handier than a harpoon."

Her gaze lifted. In the faint reflection of moonlight through the windows, she stared straight into his eyes, and he knew she was looking for answers, trying to penetrate secrets he had no intention of revealing to her. He'd never been completely honest with her. Not eleven years ago. And not now. There were some things she didn't need to know. Couldn't know.

He returned her scrutiny. Though Michael was trained to notice signs of tension and deception, he was distracted by the sweet *shush* of her breathing and the clean fragrance of her fresh-washed hair. If he tangled his fingers in that straight blond mane, he knew the texture would be as fine as silk.

In her eyes, he glimpsed a brief reflection of his own desire. He was suddenly aware of her maturity and the adult passions that burned within her. But there was also a warning. She didn't trust him.

"Michael," she said, "how well did you know Bateman? Were you friends?"

"Briefly. He was older than me. I thought he was cool. But that was a long time ago."

"Eleven years ago. I haven't forgotten."

Nor had he. Every detail of what had happened was tattooed indelibly in his brain. It was a grotesque picture, his private hell, colored in rage, regret and shame. Bateman had destroyed everything that was good in his life.

"Michael, tell me."

This wasn't a peppy little bedtime story with a happy ending. He didn't want to share the details with Annie. Eleven years ago he'd been unable to face her, and it wasn't any easier tonight.

Michael looked away, but he could still feel her gaze weighing on him. If he told her everything, her curiosity might turn to disgust. Brusquely he repeated, "We need to secure the downstairs."

"I'll go first," she said. "You back me up."

"I should be in the lead. You don't even have your gun."

"My injured wrist isn't strong enough to hold it, much less aim with any accuracy. But don't worry about me. I can handle myself."

That hadn't been the case in the parking lot outside her apartment. She'd been surprised and easily incapacitated by the assailant with the baseball bat.

Michael knew he hadn't reacted fast enough to protect her in that situation. Every time he saw the adjustable cast on her arm, he felt guilty. Her injury was his fault. "Listen to me, Annie. I don't want you to get hurt again."

"You just don't want me to be in control," she said. "Just like when we were kids. But things are different now. I'm in charge."

When she headed toward the front parlor, his only option was to follow. Muttering to himself about headstrong women, Michael took the backup position.

She moved cautiously, never stepping directly into the light, protecting her back, allowing her eyes to scan her surroundings before she proceeded. Though her nightstick and pepper spray were absurd weapons, she brandished them with confidence. It was obvious she'd done this kind of search before. She was a cop—cool under pressure, efficient, one hundred percent professional.

"I'm impressed," he said.

"By what?"

"You really know how to do this—when to stay low and when to move fast. You're good."

"I'm not a rookie, Michael. This is my job." They'd reached the guest bedroom. "Um, why don't you button up that shirt. It's chilly."

His gaze focused on the V-neckline of her satin gown,

which showed a hint of cleavage. Her nipples peaked against the satin fabric. "Are you cold?"

"Just—button up and let's get this over with."

Annie turned away from him. She felt the heat rising in her cheeks and was glad for the semidarkness that hid her embarrassed blush. Her body temperature had begun to elevate when she'd crouched beside him in the foyer and he'd stared into her eyes with such intensity. Now she was flaming hot, and she wished he'd button that shirt. The quick glimpses of his crisp black chest hair and darkly tanned flesh were driving her crazy.

She faced the uncomfortable fact that he aroused her. Oh my, this was so different from when she'd known him before and had been too inexperienced to understand her own sexuality. Eleven years ago, her attraction to him had been like a dreamy fantasy, a girl's imaginings of what it would be like to make love. When she looked at him now, her dreams were x-rated.

It was wrong for her to want him. Why had he come back after eleven years? There was more to Michael's presence than the mere intrusion of an unwanted houseguest. He might also be a threat. He had been at her apartment the night she was attacked. Now, she discovered, he was in possession of a handgun. She felt sure that his presence in her grandpa's house had far more significance than a simple urge to help out in a crisis.

She left him in the bedroom and went into the kitchen, where she took two flashlights from a drawer near the back laundry room. She checked them both. Only one was working. "I'll take this and go into the cellar alone. I know my way around well enough that I won't have to turn on the lights."

"Wrong," he said. "I'll go into the cellar alone. I have the gun."

"It's a mess down there. You'll never find anything."

"At least I can protect myself. What are you going to do if there's an armed intruder?"

She pantomimed whacking him with the flashlight and held the pepper spray up to his face.

Gently he caught hold of her wrist above the splint. His fingers encircled her arm. His grasp electrified her. Though he was careful not to hold too tightly, she could feel his hot steely strength.

"Annie, I'm sorry about this. About all of this."

"What do you mean? What—"

"Stay here." He yanked the handle of the cellar door and pulled it open. "I'll be right back."

He was halfway down the stairs before she could object, and it was just as well she didn't attempt to speak coherently. Her brain seemed muddied, drowning her common sense. Every fiber of her body was pleasantly numbed. With one touch Michael had turned her into a trembling blob of vanilla pudding.

This had to stop! She sank into a straight-back chair and rested both hands flat on the kitchen table. Moonlight shone through the upper half of the windows between the gingham café curtains and the matching valance. Crickets chirped outside the windows. If she stepped outside, Annie would be gently bathed in starlight. If she stepped outside with Michael, if he took her in his arms…

The fingers of her left hand curled into a fist and she lightly pounded the oak tabletop. Why couldn't she control her emotions? She shouldn't care about him. When he ran away and left her, he'd branded himself a liar, someone who couldn't be trusted. Michael wasn't her lover or her boyfriend. If anything, he was a suspect.

When he emerged from the basement, his white shirt was streaked with grime. "Nothing down there," he said. "The door leading to the outside was still barred shut."

She remained seated, struggling to gather her senses. She

had to find out why he had been at her apartment. "I don't think we should search outside by ourselves. We should follow proper procedures."

"Right," he said. "We'll call 911."

"Why don't you use your cell phone?" She rose and approached him so she could see his reaction in the dim light. "I know you have one."

"Do you?"

"You used it four nights ago, remember? In the parking lot outside my apartment building."

His dark-eyed gaze betrayed a total lack of emotion—a characteristic typical of a born liar. Calmly he asked, "How long have you known?"

"Why were you there, Michael?"

"I promise to explain." He went to the wall phone in the kitchen and picked up the receiver. "First I'll call the police station."

"No," she said. Her voice sounded firm in spite of the fluttering of her heart. She really wanted to believe in him, wanted him to offer a rational excuse. "I need an answer, an honest answer. If you're going to stay here, there can't be any more lies."

"Lies? I don't know what you're talking about."

"A long time ago you promised you'd never leave me. Then you were gone. You betrayed me." And it still hurt. "Now, after eleven years, you come back in the middle of another strange situation. You weren't a good Samaritan, just a stranger passing by. You were in my parking lot for a reason. What was it?"

A stillness fell between them, separating them. The gentle sounds of night—the crickets and the groans of the old house settling on its foundation—seemed deafening. Annie could almost hear the seconds ticking, widening the gulf that divided her from Michael. If he lied to her now, she could never trust him again.

"I was following you," he admitted.

He'd been watching her, and she hadn't even known. Annie felt violated and strangely excited at the same time. "Why?"

"Off and on, I'd been tailing you for almost a couple of weeks—ever since Bateman got out on parole. I knew he had a vendetta against your grandfather. Since Lionel was relatively safe in the hospital, I decided I'd better keep an eye on you."

"The standard procedure in such a situation is to follow the suspect—not the victim."

He raised one eyebrow and a slow grin curved his lips. "I figured it'd be more fun to watch you."

"Jeez, Michael. You sound like a weirdo stalker."

"I learned a lot about you."

"Like what?"

"A lot," he said. Once he'd gotten over his initial reticence about invading her privacy, Michael had enjoyed watching her. Annie had turned into the kind of woman he'd expected her to be. She had a healthy lifestyle and went jogging almost every morning. But she also had a taste for junk food. There was no special man in her life, and her partner on the Salem police force was happily married. Though her car radio was tuned to a classical station, she occasionally listened to and sang along with country-western songs.

"You could've picked up a phone and called me," she said. "All I needed was a simple warning that I was in danger."

He shrugged. "I didn't think you'd believe me. I expected you to hate me after the way I left."

"Ancient history." But her sudden frown told him that he'd guessed correctly. He wasn't her favorite person.

"Did you manage to uncover any useful information?"

she asked. "Was it Bateman who attacked me in the parking lot?"

"I'm not sure." He hadn't expected the assault. Not in the rain. "After the paramedics took you to the hospital, I went looking and found Bateman at his favorite tavern in Salem. The bartender said he'd been there all night."

"Is that a solid alibi?"

"I don't know."

"Oh, Michael, I wish you'd left this to a professional investigator. What else do you know about Bateman?"

"He had a reputation in prison as a ringleader with a lot of connections." Like a poisonous spider in the center of his web, Bateman knew how to pull strings and get other people to do his dirty work. He was surprisingly intelligent and had a natural slyness that made him adept at playing manipulative games. "He's a true sociopath, completely without conscience or any sense of right or wrong."

"I'm familiar with the profile," she said. "It explains something to me."

"What's that?"

"When I first encountered him on the street, he scared me. I don't usually get rattled, but there was something about him that triggered my fears." She hesitated. "Even though he didn't actually threaten me, my gut instinct was warning me to be careful."

"I don't know how far his influence reaches, Annie. But we can't be too cautious. That's why I don't want you going out alone on dates that might be a trap. It's best if you stay away from Jake Stillwell or anybody else."

"I'll think about it." She nodded toward the phone. "Go ahead and call the police. Please tell them not to use the siren. I'd prefer if Grandpa slept through the night."

Picking her way through the dark house, she went upstairs to change clothes before the Bridgeport police officers arrived. If the gossips in town heard she'd been wearing a slinky nightie and sleeping under the same roof as an unmarried man, they'd assume the worst, even with her grandpa there as chaperone. She had no intention of being paired up with Michael Slade again.

Before returning downstairs in her jeans and baggy gray sweatshirt, she tiptoed to her grandpa's bedroom door, intending to close it tightly. There was no need to disturb him. He needed his rest.

"Annie?" he called from the bed. "What's going on?"

Her hand rested on the doorknob. "Nothing. Go back to sleep."

A police siren screamed along Myrtlewood Lane.

"That doesn't sound like nothing," Lionel said.

She explained, "Somebody threw a brick through the window by the front door. We called 911."

"The window with roses? Your grandma's window?"

"I'm sorry, Grandpa."

"Can't be helped." He stretched out his long scrawny arm and turned on the lamp beside the bed. With a groan he forced himself into a sitting position. "Hand me a bathrobe. I won't have the local police thinking I'm an invalid."

Resigned to her grandpa's concern with his reputation, she plumped the pillows and helped him comb his hair. In spite of his emaciated body, he donned an attitude of dignity. He wasn't about to lie back quietly and accept anybody's pity.

And she was glad for his change in attitude. Pride was a whole lot better than depression. Fondly she patted his bony shoulder. "You're a stubborn old buzzard, Lionel Callahan."

"Well, I can't rest easy while you're still running around getting yourself into trouble."

Neither the attack in the parking lot nor the brick through the window were her fault. However, if it made Grandpa feel better to believe she needed his protection, Annie wouldn't disillusion him. "I guess trouble is my middle name."

"Always has been."

"By the way," she said, remembering Michael's statement that he'd come here to protect her and Lionel from possible retribution from Bateman. "Did you telephone Michael? Or was it the other way around?"

"Can't say that I recall." His expression was too innocent to be believed. "I was a little hazy after the stroke."

Hazy like a fox, she thought. Grandpa had his own special reasons for wanting Michael to stay at the house. "I hope you're not playing matchmaker."

"Between you and Michael?" He gave her a lopsided grin. "The idea might have crossed my mind. I'm not getting any younger, Annie. I wouldn't mind having some youngsters around the neighborhood."

"Great-grandchildren." She didn't like being manipulated. "Don't push me, Lionel."

"Wouldn't dream of it."

Downstairs she confronted Police Chief Derek Engstrom himself. Though he was out of uniform, his beige trousers were sharply creased. The plaid shirt under his green Bridgeport Badgers windbreaker was starched and ironed. Engstrom was a tidy person in his early forties, and he was in good physical condition. There was only a touch of gray in his thinning brown hair. As far as she knew, he'd been living alone since his mother died. "I'm surprised to see you, Chief Engstrom. I didn't think you'd be on duty this late."

"I had just stopped by the station when your call came through." He nodded to the uniformed officer. "Bobby, you remember little Annie Callahan."

"Annie was never little." Officer Bobby Janowski

smirked as he eyeballed her from toe to head. "She always was the tallest girl at Bridgeport High."

And Bobby had always been the most obnoxious bully. It annoyed her that he'd chosen a career in law enforcement. "Hi, Bobby."

"Heard you're a cop in Salem." He hitched up his uniform trousers and stood straighter, as if trying to match her height. He was only five foot nine. "That's a tough job for a woman."

"I guess I'm big enough to handle the work. Now, I suggest we go outside and have a look around."

"Agreed," Michael said.

Engstrom squinted in his direction. His upper lip curled in a disdainful smirk. "I remember you, Michael Slade."

Michael didn't need to verbally respond; his body language said it all. His eyes became cold and hooded, his chin hardened, and he thrust out his chest. He was transformed into an archetypal tough guy, a hoodlum.

"You were a troublemaker in high school," Engstrom accused. "A real punk, weren't you? You got picked up for reckless driving and curfew violations, right?"

Still Michael said nothing.

As a fellow law-enforcement officer, Annie should have taken Engstrom's side. But there was a dignity in Michael's silence. He didn't deny his past. Nor did he try to defend it.

"And drinking," Engstrom continued with the long-ago rap sheet, "underage possession and consumption of alcohol. Or maybe that was your father."

"That's right," Bobby put in. "Old man Slade was one mean son of a gun when he got drunk."

Annie couldn't stand it any longer. "Chief Engstrom, we have a problem here. An act of vandalism."

But Engstrom was on a roll. He put himself right into Michael's face. "I'm surprised to see Michael Slade in one piece. With the way he started out, I would've thought he'd be dead or in jail by the time he was twenty-five.''

"Disappointed?" Michael asked.

"You only had one thing going for you, Slade. You were the finest wide receiver who ever played for Bridgeport Badgers. I still remember that game against the Cougars." Engstrom stepped back to pantomime throwing a football. "Jake Stillwell was quarterback. You caught four touchdown passes. Stillwell to Slade. It was a thing of beauty."

This little trot down memory lane annoyed Annie even more than Engstrom's former hostility. "If you don't mind, Chief, we should check the yard for—"

"It's okay, Annie," he said condescendingly. "We're here now, and we'll protect you. Nobody's going to hurt you."

Her muscles tensed with the effort of holding back a frustrated scream. "You can't imagine how that makes me feel."

"Besides, if anyone was outside, they probably left when we pulled up."

"There might be clues," she said. "Like footprints. Or a cigarette butt. Maybe a chewing-gum wrapper. Something."

"We won't find anything in the dark," Engstrom said. "With the shadows a flashlight casts, we might miss important evidence, might accidentally destroy something."

"Hey!" came Lionel's shout from upstairs. "Is that Derek Engstrom?"

"Yes, sir," Engstrom called back. "Come upstairs with me, Bobby. Let's see how Lionel is doing."

"Wait!" Annie pointed to the chunk of brick on the floor. "This is a big fat piece of evidence. Aren't you going to do anything about it? Take it back to the station and check for fingerprints?"

"Why don't you put that brick in a grocery bag for me," Engstrom said. "We'll grab it on our way out."

Stunned by their complete lack of professionalism, Annie glared at the retreating backsides of the Bridgeport police as they ascended the stairs. To Michael she said, "I don't believe this. If I treated a crime scene this way, I'd be booted off the force."

"We're in Bridgeport," he reminded her. "The idiots are running things."

Though she wanted to speak up for her hometown, the police chief's behavior was indefensible. "Why does Engstrom have it in for you?"

He shrugged. "In his narrow mind, I'll always be Michael Slade, teenage troublemaker."

"And a damn good wide receiver."

"My only saving grace," he said. "I could hang on to Jake Stillwell's wobbly passes."

She stared down at the piece of brick. "I guess I should go to the kitchen and get a bag for this. It's probably too porous for decent fingerprints, but you never know."

"I'll wait here," Michael said.

Facing Engstrom had awakened bad memories of his small-town identity as a bad boy. The bitter ache still lingered. No matter where he went or what he did, when he came here, he was still a punk. He couldn't change that. He was still the son of an abusive drunk who couldn't hang on to his job at the lumber mill and then deserted the family for good.

Even though Michael had grown up only eight miles from here, his world had been far different from Annie's. She was a Callahan. Her grandpa was a respected man in town, and they lived in a nice house with rose-patterned windows by the door.

Eleven years ago he'd tried to be worthy of her. He'd backed away from his hoodlum friends, quit smoking and drinking. He even read a book of poetry she'd given him. He tried to be a better person, deserving of Annie's attention. And he failed.

She returned from the kitchen with a plastic grocery bag and two foil-wrapped chocolates, which she held out toward him and he declined. "More for me," she said.

She unwrapped them and popped one into each cheek, like a chipmunk. Then she picked up the brick chunk with two fingers. "Nothing remarkable about this piece of concrete."

When she turned it over, he saw markings on the bottom side. "What's that?"

Annie studied it. "Black marker. It's numbers—six, one, three—and there's a space between the six and the one."

"Six, thirteen."

"What do you think it means? A code? An address?"

"Maybe a date," he said. "June thirteenth."

It was the anniversary of the worst day of his life, the day his future died. Michael knew exactly why Bateman had thrown a brick through the window. It wasn't to signal a break-in or to offer an opportunity for a sniper.

The brick was a reminder and a threat. Six. Thirteen. June thirteenth.

Annie placed the brick in a plastic grocery sack. "What does the date mean, Michael?"

He shook his head. He didn't want to explain to her, but there seemed no way around it. It wasn't fair to withhold information. "We'll talk later."

"Today's the seventh. June thirteenth is less than a week away," she said. "Should I be concerned?"

"Yes," he said tersely. June thirteenth might be the date when Bateman intended to take his final revenge.

She eyed him curiously. "Well?"

"Not now," he said. "Not with Engstrom upstairs."

"Fine, we'll get rid of him. And Bobby. They're not acting like police, anyway."

Michael followed her up the staircase to Lionel's bedroom, where the old man was finishing a harangue about the spread of vandalism in small towns. "...the teenagers don't respect private property because nobody bothers to teach them about right and wrong."

Engstrom nodded. "You think teenagers broke your front-door window?"

"I'm not pointing any fingers," Lionel said. "But Drew Bateman was hanging around earlier."

"Bateman? I thought he was in jail."

"He's out on parole and he's got some kind of grudge."

Annie said, "I want to take out a restraining order against Bateman."

Bobby edged closer to her. "Don't you worry, Annie. I'll keep an eye on you."

"That won't be necessary," she said.

"No trouble at all," Bobby said. "I'll make a point of patrolling your block."

A growl rose in the back of Michael's throat. He was here to protect Annie and he didn't want interference. He didn't want anybody else to be close to her. Not Bobby. Not Jake Stillwell. Nobody.

And that wasn't because he was jealous, damn it. He had solid reasons, in addition to the wrenching in his gut, and the unreasonable urge to give Bobby two black eyes so he'd never look at Annie again.

Bobby said, "I'd be happy to protect you, Annie. Day and night."

"Not necessary." Michael stepped forward, placing himself between them.

"Oh, yeah?" Bobby stared up at him. "Why not?"

"I'll be here to see to Annie. She's my...fiancée."

Behind him, he heard her gasp. An instant later she jabbed him in the back with her good left hand.

"How come I don't see a ring on her finger?" Bobby demanded. "Too cheap to buy a diamond, Slade?"

"She has a beautiful ring," Lionel boomed from his bed. "These two lovebirds are honoring me by using the engagement ring that belonged to my late wife."

"You!" Annie gripped the cherry-wood rail at the foot of her grandpa's bed. She looked ready to leap over it and strangle him. "You set this up!"

"After all," Lionel continued, drowning out her objection, "you don't think I'd let a single man stay in the same house with my granddaughter if they weren't planning to be married, do you?"

"I guess not," Bobby said. But he was still suspicious. "When's the wedding?"

"Maybe in the fall." Michael took her shoulders and turned her toward him. "Maybe at Christmastime."

Her jaw clenched. Her cheeks flamed with a feverish red flush. "If you think I'm going to stand here and—"

"She wants the wedding sooner." He talked loudly to cover her words. "And you know how stubborn she can be. She'll get what she wants."

"Here's what I want," she said. "I want you to get your sorry—"

Michael pulled her close. He silenced her with a kiss.

She twisted in his grasp, but he wouldn't let go. Later she could yell at him, but right now he needed to warn off all the tomcats in town. Whether she liked it or not, he intended to keep her safe, and a fake engagement was a small price to pay.

Though he had only intended to keep her quiet, his kiss became real when her struggle calmed. She wasn't fighting him anymore. Her arms encircled and embraced him. Her lips were sweet and soft. Her supple curves molded to him, and the fire of her anger took on a passion of its own.

Her tongue flickered across his mouth, and Michael gladly welcomed her probing. He deepened the kiss, and she responded with a moan.

He was stunned by the intensity of her mature passion. Eleven years ago, their kisses had been gentle as a softly played flute. Now, Annie's kiss was a full-blown symphony.

He wanted more. But not now. Not with three other men watching. Reluctantly he broke away.

"I guess that settles it," the police chief said. "If you two aren't engaged, you should be. Congratulations."

"I'm a lucky man," Michael said.

Annie's blue eyes were dazed. Her full lips parted, but no words came out.

Before they left, Chief Engstrom promised to have Bobby and the other officers patrol the neighborhood regularly. "We'll come back in the morning when there's some light. Then we'll see if we can find anything that looks like evidence."

With Bobby trailing behind, Engstrom left the bedroom. Michael listened as the two men went down the stairs and out the front door.

From the bed Lionel chuckled. "Congratulations."

"Pretending to be engaged is the best way to keep all these guys away from Annie," Michael rationalized. "Until we know who Bateman is involved with, we can't take chances."

Lionel yawned broadly. "It's a good plan. To tell you the truth, I was worried about what people would say when they found out you were staying here. I didn't want Annie's reputation to be ruined."

"My reputation?" Annie rolled her eyes. "I don't believe for one minute that my reputation was your concern,

Lionel. You as much as admitted that you wanted me and Michael to get together. You set me up.''

"Someday, Annie, you'll thank me for this."

"Oh, yes," she said. "I want to thank you both for providing me with the single most humiliating situation in my life. Not only am I the only woman from my high-school graduating class who has never been married, but now I have a phony engagement to add to my record."

Michael didn't believe she was all that upset. There was a spark between them that couldn't be denied. "It's not so bad to be engaged to me."

She slapped his face with her left hand. Her aim was accurate and her arm was strong.

Chapter Three

The palm of Annie's hand stung from slapping the grin off Michael's face. He reacted immediately. His jaw tightened. His fists clenched. She could tell that his instinct was to slap back, but he held himself in check.

She should have exercised the same degree of restraint.

"I was wrong to hit you," she said. Physical violence never solved anything.

"Is that an apology?" His voice was cold.

"I'm sorry."

But she didn't turn tail and run. Though he hadn't physically lashed out at her, Michael and her grandfather had been bullying her emotionally, forcing her into positions that were more and more untenable.

He'd grabbed her and kissed her without permission. Though the aftershocks of that incredible kiss still trembled through her body, he'd had no right.

Annie straightened her backbone. Like an athlete who had strained a muscle, she tried to shake off the lingering effects of Michael's kiss. She had to regain control of the situation.

"I want both of you to listen carefully. I'm sick and tired of having things sprung on me." She frowned at her grandpa. "Lionel, you should have told me ahead of time that Michael was going to stay with us and help out. For that matter, you should have told me you'd kept in touch.''

''You're right, honey.'' He yawned again. Now that the excitement was over, he was ready to go back to sleep.

She dared to look at Michael. His eyes were hot. His lips invited her. It took all her willpower to confront him. ''You had no right to kiss me. And claiming to be my fiancé? It wasn't fair.''

''Agreed,'' Michael said.

''I want no more lies. No more games. This phony engagement thing will be the last decision either of you will make without consulting me first. Is that clear?''

Michael nodded. ''You're the boss.''

''Good.'' If she could get her body to stop yearning toward him, everything would be fine.

She went to her grandpa's bed and fussed with his covers while she scolded, ''You need more sleep, Grandpa, because I'm going to wake you at eight tomorrow morning. Your physical therapist is scheduled for ten o'clock, and you need to bathe before he gets here.''

''There's one more thing.'' He pointed to the bedside table. ''Open that drawer and reach way in the back. There's a cigar box.''

Now what? She removed the battered rectangular box of heavy cardboard decorated with a garish picture of a Spanish señorita with red flowers in her impossibly thick, curly black hair.

''Open it,'' Lionel said.

She eyed him suspiciously, half expecting an explosion of confetti when she lifted the lid. ''If this is some kind of joke, I will not be amused.''

''Just open the box, girl.''

Inside, resting atop a clutter of buttons and lapel pins, Annie found a three-by-four-inch sepia photograph of a smiling woman with pale eyes and long, light-colored hair swept back from her forehead in a style popular in the 1940s. She was Annie's grandmother, Elizabeth Callahan.

"The engagement ring is in there," Lionel said.

Gingerly Annie picked up a little velvet-covered box. "Grandpa, you don't have to give me this."

"Nonsense," he said. "I buried Elizabeth with her wedding band twenty-three years ago, but I kept this little diamond for you, Annie. I always thought you might like it."

Annie snapped open the box. A small bright diamond winked at her from its ornate setting of tiny, twining wild roses. "It's beautiful."

"You remind me of her. Sometimes when I look at you, I see Elizabeth." He cleared his throat. "You were only seven when she died, but do you remember her at all?"

"Her laughter." Mostly she recalled stories other people had told her about Elizabeth, but one memory belonged to Annie alone. "She took me fishing on the river in a rowboat. We didn't catch anything, but we laughed all afternoon."

"That woman had one hell of a sense of humor. She kept me from taking myself too seriously." He gave Annie a lopsided grin. "Put the ring on."

Tears stung the back of her eyelids, and she blinked to keep them from falling. This ring was a sacred symbol of her grandparents' love. Wearing it for a fake engagement seemed sacrilegious. "Grandpa, this isn't right."

"Just do it, honey. Elizabeth would've loved the joke. She would've laughed her head off if she'd seen your face when Michael said you were engaged. I never thought your eyes could pop that far out of your head."

But this moment wasn't funny to Annie. Getting married and being engaged were serious business. A lifetime commitment was not to be taken lightly. She took the ring from the velvet box and held it.

Unable to decide what to do, she rose from the bed and

walked slowly, thoughtfully, toward the bay windows. Though the miniblinds were closed, a breeze crept in. Annie wished for a strong wind to flow through her mind and whisk away all her questions and doubts.

Though she had no intention of ever falling for Michael again, there seemed to be no choice except to play along with the fake engagement. By tomorrow morning, Officer Bobby would've blabbed to somebody else, and the rumor would be all over town. To explain would be embarrassing, to say the least. "I hate lies."

Michael joined her at the windows. "The ring doesn't have to be a lie."

"What are you saying?" He couldn't possibly be proposing. After eleven years apart, they hardly knew each other. "You can't be talking about a real engagement."

"Let me help you put it on." Gently holding her left hand, he slipped the band over the tip of her third finger and paused. "This ring is my promise to you."

His nearness and the warmth of his touch soothed her troubled mind. His dark eyes shone with sincerity. Oh, how she wished she could believe his promises! She longed to curl up against his broad chest and forget her cares.

He continued, "This is my vow. I will always keep you safe. Always. As long as you wear this ring, I will protect you."

From the bed, she heard her grandpa's heartfelt sigh of relief. "Amen," he whispered.

"I accept," Annie said. Silently she added her own promise: She would protect him, too. They would be partners.

FIFTEEN MINUTES LATER, Michael sat opposite Annie at the kitchen table and watched while she polished off a ham-and-Dijon-mustard sandwich. She didn't pick at her food, mentally counting every calorie. Annie ate the same way she did everything else—without pretension.

And yet her life wasn't an open book, easily readable from page to page. Annie kept her emotions under tight control. She had erected barriers—steel walls to hide her secrets from prying eyes.

"We're partners," she said. "Just like my partner on the force in Salem."

Michael's intentions were far more intimate. He'd been watching her for days, developing a grudging admiration for her professionalism and her no-nonsense approach to life. He liked Annie Callahan. And her kiss had sparked a deeper attraction. "Partners," he said.

"As such, we should proceed with our own investigation. I suggest we start now."

As she raised the sandwich to her lips, the engagement diamond flashed like a warning signal. His promise to protect her might be more difficult than he'd expected. "Why now?"

"Because we don't want the trail to get cold." She chewed for a moment. "Engstrom and Officer Bobby aren't exactly super sleuths. I don't think they'd recognize a clue if it jumped up and bit them on the toe."

"It's their job, Annie."

"Mine, too. And I'm good at it," she said confidently. "I noticed that you're pretty handy with that weapon you were waving around. By the way, do you have a permit?"

"Yes, Officer," he said dryly.

"Why are you armed?" she asked.

"I'm here to protect you." He deflected her question. "I didn't know if Bateman would be carrying."

"Possession of a weapon would be violation of his parole." She was all cop. "Michael, may I see your gun?"

He grinned. "That's the first time a woman has said that to me and meant it literally."

"Ha-ha."

"It's double-action. Easy to cock."

"Very funny."

"Most women would—"

"I don't want to hear about your other girlfriends," she said quickly. "It's not that I'm jealous or anything. But this is the way I like to work with a partner. We stay focused on the job, which is taking care of Lionel and guarding against threats from Bateman. We don't need banter."

"Are you telling me that you and your partners don't ever talk about anything other than policework?"

She leveled a cool, blue-eyed gaze at him. "I want my male partners to think of me as a cop, not as a woman. And the best way to do that is to avoid talking about sex. Understand?"

This probably wasn't the best moment to tell her that she was cute when she was being a hard-boiled lady cop. "I bet you've got other rules."

"Only one," she said with a shrug. "But it's not worth mentioning. You couldn't possibly follow it."

"Try me."

"Always be honest. You've got to be able to trust your partner one hundred percent. There can't be any lies or betrayals."

Though he agreed with her in principle, Michael thought honesty was highly overrated. It was safer for him—and for Annie—if he continued to slide around the edges of the truth. The things she didn't know couldn't hurt her.

He reached behind his back, pulled his gun from the waistband of his jeans and placed it on the kitchen table.

Annie finished off her sandwich before she picked up the gun. "Very nice. A Smith and Wesson automatic? Is it 10 mm?"

"Yes." He knew exactly where her questions were headed. The handgun was a specially designed model issued to federal agents. Michael phrased his explanation carefully to avoid a direct lie. "It was given to me by a friend. He's in the FBI."

"That's unusual. The feds don't like to part with their weapons." Her injured right arm and wrist caused her to fumble as she removed the ammunition clip. Frustrated by her clumsiness, she flexed her fingers. "I need to practice with my left hand."

"How long before you're back to normal?"

"The swelling is almost gone. I'll probably be okay in a couple of days, but I'm going to have to wear this adjustable cast for a lot longer to protect the bones while they heal." She snapped the clip back into place and handed him the gun. "Let's go outside and take a look around."

Michael was fairly sure there were no snipers lurking in the shrubbery. Bateman didn't intend to hurt them. Not until June thirteenth.

Still, Michael insisted on basic precautions. "We're turning off the porchlight. And I want you to stay close to me."

"I'll give the orders." Grabbing the flashlight, she led the way to the front foyer. "By the way, I want to thank you for sweeping up the glass from the broken window. A lot of guys would consider that women's work."

"A lot of guys don't live for days at a time on a boat. Efficient maintenance is important."

"I guess so." She cocked her head. Curious again. "I never even knew you were interested in boats. How did you become a charter captain?"

"I guess it was a natural transition after being in the navy."

"You were in the navy?" She rolled her eyes. "Jeez, Michael, I don't know anything about you at all."

"Does it matter?"

"Well, yes. If we're supposed to be engaged, I ought to have some vague idea of what you've been doing with your life." She flicked the light switch off, and a soft darkness fell over them. "What should I say to people?"

"We'll tell anybody who asks that our relationship is based purely on sex and we don't have time to talk."

She punched his arm. It was a friendly boyish gesture. From years of hanging around with the football teams her grandpa coached, Annie had learned to act like one of the guys. But Michael knew better. Earlier, when he'd kissed her, she'd responded with the passion of a mature woman. She was hot.

"Jeez, Michael. Didn't you promise not to talk about sex?"

"As a matter of fact, I didn't."

"So you can't stop yourself from behaving like a pig?"

"Oink."

She pushed open the front door and stepped onto the veranda that stretched all the way across the front of the house and halfway around the south side. The floorboards were painted slate-blue, like the house. The surrounding rail matched the white trim, some of which was peeling badly.

The beam from her flashlight flickered across the porch swing and two wicker rocking chairs. Then she focused the circle of light on the area leading to the door.

"Too bad the ground is dry," he said. "We won't find footprints."

"Wouldn't do much good as evidence. Bateman was wearing steel-toed work boots, like most of the loggers in town."

Nonetheless, she bent low to inspect the flower beds. Though no one had been at the house to tend them, yellow jonquils and white irises bloomed in the fertile Oregon soil. At the corner of the veranda, wild red roses climbed the railing.

She raised the light and slowly swept it back and forth. "I doubt he walked up the sidewalk, aimed at the door and threw a brick. He had to sneak across the yard, staying in the shadows to avoid being seen.''

He agreed with her reconstruction of the crime. ''Tomorrow we should talk with your neighbors. Maybe somebody noticed him.''

''Grandpa won't like that,'' she said.

''He's probably not going to be real pleased about having us out here right now. You with a flashlight. Me with a drawn gun.''

''You're right,'' she said.

''However, if we find evidence that Bateman threw the brick, he'll be arrested. Lionel will like that a lot.''

She concentrated on the thick green grass underfoot. ''My probable scenario goes like this. Bateman was keeping the house under surveillance. He waited to strike until after you went downstairs and turned out the lights.''

''But he didn't wait for long.''

''Maybe he'd been there awhile and was impatient.''

Again Michael agreed with her analysis. He also knew that the most likely source of clues was the place where Bateman had hidden while he watched the house. He might have dropped something. Evidence could be as obvious as a cigarette butt or subtle as a lingering stink in the air.

Lifting his gaze, Michael scanned the spacious yard. The lawn had been recently mowed, but the hedges beside the white picket fence were overgrown. There were two tall maples and a picnic table. Toward the backyard was a white painted gazebo that Annie seemed to be headed toward.

''Not there,'' Michael said. ''From the gazebo, he could have seen the windows to the guest room, and I still had the lights on.''

''You're right.'' She altered her course and slowly paced off the distance to the taller of the maple trees. ''So, tell me about the navy.''

"It was good discipline. I joined up shortly after I left Bridgeport, as soon as I was eighteen."

"And you sailed around the world?"

"Around the Pacific, at least. I was in the Philippines right after they closed down the base."

"The navy must have kept you busy."

He glanced over his right shoulder, half turning so his gun would be aimed in the direction he was looking. There was nothing. Myrtlewood Lane was utterly quiet, not even a barking dog. The very idea of violence in a place like this seemed absurd. Yet he couldn't shake a feeling of apprehension.

"Is that right, Michael? You were busy in the navy?"

"That's right." He glanced at Annie. She was the source of his tension. The real danger came from her. These seemingly innocent conversational questions were leading somewhere, and Michael was fairly sure he wouldn't like the destination.

She circled the maple tree, covering every inch with the flashlight beam. "Is that why you never contacted me when you left town? You were too busy in the navy?"

The acid in her voice etched into his conscience. He hadn't chosen to leave her without saying goodbye, hadn't planned to leave her at all. "It had to be a clean break, Annie. I never expected to come back to Bridgeport."

"But here you are." Her wide gesture encompassed the whole town. She turned off the flashlight and faced him in the moonlight. "I have to ask. Michael, why did you leave?"

He'd known this moment was coming, the time when he needed to explain the past. "I don't know where to start."

"The beginning," she said. "Start at the beginning."

The onset of his messed-up behavior had probably been in the womb, but he wasn't about to go through a cellular genetic justification of the family patterns that shaped his existence.

He should probably start with his father, who had been the worst kind of alcoholic. A mean drunk, he had terrorized the family. When Michael was growing up, it hadn't been unusual for him to come home from school and find his mother or his six-year-old brother weeping, nursing a bruise. "For a long time I blamed my father. He was abusive. Couldn't hold a job."

"I remember," Annie said. "Who do you blame now?"

"Myself." His greatest fear was being like his father, predisposed toward alcoholism and uncontrollable rage. "I take full responsibility for my own actions."

She went to the picnic table, stepped on the bench and sat on the tabletop. "Tell me why you left Bridgeport."

He sat beside her, not facing her. Somehow it seemed appropriate to be sitting in the quiet hour before midnight with a gun in his hand, finally talking to Annie. So many times he'd visualized this moment when he hoped to explain what had happened, to look at her and find forgiveness in her eyes. "It was during the football season when I was a senior in high school. In November. That was when my father left."

"He deserted your family?"

"Like a rat leaving a sinking ship. But I was glad to see him slink away."

"You never said a word about it," she said. "And you were over here a lot that year."

"I liked being here." He remembered Christmastime, when they'd strung lights from the gazebo. "Your grandpa was more to me than a coach. I guess I'd call him a positive role model, but back then I didn't understand terms like that. All I knew was that Lionel Callahan was the sort of man I wanted to be. Honest, responsible and brave. He never backed down, but he never took unfair advantage."

"I feel the same way," she said. "I was lucky he took me in after my parents died."

Again he couldn't help wondering at her definition of luck. She'd lost both parents. Most people would've been emotionally destroyed, but he'd never heard Annie complain.

"Anyway," he said. "Everything turned out okay. My mom has an apartment in Seattle. My brother is in college."

"You're taking care of them?"

"It's the least I can do."

She stamped her foot on the bench. "Oh, Michael. I wish you'd told me about your father leaving."

"I'm surprised you didn't know. It felt like my family troubles had been broadcast on the Bridgeport grapevine."

"I wasn't very well connected. Most of my free time was spent with Lionel. Or playing sports." Her chin lifted. "I was pretty much a loner."

"You were pretty much terrific."

"Come on, Michael. I was a nerd. A six-foot tall female jock who ran track, played volleyball and starred on the basketball team. Nobody could believe it when *cool* Michael Slade took me out on a date. I couldn't believe it myself."

"Four dates," he said.

"Five if you count the time we went for a picnic on a Saturday afternoon in May and got rained out."

"You didn't even let me kiss you until the third date," he remembered. "I was beginning to think you didn't like me."

"Just inexperienced," she said quietly. "That was my first real kiss."

It was his turn to be surprised. "Impossible. You were sixteen."

"I was also the granddaughter of the football coach who

threatened every guy on the team with dire consequences if they came near me.''

''Those were Lionel's laws for the team,'' Michael said. ''Don't smoke. Don't drink. And don't even think about touching Annie.''

''So why did you ask me out?''

''It was after football season. And I used to like breaking the rules.''

Dating Annie represented the sweetest, simplest part of his young life. She was his best memory.

''Michael.'' She cleared her throat. ''I always wondered why you didn't ask me to Prom.''

''I couldn't afford it.''

''But that's ridiculous. I would have—''

''Don't finish that sentence,'' he warned. ''I didn't want charity from you or anybody else. After dear old Dad left, I was desperate for money, and I got hooked up with a bunch of guys from Wayside. Kind of a gang.''

''With Bateman?''

''He was the ringleader.'' Sick memories flooded his brain. He heard the echo of cruel thoughtless laughter. In his mind he saw the harsh neon lights, beckoning to him, urging him to take risks. ''Things are different in Wayside than they are here. It's a beach town with a lot of tourists and nightspots. On the beachfront you meet people and never see them again.

''I started panhandling, and I got real good at conning the tourists out of their money with stories about how my car had broken down. Maybe they believed me because I had that clean-cut, all-American football-player look. I didn't care. I just wanted their cash.''

Those lies were his first step toward crime. He shoplifted a birthday present for his six-year-old brother. He swiped a bottle of wine. ''I should've gotten a job, but it was easier to cheat and lie and steal. There was also something cool about the gang. God, I was an idiot. Toward the end, I wanted to break off with them."

"I'm glad," she said. "But why the change of heart?"

"Because of you." He avoided her gaze. Talking about his feelings had never come easy. "Even though everybody else in town said a Slade would never be good enough for a Callahan, you believed in me. I wanted to be worthy of your expectations."

"I never wanted you to be anybody but yourself."

"You didn't know me, Annie."

It was just as well he'd left when he had. They'd had no future. At that time in his life Michael had nothing to offer. He'd been almost as bad as the police chief remembered— a troubled teenager on his way to disaster. "It was June thirteenth. Six. Thirteen. Bateman planned a robbery in Wayside. I don't need to go into details, but we all had a part to play. Afterward we planned to meet by the deserted bridge across the Yaquina to split up the take."

"I remember something about this." Annie stared through the night at his profile, wishing she could clearly read the expression on his face. "There was a story in the newspaper."

"Not much publicity," he said. "One of the guys had a powerful father who kept our names out of the press."

She had never connected the incident with Michael. However, at the time, she hadn't been thinking clearly. His disappearance had consumed her, made her half-crazy. She hadn't been able to eat or sleep. World War III could have broken out, and she wouldn't have noticed. "Your mother wouldn't tell me where you were or what had happened. Then, only a few days later, she was gone, too."

"It was better that way." He stared down at the ground, at the pewter-colored gun in his hand. "Bateman's plan went off without a hitch. At least, that's what we thought until we met at the bridge. The county sheriff in Wayside had put together a sting. The cops were waiting for us.''

Again Annie should have been rooting for the police. Michael and his friends were petty criminals who needed to be taken off the street. But she couldn't help feeling sympathy for him. He'd been young and confused, wounded by his father's mistreatment. So many teenagers were misunderstood. So often they made mistakes that would haunt them for the rest of their lives.

''I didn't know Bateman had a gun,'' he said. ''When the cops moved in to make the arrests, he started shooting. A deputy was wounded. They returned fire.''

The details of the long-ago story came back to her. ''Someone else got in the way of the bullets. An innocent person who wasn't connected with the gang.''

''Her name was Marie Cartier.''

And she was killed.

Michael's poor judgment had ended in homicide.

Annie looked upward to the shimmering galaxies, unchanging and yet so different. When she was sixteen and Michael broke her heart, she came out here to cry so her grandpa wouldn't hear. She'd been sitting in this very spot, looking up at the stars and seeing nothing but a reflection of herself, her own teenage angst. She hadn't known the truth of what had happened.

Now the starlight fell on Michael, too. In spite of the cloaking darkness, she clearly saw his remorse. She wished she could go back in time, reach out beyond her own pain and comfort seventeen-year-old Michael Slade. ''You can't blame yourself for what happened.''

''It should've been me who died. Every day I'm alive is a day stolen from Marie Cartier.''

Abruptly he rose from the picnic table and strode a few paces away from her. She sensed that he was holding back. What was he hiding? ''What else, Michael?''

"I hate talking about this."

"About Marie?"

"If everything had gone the way we planned, it would've been simple. They promised me nobody would get hurt."

They? "Who promised you?"

"Bateman," he said quickly. "Drew Bateman. He was the only one with a weapon, and he was tried as an adult. Two of the other guys went to jail for assault and got much shorter sentences."

"And you?"

"I got off easy, partly because I was only seventeen and I was ready to tell the truth. There were three of us who testified in the judge's chambers, and the records were sealed."

Annie had been involved in police work long enough to know about codes of silence. Any criminal who testified against another faced the threat of revenge, even if the court documents were sealed. "Did Bateman blame you for speaking out against him?"

"I don't know." Michael shrugged, trying to ease the burden of the past. "I never spoke to him again. Not until today."

"If he was after you, the brick through the window makes more sense. Six-thirteen would be a warning to you. A threat."

"You're probably right. The fact that I'm staying here with you is a bonus for Bateman. He can harass all of us at the same time."

He heard the creak of the picnic table as she climbed down. He sensed her presence right behind him. "I'm glad you finally told me the truth, Michael."

It wasn't the whole truth, but it was all he could stand to tell her now. Turning, he faced her. The starlight struck silvery highlights in her hair and burnished her features with a mystic glow. He saw bittersweet sadness in her eyes, a reflection of his own regret.

His fingers itched to touch her, to stroke the line of her jaw and tuck a strand of hair behind her ear. But he had no right.

She continued, "I shouldn't say this, because it's not very coplike. But it's easier for me to forgive your crime than to forget about the hurt you caused when you left. I've lived with this anger for a long time."

So be it. He wouldn't beg for her forgiveness. "Let's go inside. We're not going to find anything tonight."

"Okay, as soon as we check the gazebo."

Though he thought the gazebo was in the wrong place for surveillance, Michael didn't object. He was quickly learning that, when Annie had her mind set on doing something, it was easier to fall into line.

The latticework gazebo, overgrown with grapevines, would have made a comfortable hiding place for Bateman while he watched the house. There were curved wooden benches against two sides. The floorboards squawked when they stepped inside. Dead leaves lay scattered where the wind had blown them.

"This place needs a good sweeping out." Annie shone the beam around the edges and underneath the benches.

"It doesn't look like anybody has been in here," he said.

"I'm not so sure." She focused on one of the benches. "Doesn't it look like that spot has been cleared away? As if somebody was sitting there?"

"Maybe."

"Do you think we should dust for prints?"

"Even if you were carrying a fingerprint kit with you…" And he really hoped she wasn't. That would be dedication above and beyond the call of duty. "I suggest we let Engstrom do his job tomorrow."

"You're right," she said. "It's been a long night."

She left the gazebo first, making a beeline for the back door as Michael stood watching. Though he was still holding his gun, ready to protect her, her long-legged stride distracted him. Her natural athleticism combined with a feminine twitch of her hips. He could watch her forever.

Dragging his foot through a small pile of crumbling leaves, he felt his toe bump something hard. He leaned down, pushed away the dust and found a tiny glass figurine of a woman in a fancy blue ballroom gown. Cinderella?

He picked it up and smiled, pleased to think that the cheap little statuette belonged to Annie. In spite of her cop attitude, she still enjoyed feminine fantasies, like Cinderella. Maybe she even imagined herself in a fancy ballgown, meeting Prince Charming.

"Michael," she called out. "Are you coming?"

"I'll be right there." He stuck Cinderella into his pocket and followed Annie into the house.

Chapter Four

Annie's grandpa had taught her how to throw a football, how to pump her arms when she ran and how to shoot hoops. What she hadn't learned was how to run a house properly. By ten o'clock the next morning, she felt like a one-armed traffic cop on a six-way intersection.

Because she'd overslept, she hadn't had time to wash her face or fix her hair. The breakfast dishes lay unrinsed in the kitchen sink. While Michael was helping Lionel bathe, she'd snatched the sheets off her grandpa's bed only to discover that she had no clean linens because she'd forgotten to run the washing machine last night. A technician from Ace Security Systems, hired by Michael, had just blown an electrical fuse. And someone was knocking loudly at the front door.

Annie snatched it open and stared down into the wide bright eyes of a young woman who couldn't have been more than five feet tall. This little brunette gamine wore a snug white T-shirt over breasts that were full and impossible not to notice.

"You must be Ms. Callahan," she said, consulting the pink copy of a work order. "I'm your grandfather's physical therapist."

Though Annie would be the last person on earth to oppose a woman's right to any occupation, she had requested a male therapist. Lionel made it very clear that he wanted to do his workouts with a man. "I thought your name was Sam."

"Short for Samantha," she said. "Where's my patient?"

"My grandfather is a big man. He used to be a football coach," Annie tried to explain. "I don't know how you'll be able to support his weight."

"I'm a lot sturdier than I look." As if to prove her statement, Samantha picked up the large gray plastic case containing the implements of her trade. "I need to get started. I have another appointment at noon."

"Of course."

Annie held open the screen and directed her toward the staircase. Michael was with Lionel. Let him handle the Sam-who-was-really-Samantha issue.

A screeching throbbing alarm signaled that the electricity had come back on. The security-system technician yelled, "Sorry."

"Turn it off!" Annie clapped her hands over her ears. "Now! Please!"

Mercifully the noise died. And the telephone started ringing. She grabbed the mobile from the nook in the hallway. "Hello?"

There was no answer. Only a faint static.

"Who is this? Hello?"

Was it Bateman? She knew better than to engage in conversation with a crank caller. Vigorously she pushed the disconnect button—a gesture that was nowhere near as satisfying as slamming down a receiver.

And the parade of problems continued as Chief Engstrom and two other officers took Sam's place at the front door. Engstrom's badge, exactly like the five-pointed star she wore in Salem, glistened. From his polished shoes to his starched uniform collar, he looked every inch the professional lawman. Apparently he took his personal appearance far more seriously than his investigative work.

"Good morning, Annie." He pulled open the screen door and scowled at the broken window, patched over with cardboard and duct tape.

"Good morning, Chief." She pointed down the hall toward the kitchen. "There's coffee made. Help yourselves."

No sooner had the cops left the foyer than she whirled and faced Michael who was coming down the stairs from her grandpa's bedroom. This morning he wore a black polo shirt tucked into his jeans. Clean-shaven and neat, he looked annoyingly calm.

She asked, "How's Grandpa taking the news that his therapist is a woman? Will he work with her?"

"He grumbled for half a minute, but Sam moved right in and started unpacking her gear while she gave him a lecture on nutrition." Michael flashed a devilish grin. "That's when Lionel had a chance to get a good look at her. That little lady has an amazing body."

"That's not a qualification." Annie fought the impulse to glance down at her own average-size breasts. She was *not* jealous. "Just because a woman is, um, full-figured…"

"It helps for a physical therapist to have a decent physique," he said. "I think Lionel and Sam are going to get along just fine."

For future reference she filed away the information that her grandpa preferred working with young, well-endowed females. What man didn't?

"I like yours," Michael said.

"My what?"

"Your breasts." He lifted an eyebrow, teasing again. "They're in perfect proportion. Round and high. Very sweet."

She hated the warm flush she felt creeping up her throat. He had no right to be examining her breasts or any other part of her body. Unfortunately she doubted that another lecture on why partners shouldn't be sexually involved would be effective. Instead, she informed him, "Engstrom is here."

As if on cue, a shout came from the kitchen. "Hey, Annie. You're out of coffee."

"I'll be there in a minute," she hollered back. Through the front screen door, she saw another person approaching the house. It was Edna from the mini-mart and she carried a big stainless-steel pot. Annie could only hope Edna's cauldron contained a witch's brew that would knock her unconscious.

"It never stops," she muttered. "I'm not cut out for this kind of work."

"What do you mean?" Michael asked.

"Housekeeping," she said. "It's all loose ends. A little here. A little there. Total chaos."

"You're doing just fine."

Couldn't he see she was totally overwhelmed? "I'd make a terrible housewife."

"Yoo-hoo!" Edna called through the screen door. "I brought some of my special chicken soup for Lionel."

"How nice." For lack of any other recourse, Annie welcomed her inside.

Edna's pug nose wrinkled with delight as she peered over her half glasses at Michael. "And here's your handsome fiancé. Shame on you, Annie, for not telling me. If Officer Bobby hadn't stopped by the mini-mart last night before closing, I might never have known."

Annie had almost forgotten the engagement. It was the icing on her stress. "Do you remember Michael Slade?"

"How could I forget the best wide receiver in the history of the Bridgeport Badgers?" Edna tried to gesture with the cauldron, and a dribble of yellow viscous liquid spilled between the loose-fitting lid and the edge. "You know, Michael, my daughter had a big crush on you in high school. Remember? She was captain of the cheerleading squad.''

"Candace," Annie said. "She married Jake Stillwell."

"And divorced him," Edna said.

Her gaze stuck on Michael. She was appraising him, taking his measure and deciding his net worth. But why? Supposedly Michael was already spoken for.

Edna continued, "Candace has two beautiful children from the marriage and a decent amount of alimony. But what she really needs is a new husband."

Aha! Now Annie understood the rules. Until the marriage vows were spoken, Michael was considered fair game.

"The poor kids," Edna said. "They need a new daddy."

"Mm," Michael said.

"The oldest is a boy. Seven years old and quite the athlete. If you had the time, Michael, you might give him some football pointers."

"Er..." Michael said.

"Anyway, Candace wants to throw an engagement party for you two. She'll probably stop by today or tomorrow."

Candace Grabow Stillwell, the most popular girl in high school, was coming here? Annie shuddered at the thought. Her self-esteem always dropped several notches when she was in the same room with the former cheerleader. "I suppose Candace is still full of energy."

"She's doing as well as can be expected after a divorce." Edna frowned. "If you ask me, she spends far too much money on clothes. But she says it's so hard to find nice things in a size six."

"Six?" Annie cringed. She hadn't worn a size six since fourth grade.

"Annie!" The policemen in the kitchen were restless. "Can we get some coffee back here?"

Though she felt ready to toss up both hands in surrender and crumple to the floor like a used tissue, Annie was too stubborn to admit defeat. "I need a little help," she said. "Edna, could you take your soup to the kitchen, then brew up some coffee for Chief Engstrom and the other officers?"

"No problem, sweetie." She started down the hallway with her soup sloshing dangerously. "And I'll make some coffee for Lionel and take it up to him."

Not a good idea! Seeing Engstrom and the boys last night was a good start, but Lionel wasn't ready for a parade of visitors. "He can't be disturbed, Edna. His physical therapist is here, and they're in the middle of a session."

"Nonsense, Annie. He'll see me." She tossed a little wink over her shoulder. "I think he's always been a little bit sweet on me."

"Oh," Annie said. That was just what she didn't need— her grandpa starting a romance with Candace's mother.

When Michael rested his arm on her shoulder, she instinctively recoiled. Then she remembered that they were supposed to be engaged.

"What can I do to help?" he asked.

"Keep an eye on things." She told him about the dishes in the sink and the sheets in the dryer. "And tell Engstrom that he should check for fingerprints in the gazebo."

Apprehensively he glanced toward the kitchen where the conversation level had risen to a roar. "What are you going to be doing?"

"Taking a shower."

Without waiting for him to object, she hiked up the staircase and into her bedroom where she grabbed a pink cotton shirt from the closet and a pair of jeans from her dresser drawer, then raced next door to the bathroom where she scooped a bundle of wet towels off the tile floor and into the hamper.

She slammed the door, waiting for calm. It still wasn't quiet. The old house reverberated with the activity of so many people doing so many different tasks.

She flipped the lock on the door, turned on the hot water in the shower, and something magical happened. The noise of pelting water masked the other racket in the house. A cloud of steam reached out to envelop her, and the warm moisture penetrated her pores, creating an illusion of privacy. "Sanctuary."

She breathed deeply—inhale, exhale. Her racing heartbeat slowed to a normal level. The tension in her upper back released. She hadn't even been aware she'd been hunching her shoulders.

Taking her own sweet time, she unfastened the Velcro strips on her splint and removed it. The grotesque black-and-blue bruising had faded to a sickly yellow at the edges. Though the swelling had gone down, she still couldn't make a tight fist without feeling a sharp pain. Her wrist was stiff, and she was unable to rotate it freely.

Though the doctors in Salem had advised her to rest the arm and allow time to heal, Annie was impatient. She needed to be able to use her gun hand. A can of pepper spray simply wasn't going to be sufficient protection against Bateman.

Before stepping into the shower, she twisted her long blond hair into a knot on top of her head. Then she carefully removed her grandma's engagement ring and placed it on the edge of the sink. The delicate gold setting seemed too fragile to hold the diamond, and Annie would rather die than lose the precious gemstone.

Hot water sluiced over her body, washing her tension down the drain. In her new role as Lionel's caretaker, she needed to remember to do these simple special things for herself: a soothing shower or bath by candlelight; a morning jog when the sun was rising; private moments for reading; or time to contemplate the buttery yellow of a blooming jonquil.

During the past three and a half years of living alone in

Salem, she'd had no trouble arranging the necessary time
to unwind. Now she needed to make a conscious effort, or
else she'd be tense as a cocked pistol. And tension led to
mistakes.

Annie couldn't afford to mess up until the threat from
Bateman was over. At the same time, she needed to be
mindful of her grandpa's status in town, taking care not to
embarrass him. At the moment it seemed far more difficult
to deal with the citizens of Bridgeport than to face constant
harassment from a sociopath with a grudge. The phony engagement meant she'd have to lie and lie and lie. Her frustrated sigh mingled with the steam from the shower. Deception was unnatural for her. She'd never learned to fake
it.

And she still didn't trust Michael. The story he'd told
her last night went a long way toward explaining why he'd
left town eleven years ago, but there were still holes.

If his testimony against Bateman was sealed and secure,
why hadn't he returned to Bridgeport after the trial? Why
had his mother and brother also left town? Though Michael
swore that Bateman didn't want revenge against him, she
didn't believe it.

She toweled dry and dressed in her pink cotton shirt and
jeans. There were other questions, too. Why was Michael
carrying a gun that was FBI issue?

Most important of all, how had he known that Bateman
would be coming after her and Lionel?

Taken altogether, Michael seemed to have too much information about Bateman, including details about his life
in prison. Therefore, Michael had inside connections. The
inmates at the state prison? While she wanted to believe
his life in crime had ended when he was seventeen, she
wasn't certain.

She slid the engagement ring onto her finger and returned
to her bedroom, glancing into the mirror over her dresser.

She looked tired, so she applied dabs of concealer to the dark circles under her eyes. Annie firmly told herself that she wasn't making this extra effort to impress Michael— she didn't care what he thought about her appearance. She swept her pale lashes with mascara. The only reason she was putting on makeup was to avoid looking drab and lifeless in case Candace showed up.

After she brushed her hair and fastened a ponytail on top of her head, she was ready to face the world. "You can do this," she whispered to the face in the mirror.

Her grandpa had always told her she could handle anything, and she had the sports trophies to prove it. Though she'd packed most of them away, she kept one for each sport she excelled in: volleyball, basketball and track. They stood arrayed on the corner of her desk. Fondly she picked up a two-foot-tall column topped by a gold runner that symbolized first place in all-around track. This trophy was tangible proof that she was a winner. She could cope with the housework, manage Bateman's threats and deal with the lies.

Then her gaze fell on the little statuette that stood beside her glittering awards. It was a cheap figurine, a tiny dancer in a blue ballgown that reminded her of Cinderella. Mindful of fingerprints, Annie lifted Cinderella by her tiny waist.

Back in Salem she'd received three other statuettes that were disturbingly similar to this one. When had it started? Ten days ago, or two weeks. The timing coincided with the date Bateman was released on parole. But why would he leave these strange souvenirs? If this was supposed to be a message, she didn't get it.

She did, however, understand the threat. He'd been here. In her bedroom. He had violated her private sanctuary with his loathsome presence.

Disgusted by the thought of Bateman moving through her room, she wanted to scrub the floors. What had he touched? Had he sat on her bed? Her nostrils quivered with the remembered stink of fruity chewing gum and sweat. Every surface in this room needed disinfecting. Glaring at Cinderella, Annie wanted to snap the figurine in half and bury the pieces ten feet under. She opened a desk drawer and took out an envelope, which she dropped Cinderella into before placing it in the center drawer of her desk.

Suddenly Michael burst into her room and charged toward the window. "Come over here. Quick."

She closed the drawer and joined him as he eased the white lace curtain to one side.

Parked at the curb, opposite her grandpa's house, was the beat-up black pickup. Bateman himself leaned across the hood. At first she thought he was smoking, then she realized he was sucking on a lollipop.

He seemed to be staring up at the window, watching and silently gloating about his ability to come into the house, into her bedroom, without detection.

Though she should probably tell Michael about the statuette, Annie hesitated. She wanted to maintain her control of this investigation. After all, they weren't really partners. He was a charter-boat captain. It might be better to keep these little figurine clues to herself.

"I hope your security system works," she said.

"Damn right, it will," he said. Michael's blood boiled. Yesterday he had warned Bateman to stay away from Myrtlewood Lane. "What does that bastard think he's doing?"

"Standing on the street," Annie said. "He can't be arrested for that."

"I want him gone."

His rage was a fire, searing from deep inside his soul, demanding release. But she was right. Bateman hadn't trespassed. There was nothing Michael could do but stare through the window. This inability to act, this damned pathetic impotence, fed the flames within. Struggling for control, he squinted his eyes nearly closed and tried to think of cool rivers and cascading waterfalls—anything to douse the unbearable torturous heat.

Anger was Michael's curse, the legacy from his abusive father. And he fought to control his rage, to distance himself from it. When he'd played football, he used the anger for energy to score. In the navy, his commanding officer had discovered Michael's secret fury and had exploited it. Michael's anger was what had caused him to be recruited into the elite U.S. Navy SEAL program. Their intense training helped him manage the impulse to lash out until his anger was honed to a laser point of attack.

He watched as Bateman's car drove away, and his fury began to cool. The constricting tension loosened its grip.

"I'd better get that restraining order filed with Engstrom," Annie said as she turned away from the window. "Is he still here?"

"The cops show no sign of leaving. They've gone through a pot of coffee and eaten half the cake that was in the fridge."

"Good thing I don't have doughnuts. They'd be here forever."

Annie giggled, and the sound was so uncharacteristic that he took a closer look at her. Her gaze darted nervously, and she turned away from him as if she had something to hide.

"Annie, what's wrong?"

"Nothing," she said too quickly.

He didn't think she was frightened by Bateman. Though she'd seemed shaky when he first saw her yesterday, she'd proved her courage last night when she'd investigated every room with cool competence.

Still, the diffident set to her shoulders and her refusal to directly face him betrayed a certain anxiety. "Talk to me, partner."

"Not right now. I need to think."

When she reached up to push a strand of hair off her forehead, he saw the bruise on her forearm. The ugly purple discoloration took his mind off all other concerns.

With infinite gentleness, he held her arm and inspected it. "I should've come to your rescue sooner."

"What's done is done."

"Annie, I'll never let anything like this happen to you again. Never."

"Oh, please. I'm a cop, Michael. It's my job to stand in harm's way."

And he hated her job choice, her career. He didn't want to think of Annie putting herself in danger. "If I had anything to say about it—"

"You don't." Her blue eyes flashed as she finally looked up at him. "I like my work. It gives me a chance to make a difference. Sometimes I can really help somebody in trouble."

"There are other ways to help."

"Not for me," she said. "I've had this conversation with my grandpa. Many, many times. He thinks I should be a social worker or a counselor."

"Good advice," Michael said.

"But that isn't the path I've chosen—at least, not for now. I'm a cop and a darn good one."

Though her voice remained calm and matter-of-fact, he heard the stubborn note of conviction. Her message was clear. Annie made her own decisions and she stuck by them, right or wrong. Neither he nor Lionel nor an army of logicians would change her mind. This was a battle best saved for another time—after she'd learned to trust him.

When she picked up her adjustable splint and began her struggle to fasten the Velcro strips, he stepped forward. "Let me help you put that on."

She nodded and held out her poor injured arm. Carefully he wrapped the splint.

"It needs to be more snug," she said. "For support."

Michael adjusted the strips. Being close to her sparked his protective instincts. He wanted to lock her away in a quiet safe place where no one could ever hurt her again. Somewhere they could be alone, where his touch would unleash her passions...

He glanced toward the desk where he'd left the little Cinderella statue next to her sports trophies. The incongruity of a blue-gowned princess standing amid the glittering athletes had amused him. Apparently Annie didn't agree because the Cinderella was gone.

He finished with the splint and allowed his hand to linger above her elbow, lightly holding her arm, feeling the wiry strength beneath her skin. When she looked up at him with questions swirling behind her eyes, he wanted to kiss away her doubts.

"Thanks, Michael. It's hard to get that thing adjusted for proper support without being too tight."

"I'm here to help." With the slightest encouragement, he would kiss and caress and whisper heartfelt compliments in her pink shell-like ear. "What else can I do for you?"

Her gaze softened. The worry lines around her eyes faded, and she looked more complaisant. She wore a touch of makeup today, but she didn't need it. Her skin glowed, soft and delicate as a rose petal.

"You've done enough," she said.

"Annie, I haven't even started to—"

"Enough." To emphasize her one-word statement, she took a step back, away from him. "This isn't the right time. I have a houseful of people to deal with."

He smiled, pleased at the implication. If this moment wasn't right, it meant that another time might be. Though he wasn't a patient man, Michael was willing to wait. "We ought to take advantage of all these people being here."

"Tell me how."

"They can keep an eye on Lionel, make sure he's safe, while we go to the hardware store to pick up glass to fix the front-door window."

"Good thinking." She nodded. "With any luck we'll be gone when Candace shows up."

Michael wasn't anxious to see Candace, the ex-wife of Jake Stillwell. Her mother had made it fairly clear that Candace was on the lookout for husband number two whether or not he happened to be engaged at the moment. However, he said, "If she wants to throw us a party, we should consider it."

"Why?"

He needed to make contacts in town, needed to find out if Bateman was working with anybody else. "Might be fun."

"I'd rather walk barefoot on broken glass."

"That sounds a tiny bit antisocial."

"I don't mean to be." Annie fidgeted. She glanced in the mirror, adjusted her ponytail and began fussing with the bottles and cosmetics on top of her dresser.

"Do you have a problem with Candace?"

"No problem." Her hand rested on the doorknob.

"I thought we were supposed to tell the truth, partner."

She leaned her back against the door. A dozen different emotions flitted across her expressive face. Then she sighed. "The truth. In a nutshell. I liked growing up in Bridgeport. There's a special kind of security that comes from knowing so many people and having them know you. And I really appreciate all the concern for Lionel. The casseroles. The get-well cards. Even Edna's chicken soup. But there's something awful about a small town when you don't fit in and fulfill expectations."

"What do you mean?"

"I never got married and had kids, never settled down."
She gave an angry little shake of her head. "It sounds so
old-fashioned to be worrying about things like that."

"It's this damn town," he said.

Like Annie he had a life outside Bridgeport. He'd
achieved a certain amount of success. But here, to the cra-
dle of his youth, he became a bad boy, a troublemaker. The
seeds of the past sprouted faster than weeds in a garden,
choking out the sunlight.

"When I was growing up," she continued, "I was never
one of the popular girls. Not a prom queen or a cheerleader.
I didn't have many girlfriends because I spent all my time
with Lionel and the jocks. I was one of the guys. A tomboy."

"I never thought of you that way," he said.

"You sure did. Don't you remember playing one-on-one
basketball with me? We were about twelve."

Though it was almost twenty years ago, he remembered
as if it were yesterday. They were playing on the court after
school. Annie was a little bit taller than he, and she was
good—fast on her feet with a neat layup shot he couldn't
defend against. Their casual game had turned into an intense rivalry, and neither of them would quit until it was
too dark to see the hoop. "I seem to recollect that I won."

"Hah!" Her competitive nature flared. "It was a draw.
But that's not my point."

"What is?"

"While we were playing, did you think of me as somebody you'd like to date?"

There was nothing wrong with being different. "I've
never thought of any other woman the way I think of you."

"What does that mean?"

"I've never wanted any other woman the way I want
you. You're different, Annie. And you're beautiful."

Her shoulders straightened, and he could see her almost physically adjust to his compliment. It amazed him that she didn't realize what a truly spectacular woman she was.

Almost shyly she said, "Even if I don't fit in."

"*Because* you don't fit in. I'm not attracted to all the paper-doll cheerleaders and prom queens."

"Oh, Michael, I wish you hadn't left town. It would have done my teen-aged self-esteem a lot of good to hear you say these things."

He should have been here for her. He should have held her hand and escorted her through adolescence and into womanhood. Michael regretted their years apart, the happiness that could have been theirs. He crossed the room and closed the space between them. "It's not too late."

"Some things are gone forever. Like having a steady boyfriend on Saturday night." She shrugged. "I can never go back in time and have a date for the senior prom."

It had never occurred to Michael that she wouldn't be swarmed by boyfriends. Most of the guys in Bridgeport knew her and liked her. Had she pushed them away after he left?

Again he thought of the little Cinderella statuette. Never went to the prom? That was a shame. Every woman should be a princess at least once in her life.

He lifted her hand to his lips and brushed a kiss across her knuckles. When he looked into her eyes, the diamond sparkled between them. "We're engaged. That's at least one step beyond going steady."

"However," she said, "it's a lie."

Chapter Five

There were all kinds of lies. Almost every day Michael stretched the boundaries of truth. And it had all started here in Bridgeport.

As he escorted Annie to the street where his pearl-gray BMW was parked, he acknowledged to himself that the fine automobile was a lie. He couldn't really afford a car like this, but the Beamer came with the boat. Besides, it pleased him to drive a classy vehicle. Every time he slid behind the wheel, it contradicted the opinions of all the people who'd predicted he'd never amount to anything. The rumble of the engine when he turned his key in the ignition sounded like a well-tuned triumph.

Some lies were okay.

In minutes they were cruising on Main Street. It looked much the same as it had eleven years ago. The wide two-lane thoroughfare was bordered on each side by storefronts that edged up to the sidewalk, with cars parked at the curb.

A gray aura of weariness clung to the streets. Graffiti marred the sides of the two-story buildings. A trash can overflowed. Some of the stores were vacant. Bridgeport was like a sad tired woman who neglected her appearance because she didn't think anybody noticed or cared.

"The tavern seems to be doing a brisk business," Michael noted.

"They say the bars and the hookers are always the last to go." She shook her head in dismay. "I remember when people used to take pride in the town. They shopped on Main Street, instead of driving to the big superstores. Everybody you met was a neighbor."

He pointed to the movie house with one word on the marquee: Closed. "I used to spend hours in that place, eating popcorn and licorice until I got sick."

"Now everybody goes to the eight-screen multiplex."

The decline had started many years ago when the bridge outside town was condemned, and a new bridge across the Yaquina River was constructed in Wayside. Tourist traffic was diverted. Then three of the four lumber mills closed down, and a lot of people, including Michael's father, were laid off.

Though Michael resented the town, the slow deterioration pained him. Dropping a few grenades on Main Street would've been kinder.

He turned at the stoplight—the only stoplight—on Kreiter Street and parked in the lot behind Main Street Hardware. At the edge of the asphalt—which was marked in fading stripes with more spaces than were ever used—the towering trees and thick bushes formed a natural wall. When he was a kid, he'd spent hours in the forest, climbing over logs, wading in swampy waters and catching tadpoles.

"The trees are so green," Annie said wistfully. "There's nowhere in the world that can match the Oregon woodlands."

"Semitropical rain forests," he said.

"Have you been there?"

He wasn't at liberty to tell Annie about the top secret SEAL mission in El Salvador. "There were a lot of snakes."

"Eeew." The rough tough lady cop gave a very girlish little shiver. "I prefer Oregon."

"There are snakes here, too."

"But mostly the two-legged kind. Like Bateman," she said. "Do you think he's staying in town?"

"Either here or in Wayside." Later tonight Michael would find out.

In the hardware store Michael gave the windowpane measurement to a clerk, a clone of the man who'd worked there eleven years ago. Mopping his shiny forehead and bald pate, the clerk dithered nervously. "You're going to have to give me fifteen minutes on this. It's the noontime rush, you know."

Michael could have pointed out that there were only three other people in the store, which hardly constituted heavy traffic, but he wasn't in a hurry to return to the house. "Take your time. We'll be back in a while."

He directed Annie toward the front door and outside onto Main Street. "How about a cup of coffee? My treat."

She grinned. "Is this a date?"

"You bet." Teasing, he added, "We probably ought to hold hands. To give the appearance of an engaged couple."

"Our cover story," she said. "Do you think anybody will believe it?"

"You should probably give me a long loving moonstruck look. Maybe plant a little kiss on my cheek."

"Don't push it, Michael."

But she didn't object when he laced his fingers through hers, and they strolled casually along the wide sidewalk. He liked walking with Annie, liked the way her long-legged stride matched his. They seemed to fit together. Their engagement was a lie, but it felt so right. "So where's the Starbucks?" he asked.

"We're in Bridgeport," she reminded him. "This is possibly the only town in the entire Pacific Northwest without a coffee shop."

"Amazing."

"I'd rather have a root-beer float, anyway."

At the corner drugstore on Main Street, there was a soda fountain with six stools, three of which were occupied. He ordered two root-beer floats to go from the kid behind the counter. Of course, Annie wanted chocolate ice cream in hers. Outside, they sat on a black wrought-iron bench facing the street.

Annie took a long sip from her straw. "Yum. There's nothing like real ice cream, real *chocolate* ice cream with one hundred percent pure butter fat."

"You don't need to worry," he said. "Not with that lanky body of yours."

"Hey, pal. This Gumby-like physique doesn't come easy. I've done my share of dieting."

"Ever consider giving up chocolate?"

"Not a chance. It's my favorite vice."

He remembered something about chocolate being considered an aphrodisiac. "You know what they say about chocolate and sex."

She grinned. "Chocolate's better?"

A light springtime breeze kicked along Main Street. Sunlight sparkled through the high tree branches, which were visible above the two-story buildings. For a moment the dismal cloud over tired old Bridgeport lifted, and he saw the past through the rosy glow of nostalgia. He slipped backward in time to a gentler era, when he was the star wide receiver for the Bridgeport Badgers and Annie was his girl, his honey, his special date on Saturday night.

He wished he could go back and reclaim his innocence. There were a hundred things he'd do differently, and most of them revolved around Annie.

A Lincoln Town Car double-parked in front of them, and a tall blond guy popped up from the driver's side. "Michael Slade? What the hell are you doing back in town?"

Michael nodded. "Jake."

Jake Stillwell hadn't changed much. He still acted like he owned the whole damn town. Two cars backed up behind him on the street. "And Annie Callahan. You look great!"

"Thanks," she said coolly.

"What's the deal, Annie? I thought you didn't have time to go out on dates."

Michael rose to his feet. "This isn't a date. We're engaged."

Jake slammed his hand on the roof of his car. "No way."

On a rational level Michael knew that his surge of masculine pride was absurd—definitely another lie. But it felt good to be one up on the rich kid who had everything. "Show him the ring, Annie."

She held up her hand and wiggled her graceful fingers.

Jake's brow furrowed. He looked like he was going to charge over and demand explanations, but the cars behind him began to honk.

"I'll give you guys a call," he said as he slipped back into his car and continued down the street.

Michael's self-satisfied, cheese-eating grin lasted only an instant. On the opposite side of the street, he spied Drew Bateman, leaning against a storefront. Bateman had the gall to give him a casual wave, erasing the pleasant sheen of the afternoon.

Not wanting to upset Annie, Michael stepped in front of her, shielding her view. "We should pick up the window glass."

"I already saw him," she said quietly. "There's nothing we can do, Michael. Bateman has as much right as the next sociopath to hang around on a public street. As long as he stays over there, I don't care."

"I do." Michael was seething. He didn't want Bateman to even look at her.

"If we let him bother us, he's won." She wasn't fond

of being stalked, either. But Annie was stubborn enough to brazen it out. "I'm not going to hide from him. I intend to sit right here with my legs crossed and the sun on my face while I finish my root-beer float."

She dipped a plastic spoon into the softened ice cream and forced a conversational tone. "Grandpa has some big plans for Bridgeport."

"Tell me."

"Over the years he's bought up a lot of land, and he wants to build something that would draw people to the community. Like an apartment complex."

"That's an ambitious project."

"I haven't been encouraging him," she said. Her grandpa's project seemed too big an undertaking for someone his age. "But I might be wrong. He needs to get involved in something."

After the last sip of root beer, they returned to the hardware store, where they picked up the glass, neatly wrapped in brown paper. Annie did a bit of additional shopping, buying batteries for the flashlights and taking a handful of samples for the larger task of painting the house.

"What do you think, Michael? Eggshell or ivory?"

"White is white," he said.

"I'd like something a little more interesting. Maybe alabaster."

The idea of getting her grandpa's house into shape cheered her. A fresh paint job, inside and out, would be a major improvement. After that, the hardwood floors needed a good buffing. Possibly she could even convince Lionel to get rid of the old furniture. Feeling almost optimistic, she led the way out of the hardware store and into the parking lot in the rear.

As soon as she saw Michael's car, her sense of well-being faded. All four tires were flat.

"Damn." Michael fumed and paced in a belatedly protective circle around his car. "I can't believe this."

Annie proceeded to examine the deflated tires on the BMW. Though she wasn't happy about the continued harassment, she wasn't frightened by this new assault. Her head was clear. She was in control. This parking lot was a crime scene, and her police training taught her how to deal dispassionately with an investigation.

She crouched to inspect the right front tire. The inflation valve cap had been unscrewed. A twig wedged into the stem forced the valve to stay open and allowed the air to escape. Simple and very neatly done.

She removed the twig. "There doesn't appear to be any damage to the tires."

Michael leaned over her shoulder and growled, "Nobody touches my car."

"Oh, right." She rolled her eyes. "How could I have forgotten the sacred bond between a man and his car?"

"This is no time for sarcasm."

"I'll bet you'd rather take a bullet in the neck than have somebody scratch your fender." She went to the rear tire and plucked the stick from the inflation valve stem. "This is really no big deal. We'll go back to the hardware store and get some of that stuff that temporarily fixes flat tires. Then we drive to the gas station for a fill-up."

"What about the valve caps?" he demanded. "They're gone, aren't they?"

"I don't see them."

"There might be other damage," he grumbled. "Don't touch anything else."

"Fine."

Leaving the last two tires with the twigs still in place, she stood upright and scanned the parking lot for clues. There was nothing unusual. No footprints because the lot was asphalt. No decent fingerprints could be lifted from a twig. Since the whole job of deflating Michael's tires had probably only taken five minutes, she doubted there would even be a witness. How ironic! It seemed to Annie that her every breath was observed by dozens of curious townspeople, but Bateman had struck twice without anybody coming forward to say they'd seen anything out of the ordinary.

If her nature was more paranoid, she'd suspect that the whole town was in collusion, conspiring to make her life difficult by deflating tires, throwing bricks and leaving little figurines on her desktop.

Michael yanked open the hood and glared at the engine. "I should've attached the car alarm."

"Let me get this straight," she said. "You have a car alarm, but you decided not to use it?"

"It's not hooked up. I leave my car in a garage when I'm taking a charter out. Sometimes I'm gone for weeks." He tugged at the sparkplug connections. "The alarm kept going off and the guys at the garage disconnected it."

Annie glanced at her watch. It was twenty minutes before noon, and she'd hoped to be back at the house in time to talk with Sam, the physical therapist, before she left. "I'll leave you here with the car and walk home."

"Not alone," Michael said. "You're not going anywhere by yourself."

"Don't be silly. It's only a little more than a mile."

"I said no."

His dark eyes sparked with an anger that far surpassed annoyance. His intensity startled her. Another person might not have noticed the change in him. Michael hadn't transformed from Dr. Jeckyll into Mr. Hyde. But Annie was trained to read people's moods and recognize the signs of danger. More than that, she was attuned to Michael, and she saw the fury burning deep inside him.

The muscles in his jaw twitched. His already tanned

complexion turned even darker. "Michael? Are you all right?"

He swung away from her and from the BMW, but she could still see the tension in the set of his broad shoulders and the tilt of his head. He looked as if he might lash out at any moment.

As an athlete and a cop, she understood the rush of adrenaline that came from provocation, but Michael's fury was different, more dangerous than a burst of energy on the football field.

The sensible thing to do was to stay away from him, but she was fascinated by his unbridled emotion, his passion. Waves of masculine energy emanated from him, and Annie felt herself being drawn closer, wanting to soothe his rage, to care for him. She wanted to be the woman who tamed this strong powerful man and gave him peace of mind.

But that was a mistake. She needed to keep her distance. Only a fool tweaked the tiger's tail. "Calm down, Michael. It's just a car."

"Last night, it was only a window. But a few days ago he came after you." By the time he faced her again, he had reined in the fury. "We need to be careful, Annie."

She watched in amazement as his features returned to normal. It must have required tremendous willpower to bring that rage under control. She hated to think of what might have happened if Michael had caught Bateman in the act of letting the air out of his tires.

Another car pulled into the lot. The Lincoln parked nose to nose with the BMW, and Jake Stillwell stepped out. "Looks like you've got a problem, Slade."

Though he was the same age as Annie and Michael, Jake looked older. His blond hair was thinning, and his body had softened. His shoulders were rounded, and he had a little pot belly. When he shook hands with Michael, the contrast was blatant. Michael's deep tan and muscular physique bespoke hours working outdoors on his boat. Apparently Jake's only exercise was riding a desk at the lumber mill.

She held out her hand for a greeting, but Jake enveloped her in a hug that lasted a few seconds too long to be comfortable. At least he smelled terrific—some expensive aftershave.

He gazed at her with bloodshot eyes. "How's Lionel? I heard he wasn't doing well."

"He's improving," she said. "What about you, Jake? What's going on in your life?"

"The lumber mill takes all my time. Ever since my father retired, I've been running the whole show. It's a lot of pressure, but I'm handling it. I've even considered expanding operations."

"That would be wonderful for the town," she said.

"Yeah, sure."

His gaze slid away from hers. Though she didn't want to leap to conclusions, Annie was fairly certain Jake didn't give a hoot about Bridgeport. Like his father before him, Jake ran the lumber mill for profit—*his* profit.

"How are your parents?" she asked.

"They spend most of their time at the condo in Portland. My mother still hangs around at the galleries and spends too much money on art."

The Stillwell home was a veritable treasure trove of fine paintings and sculpture, and Jake's mother had been generous about showing her collection. "She was always trying to bring culture to Bridgeport."

"Talk about a waste of time."

Annie didn't like the way Jake had turned out. When he was younger, he'd been brash and confident. Now he was just smug and more than a little snobbish.

"So," he said, "you two are engaged."

"Yes, we are," Annie heard herself say. Oh, Lord, she was actually getting into the lie. "And we're very happy."

"That's sweet." But his tone was disdainful, sneering. "I never figured you two would end up together. She was always too smart for you, Slade. And now she's too pretty. Like a fashion model."

In high school Jake had barely noticed her. Annie suspected the real reason for his sudden interest had something to do with making Michael angry, playing a game of one-upsmanship.

"I mean it," Jake said. "You look fantastic. Are you sure you want to marry this criminal?"

"Criminal?" Was this a thoughtless reference to Michael's past? "What do you mean?"

"Good old Michael was always a troublemaker. You'd be better off with somebody stable like me."

"Guess you haven't been paying attention," Michael said, stepping up to confront him. "Annie's taken. Her dance card is full. She's engaged to me."

"Until the minister ties the knot, nothing's final. You're not afraid of a little competition, are you?"

"From you? Not hardly."

They stood glaring at each other, and Annie was reminded of a couple of bull elk who rammed heads and tangled antlers until one was recognized as superior.

Without backing down, Jake nodded toward the Beamer. "Nice wheels. Did you steal it, Slade?"

"Did you let the air out of the tires, Jake?"

"What? Why would you think that?"

"Because it's a childish stupid prank."

"Believe me, Michael, I've got better things to do." Jake turned to Annie. "Can I give you a ride someplace while your fiancé fixes his flats?"

For once she agreed with Michael. She didn't want to be alone with Jake Stillwell. She was afraid his smarminess would rub off, and she'd have to take a shower again. "No, thank you."

"Fine."

"I'll run back into the hardware store and get some stuff to fix the flats," she said.

"Hurry back," Michael called after her.

Then he turned his full attention on Jake. Even though they'd played on the same team, they'd never been friends. Jake had also been involved in the incident at the bridge. His wealthy father had helped shield the boys' identities.

"This is the first time you've showed your face in Bridgeport in years," Jake said. "Why?"

"I came back for Annie." Though that hadn't been the stated reason, he realized it was the truth.

"You know, Slade, I always had kind of a thing for her."

"Did you date her?"

"No. I was stuck with Candace. Besides, Annie wouldn't get serious about anybody after you left town. I never knew where you went, Slade."

"The navy."

"What are you doing now?"

"I captain a charter boat out of Seattle."

Though Michael saw a glimmer of envy in Jake's bloodshot eyes, he knew better than to expect acknowledgment.

"Physical work," Jake said. "Maybe I could hire you for a weekend."

"It's a seventy-foot sailing yacht with full accommodation for four to six passengers," Michael said. "You couldn't afford me."

"After you get married—if you get married—is Annie going to live with you on the boat?"

"I've got a condo in Seattle." But Michael hadn't thought that far ahead in their fake engagement.

"Leaving her alone while you're out to sea? That's not a good plan. She'll get bored. She'll be easy pickings for somebody like me who can be with her all the time.'' He gave a short laugh, but he wasn't joking. ''You could never understand a woman like Annie. She needs a place to settle down. She lives in Salem for the moment but, at heart she'll always be a small-town girl.''

Though Michael hated Jake's attitude, the comment held some truth. Annie would be happiest in a place like Bridgeport. ''We'll figure it out.''

''You do that.'' Jake circled to the side of the car. ''As long as I'm here, I might as well help you with the tires.''

''You don't need to ruin your pretty manicure.''

''Very funny, Slade.'' He bent down to inspect one of the tires. ''A twig in the air valve. We used to do stuff like this.''

''We used to be jerks.''

Jake pulled out the twig. ''I heard Bateman got out on parole.''

''Bad news for everybody,'' Michael said. He was fairly sure Jake had something up his sleeve, an ulterior motive. A connection to Bateman? ''Have you seen him?''

''On the street.'' Jake removed the last twig from the valve stem and stood. ''There's something attached to this stick.''

He unrolled a scrap of paper and read it to himself before looking up sharply. ''Is this supposed to be some kind of joke?''

''What does it say?''

'''June thirteenth. You can't get away.''' Jake looked up. ''You think this is funny?''

''I'm not laughing.'' Michael held out his hand. ''Give me the note.''

''Why?''

''I'll pass it on to Chief Engstrom. He can test for fingerprints.''

''Yeah? And you know whose prints are on this? Mine.''

Jake shredded the note and tossed the pieces to the ground. "You're trouble, Slade. You always have been."

But he had the story backward. It was Jake who'd introduced him to Bateman and the gang in Wayside. It was Jake, the quarterback, who goaded him into taking risks. Michael could've hated him for that, but he took responsibility for his own mistakes, his own failures. He wouldn't blame Jake Stillwell or anybody else.

In cold silence Michael stood and watched as Jake climbed behind the steering wheel of his Lincoln, fired up the engine and backed away, leaving a cloud of dust and a lot of questions. It seemed crazy to suspect him of complicity with Bateman, but Jake wasn't particularly scrupulous when it came to getting what he wanted. And if he wanted to bring Michael down a few pegs...

Seconds later Annie emerged from the hardware store. "Oh, good. You got rid of Jake."

But Jake Stillwell wasn't gone for good. Michael's gut told him Jake was part of the situation with Bateman.

"Michael? Is something bothering you?"

He watched as the spring breeze picked up the pieces of the note and whisked them away. He didn't want to worry Annie by telling her what had happened. It was his job to protect her from Bateman and Jake Stillwell and everybody else.

"Nothing," he said. "Nothing's wrong."

BY THE TIME they returned to the house with the tires repaired, every one had gone except the technician who was installing the security alarm. He helped Michael install the new glass while Annie ran upstairs to check on Lionel.

Her grandpa was propped up on the pillows, breathing steadily and watching baseball on the television at the foot of the bed.

"How was the physical therapy?" she asked.

He raised his left hand to show her his progress. "I think I'm going to be all right."

She leaned down and kissed his forehead. "Did you have some lunch?"

"A sandwich," he said. "That little Sam is real big on nutrition. She says I should drink more water, but I'm not going to. Not yet. I don't want to be running to the bathroom every five minutes."

"Should I help you over to the window so you can sit in your easy chair?"

"I'm content to lie right here and watch the Mariners. It's a doubleheader."

She joined him for a few minutes before returning downstairs. Michael and the security technician were standing in the hallway, where a digital keypad had been mounted on the wall.

"Good timing, Annie. We're ready to enter the codes."

"The codes? That sounds very high-tech for an old house on Myrtlewood Lane."

The technician launched into his explanation. "When you're ready to leave the house, you press the 'on' button to set the alarm. Then you have one minute to leave the house and lock the door."

"What if I want the alarm on while I'm in the house?"

"Make sure everything is locked up and turn it on."

"Okay." Annie was familiar with many types of alarm systems. This one seemed simple enough.

"When you come back inside after being gone, you have sixty seconds after you open the front lock to disarm the device by punching in a code."

"What happens if it takes longer?" she asked.

"The sirens go off and an alarm rings through to the police station and to our office. You turn off the siren by inputting your code. Then our office will call, and you need a key word to identify yourself."

"It's a good system," Michael said. "I have the same thing on my boat."

"On a boat?"

"It's a nice vessel. I don't want anybody breaking into the cabins while we're at dock."

He certainly was cautious about his security. A car alarm. A boat alarm. And he carried a gun. Maybe Michael was a true paranoid.

The technician said, "Now I need a number code. Five digits. Something you can remember, but nothing obvious like a birthday."

"Six, twenty-five, seventy-six."

The number popped into her head with startling ease. It was the date her parents had launched their sailboat. Annie hadn't thought of that day in years, and her memory was a blur of laughter and excitement and splashing sunlit seas. She couldn't have been more than four or five years old, too young to read. But she knew her numbers, and she remembered the date printed on a brass plaque, fastened to the cabin wall. She'd traced it over and over with her small fingers.

The technician repeated the numbers and did some computerized wizardry. "Now I need a code word for your identification in case the office has to contact you."

She turned to Michael. "What's the name of your boat?"

"Rosebud," he said. "That's the name she came with, but I kind of like it."

"That'll be my code word. Rosebud. It's perfect."

"Why?" he asked.

Because she wanted him to be a part of her life. After he was gone, she'd say the word and think of Michael, sailing around the world in his charter boat. "You're my protector. You should be part of the security system."

"I can't argue with that."

The rest of the day passed uneventfully, and Annie was

curled up in bed by ten o'clock. At eleven she still lay awake, staring at her digital alarm clock and watching as the minutes changed.

There was no good reason for this insomnia, but she tossed and turned, unable to get comfortable. Remembering the bag of chocolates downstairs in the kitchen, she threw off the covers, tossed a silky kimono over her lacy white gown, put on slippers and headed for the staircase.

At the end of the hallway she paused. There was an odd tapping noise. Peering through the darkness, she saw Michael's silhouette. He stood at the security alarm keypad, punching in the code numbers to disarm the device.

"Cancel," he mumbled under his breath. "What was it again? Six, two, four. Damn."

What was he doing? Trying to turn off the alarm? He hadn't noticed her, and she sidled around the archway into the front parlor. There had to be a simple explanation for what Michael was doing. If he turned off the alarm, he could leave the house. But why?

"Got it," he said quietly. "Now, rearm."

He hurried past the parlor to the front door, unlocked it and went outside.

After the latch clicked, she only had a few seconds to follow, or else she'd have to go through the disarming and rearming process all over again. Annie made a lightning decision.

She was out the door. Standing on the unlit veranda in her kimono and gown, she realized that the security alarm was already reactivated. And she didn't have a key.

Chapter Six

In the pale light of a waxing moon, Annie poised on the top step of the veranda like an exotic night bird. The drooping sleeves of her pink-and-orange kimono, decorated on the back with a giant purple dragon, fell winglike from her wrists. It wasn't the most subtle outfit she'd ever worn.

For a moment she thought Michael would turn around and see her. How could he miss seeing her? But he was intent on his own path, striding purposefully along the sidewalk headed toward Main Street. He looked as if he knew where he was going, and she suspected it wasn't to the mini-mart for a midnight snack.

Since she couldn't go back to the house without setting off the screaming alarm, there were two options. She could stay here on the porch, prudently awaiting Michael's return. Or she could follow him.

Cinching the belt on her kimono, she alit from the veranda and padded after him. This might be the only way she'd learn Michael's secrets. Besides, he'd spent considerable time spying on her in Salem. Turnabout was fair play.

Her flimsy ballet slippers offered little protection against the rough sidewalk, especially since she had to jog to keep him in sight. The silky fabric fluttered around her knees and elbows. Her hair tossed. There wasn't the slightest doubt in her mind that she looked like a crazy woman.

Fortunately no one else was on the street. After eleven o'clock all the sane citizens of Bridgeport were safely tucked away in bed, even though it was Saturday night.

Two blocks from the house she tripped against the curb and sprawled forward. Careful not to land on her injured arm, she tumbled to the right and landed first on her knees, then on her right arm. She rolled onto her back and stared straight up at the cloudy skies. The first heavy raindrop splattered on the tip of her nose.

"Swell." Now she would be a drenched exotic bird, a complete eccentric, a certifiable candidate for the Isadora Duncan wing of the loony bin.

Regaining her feet, she hurried along the sidewalk. Michael was moving quickly, and she had to run again. The rain was nothing but a trickle, but lightning zigzagged across the skies and thunder crackled. The sound masked Annie's noisy pursuit, her feet slapping on concrete and her breath coming in labored gasps.

As they neared Main, a pair of headlights rounded the corner, and Annie leaped off the sidewalk and hid behind a yellow-flowering forsythia bush.

After the car passed, she peeked out. Michael was nowhere in sight. "Shoot!"

Emerging from the bushes, she took off at a run. At the end of the next block was the central business district, and she couldn't risk trotting past that well-lit area where there were still a number of cars and pedestrians. If she couldn't spot Michael from here, she'd have to abandon her quest.

Then she saw him. He stood in a public phone booth at the gas station.

Annie ducked behind one of the black wrought-iron benches that had been placed throughout town as part of a civic project. She watched as he spoke into the receiver.

This was very odd. Surely he could've called from the house or used his cell phone.

The only reason she could imagine for his extreme precaution in seeking out a public phone booth was to secure a completely neutral line. For some reason he needed to make an untraceable connection.

She remembered his inside information about Bateman's prison life. Added to that was Michael's vaguely nefarious past. But why go to all this trouble? Petty criminals generally didn't care about special phone connections. Was he involved with organized crime?

So many things about him didn't add up. He'd come from a poor background and had been in the navy, which wasn't a high-salaried career. And yet, Michael was a skipper on a charter boat. And he drove an expensive car. Where did he get the money?

As he left the phone booth, she craned her neck around the edge of the iron bench, trying to see where he was going. But a young couple was headed down the street toward her, and Annie needed to find a better hiding place. She slipped through the gate of a chain-link fence.

Immediately she heard ferocious barking from behind her right shoulder. She could either stay here and be torn limb from limb by Fido, or she could return to the street and hope she'd make a getaway before anyone noticed her. Or maybe she'd catch a break. Maybe the barker was a small dog—a sweet-tempered little poodle.

No such luck. A piranha-jawed bulldog charged toward her.

"Back!" she shouted as she burst through the chain-link gate and ran directly into the young lovers.

The woman screamed.

"Excuse me!" Annie shouted.

"Hey, you!" The man made a grab for her. "What the hell are you doing?"

She hiked her kimono above her knees and sprinted at top speed, praying that none of the local cops was patrolling in this area. With her luck it would be Officer Bobby, the former bully with a big mouth.

Her grandpa would never forgive her if she got picked up on the street wearing her nightie and a kimono. They'd have to pack their bags and move away from Bridgeport in shame.

Dashing through yards and hopping fences, she made it back to Myrtlewood Lane. Though the rain had not become more than a drizzle, she was drenched, the silky kimono plastered to her thighs.

When she saw another set of headlights, she was almost too exhausted to care. But it would be a shame to come this far and wind up getting caught by her grandpa's next-door neighbor.

With a last-ditch effort, Annie dragged her soggy body behind a neatly trimmed hedge and dropped to the moist earth in the yard beside her grandpa's house.

The headlights belonged to a familiar old black pickup. It parked at the curb, and when the driver's-side door opened and the inside light came on, she clearly saw Drew Bateman. He stepped out into the heavy mist and closed his door so quietly she heard only a slight click.

Though he wore work boots, he moved quietly and stealthily, coming three steps up the sidewalk toward the front door of her grandpa's house.

From her hiding place, she saw him clearly, and she dared to hope that he'd perform some act of vandalism. She'd be a witness. She could press charges.

But he came no closer. He stood, staring and silent as a dark sentinel.

Lightning split the sky and in that brief flash she saw his face. Horrible! His lips were twisted, baring his teeth. His brow was lowered. His eyes seemed to glow with an almost inhuman intensity.

Slowly he raised his arm. His fingers clenched. Fiercely he shook his fist at the house.

He made a guttural feral noise in the back of his throat.

"For what you did to me," he growled. "You will die. You'll all die."

A thunderclap underlined his words. He turned, got back in his pickup and drove away.

Annie huddled on the ground in her kimono. She was stunned by Bateman's ferocity. The wet leaves of the shrubbery brushed her cheek. The raindrops felt like tears. Never before had she seen such raw hatred.

MICHAEL WALKED swiftly through the night. Though it was a little rainy, the darkness felt as comfortable as a black velvet robe, soothing as a calm sea. He had always preferred starlight to the glare of the sun. Life was a lot more interesting in the shadows.

Unfortunately all he had discovered tonight was darker shade of gray—no answers. His phone call had been unproductive. When he'd paid a visit to the local tavern, he learned that most people in town feared Bateman and avoided him. No one admitted being in contact with him, and there were no indications that anybody knew about the harassment of Annie and her grandfather, who was probably the most well-liked man in town.

Still, Michael's instincts told him Bateman wasn't working alone. He didn't believe Bateman was the one who'd attacked Annie in Salem, and he wasn't sure about these other incidents of harassment.

Not that Bateman was innocent. Far from it. But his style was to goad others into doing his dirty work. In a strange way, similar to Charles Manson, Drew Bateman was a leader. He had a dark charisma that made weak men seek his approval—weak men, like Jake Stillwell.

According to the gossip in town, the lumber mill wasn't doing such great business. Jake had lost a lucrative contract for wood chips from a Japanese supplier, and loggers were being laid off. One of the men who'd lost his job was Officer Bobby's brother.

Michael had to wonder about Bobby Janowski. Though the night cop hadn't been connected with the incident at the bridge, Bobby had been a bully in school. He was the dull-witted cowardly type who would align himself with Bateman.

On the sidewalk leading to Lionel's front door, Michael walked softly, not wanting to wake Annie or her grandpa. The floorboards on the veranda creaked as he approached the screen door with his key in hand.

"It's a little damp for a walk."

Startled, he turned and saw Annie sitting on the porch swing. She was wearing some bizarre costume and her hair was wet. "What are you doing out here?"

"You took the words right out of my mouth. Where did you go, Michael?"

"It's no big deal." Though he felt guilty as a teenager out past curfew, Michael tried to be nonchalant. "I went into town for a drink at the tavern."

"I don't believe you." Her voice rasped with irritation. "You take your bodyguard duties far too seriously to sneak off for a nip."

"I figured you'd be safe," he said. "That was the whole point of the alarm system."

"I'm tired of your lies. Why did you go into town?"

Since she obviously wasn't buying his casual attitude, he needed to level with her. The whole truth was unnecessary, but she needed a piece. "I decided to do some investigating on my own. I wanted to find out if anybody around here was involved with Bateman.''

She was quiet, considering. Though he could barely see her features in the dark, he knew she was judging his statement and testing it against her internal truth meter. Finally she said, ''It's customary for partners to keep each other informed about their investigative activities. *All* of their investigative activities. That's the advantage of a partnership. Two heads are better than one.''

He eased onto the porch swing beside her, starting a gentle rocking motion. ''I wish I had information, but I didn't learn anything important. The lumber mill is experiencing a slump due to a cutback in purchases from the Pacific rim. But that's not news.''

''What else did you do?''

He peered at her through the darkness. This was one bedraggled woman. Her bathrobe was brightly colored and smeared with mud. One sleeve was torn at the shoulder. ''What happened to you?''

''You have the most infuriating habit of answering a question with another question,'' she said. ''But I will *not* be distracted. Besides going to the tavern, what else did you do?''

She must have followed him. Though Michael found it hard to believe that Annie would streak through town in her bathrobe, that was the only explanation for how she'd gotten so wet and raggedy. And she must have seen him at the telephone booth.

Once again, he realized, it was time for a lie. He feigned concentrating. ''Let me think. I walked downtown because I wanted the exercise and the chance to think. And it occurred to me that I ought to check in with my first mate, because we have a one-day charter scheduled for tomorrow morning. So I stopped to call him from the phone booth by the gas station. Then I went to the tavern.''

Her steady gaze focused upon him, and he struggled not to fidget. Though Michael's livelihood depended on his ability to lie effectively, his facade wavered in the face of her relentless scrutiny. He could tell that she wasn't entirely appeased by his answer.

"Let's get you inside, Annie. You must be cold."

When he reached for her, she sprang off the porch swing, causing a vigorous lurch. "Don't even think about touching me."

What? Earlier today she'd relaxed her guard against him. They'd reminisced. She'd held his hand. This afternoon had been easygoing and downright pleasant. Now they were back to square one. Her change in attitude was unacceptable. Michael wasn't accustomed to taking two steps forward and one step back. "You're the most stubborn difficult woman I've ever known."

"And you're a liar."

"What do you mean?"

"Telling half a story doesn't count as the truth." Bristling, she stalked toward the door. "Would you open this, please?"

"Not until you answer my question. What the hell are you doing out here?"

"I accidentally locked myself out, and I couldn't sneak back in through a window because of the blasted alarm system." She shivered. "I'm freezing. Unlock the door."

Michael knew there was something more, something she wasn't telling him. But it would be cruel to keep her outside any longer than necessary. He fitted his key into the lock.

As soon as the door swung open, she darted down the hall to the alarm and punched in the code to disarm the security system. When the door closed, she reactivated it.

The back side of her robe, Michael noted, was even more bizarre than the front. A purple dragon crawled up her spine and snarled at him.

Michael snarled back. He didn't like the scornful attitude of this dragon's mistress. Once again Annie had warned him not to touch her and had called him a liar.

But when she whirled and faced him, he couldn't stay angry. Her competent-cop expression didn't match the smear of mud across her cheek and twigs sticking out of her hair. In the flamboyant robe, she looked more like a circus clown than a policewoman. He grinned.

"What's so funny?" she demanded.

"Where did you get that robe?"

"For your information, it's a genuine Japanese kimono, the kind a geisha would wear."

Tall, blond, long-legged Annie with sticks in her hair was about the farthest thing from a geisha he could think of. But Michael knew better than to comment. Her stubborn eyes and out-thrust chin warned him not to tease. Calmly he said, "Tell me what happened to you."

"While you were gone, Bateman came by."

"Damn it!" Another assault from Bateman while he was missing in action. "Did he do this to you?"

"He didn't even see me. He didn't do anything. No acts of vandalism. He stood on the sidewalk and shook his fist at the house."

She demonstrated the vigorous motion, flicking droplets of moisture from her sleeve. Then her arm dropped limply to her side, and her voice became quiet. "He looked demonic, Michael. Completely deranged."

And she'd been outside, beyond the alarm system and vulnerable. How was he going to protect her if she kept taking risks? "Did he say anything?"

"He vowed that we'd die. All of us."

Her shoulders drooped. Her head lowered and she stared forlornly at her slippers. He longed to comfort her, to kiss away her fears and make her feel safe again. He wanted so badly to take care of her. "Let's go to the kitchen. I have a robe you can change into, and I'll make coffee while you tell me the whole story."

"But there's nothing else to say."

"What about a profile for Bateman? You're a cop. You know about the criminal types."

"I've taken a couple of workshops, but I'm no expert on criminal psychology." She looked up at him. "Do you really think profiling would help?"

"We've got nothing else to go on. No evidence. No witnesses."

"Only his threats." The confidence had begun to return to her eyes. "And our own suspicions."

He left Annie in the kitchen and grabbed his navy-blue terry-cloth bathrobe from the guest bedroom. When he returned, she stared down at the brightly colored robe in her hands. Underneath she wore a sleeveless white cotton gown with lace around the square neckline.

When she held up the kimono, the moist white fabric clung to her breasts. Her slender arms moved gracefully, and he was captivated by her unmindful elegance.

"Ruined," she said mournfully. "I loved this kimono."

He took it from her. "Must be one of a kind. I can't imagine there are two people who'd love this thing."

"Then you have no imagination. Obviously you don't spend much time in lingerie stores."

"Not much."

"It's a weakness of mine," she confided. "Since I'm wearing a boring uniform all day, I like to dress up at night. Silk and satin feel so cool and wonderful against my skin."

She was dead wrong when she accused him of having no imagination, because her words plunged him deep into fantasy. He envisioned smooth fabrics rubbing intimately against her lean body, sliding over her breasts, caressing her inner thighs.

When she reached for his robe, he held it away from her, drawing her closer toward him.

"Michael?"

Her eyes held a question, and he had the answer. "Yes, Annie."

She met his gaze, and electricity arced between them. Their attraction was an undeniable force of nature. God, he wanted her. At the slightest signal of acquiescence, he would sweep her into his arms and carry her into his bedroom.

Instead, she purposely broke the connection. She grabbed his robe and wrapped it tightly around her. "Michael, weren't you going to make coffee?"

Fully aroused, he walked stiffly to the coffeemaker beside the sink. He'd enticed her into the kitchen to talk about something, but the subject had fled his mind.

"Bateman," she said. "You called him a sociopath, but I think he's way more dangerous."

While he measured scoops of coffee into the filter, she went into the bathroom. Still talking, she said, "His face tonight was horrifying, like a gargoyle, a creature from hell."

She returned to the kitchen with a towel wrapped around her damp hair. With the end she wiped her face. The color had already begun to return to her cheeks.

"Here's what I think," she said. "Bateman isn't the clever mastermind you seem to think he is. He's vicious and unpredictable, motivated by pure unadulterated hatred."

Michael forced himself back to the unpleasant topic of Drew Bateman. "But he's not out of control."

"Not usually."

With a shudder, Annie remembered the dark threat of violence in Bateman's gestures. As a cop, she'd seen worse.

The difference was that Bateman's revenge was directed at her and her grandpa.

Sinking into a chair beside the kitchen table, she wished she could completely trust Michael. And trust would be the first step. Denying her physical attraction to him was becoming almost impossible.

"He's been clever enough to play games with us," Michael said. "Making his presence known without breaking any laws. Engaging in petty vandalism."

His words made sense. But as she watched him opening the cupboard beside the sink, her mind slipped off on another track. His shoulders were so broad and strong. She wanted to feel his arms around her, holding her tightly, crushing her breasts against his chest.

"...an obvious threat," he finished his statement.

"What did you say?"

"The date he wrote on the brick was an obvious threat. Kind of like a serial killer who sends clues to the police, wanting to be caught before they kill again."

"Teasing us," she said.

Michael poured the coffee into two mugs and joined her at the table. "There was another threat this afternoon. A note was wrapped around one of the twigs stuck in the tire valves. It said something about June thirteenth and we couldn't get away."

His words erased her thoughts of passion. Once again, Michael was withholding information.

"Why didn't you tell me about this sooner?"

"I didn't want you to worry."

Exasperated, she said, "I wish you'd treat me like a partner, Michael. The note is a piece of evidence. Even if Engstrom can't take fingerprints from it, the reference ties it to the brick. It's proof that your flat tires are connected to Bateman. So where is it? Where's this note?"

"Jake shredded it."

"Why?"

"Because he was the one who found it, and his finger-prints were on the paper. He didn't want to get involved. A juvenile criminal record isn't good for business."

"Jake?"

"He was arrested along with the rest of us on June thir-teenth."

Now she understood why Michael had objected so ve-hemently when she'd considered making a date with Jake. "I guess it's not so hard to believe. He was always com-petitive and liked to think he was tough."

"He got the same deal I did. Sealed court record and no charges."

"Do you suspect him, Michael? Do you think he's still involved with Bateman?"

He lifted his coffee mug to his mouth before answering. "I can't think of any good reason for Jake to bother with somebody like Bateman. Not unless there's a profit."

"And I don't think he wants revenge. He's always liked my grandpa."

Or had he? During Jake's senior year as quarterback when Michael hadn't been there to catch his passes, Jake and her grandpa had argued furiously about the game plans. If she remembered correctly, Jake had wanted to get Lionel fired. But that was years ago. Surely he didn't still bear a grudge.

It amazed her how much had happened right under her nose, and she'd been unaware of the undercurrents, the in-trigues, the turmoil. Lionel had kept her shielded from all these disturbing events, including the incident on June thir-teenth. He'd always kept her safe.

Annie owed him her youth, her innocence, her steadfast belief that the world was essentially a good place. When she thought of Bateman threatening her brave, strong, kind-hearted grandpa, she wanted to scream.

Instead, she sipped her coffee, allowing the rich hot brew to soothe the chill inside her. "Are there any other former gang members I should know about?"

Michael shook his head. "None of them live in this area anymore. And nobody seems to know where Bateman is staying."

"We can get an address from Chief Engstrom tomorrow." Immediately she corrected herself. "Not tomorrow because he's probably not working on a Saturday. What's the date?"

"Tomorrow is the ninth."

Only four more days until the thirteenth. She tasted her coffee again, allowing her suspicions to form into coherent thought. "Here's something that puzzles me. Bateman keeps sneaking around, harassing us. But his notes seem to say that nothing will happen until the thirteenth."

"He could be trying to put us off guard," Michael suggested. "If we don't expect him to attack until the thirteenth, we might be less cautious now."

"It's almost like he's two different people. One of them is a cruel bully, taking his revenge by scaring us. The other is cool and calculating, waiting patiently to make his move."

"I vote for cool and calculating. He's crafty, a lot smarter than you think."

"You didn't see his face tonight." She flinched at the horrible memory. "He was anything but cool."

She didn't want to meet either one of Bateman's personalities in a dark alley. Whether he was driven by psychotic rage or cleverly plotting his vengeance, Drew Bateman was a dangerous man.

Whether or not Michael was standing nearby, she needed to be prepared to protect herself against him.

THE FOLLOWING DAY, Saturday, in the afternoon, she took her gun down from the upper shelf of her bedroom closet.

Her injured arm was strong enough to hold the Glock automatic, but she needed to work on some target practice.

Now was a good time. Lionel was taking his afternoon nap. She and Michael had been outside on the front veranda, scraping away the old peeling paint to prepare for a touch-up job on the trim. But Annie had finished all the parts she could reach, and they only had one ladder, which Michael said he'd use.

Though he wouldn't like the idea of Annie going into the forest alone, she'd rather have Michael stay here and keep an eye on Lionel. Also, she wasn't sure how steady her aim would be, and she simply couldn't stand any more humiliation. The young couple she'd crashed into last night had blabbed their story, and Annie had already received a phone call from Edna Grabow, Candace's mother, warning her to be careful of a crazy bag lady who was attacking people on the streets of Bridgeport.

Bag lady, my foot. That had been a gorgeous kimono. With a quick yank, Annie adjusted the ponytail on top of her head. She packed her gun and several rounds of ammunition in a backpack and left the bedroom.

From the upstairs landing Annie heard the doorbell ring. The front door was open and the alarm was turned off because Michael had been working outside. A voice called through the screen door. "Annie, it's me. Candace."

She froze, staring down at the foyer as Michael came down the hallway from the kitchen carrying a glass of water. He opened the screen.

A beautifully tanned woman with wispy red hair leaped into his arms. Candace, the former cheerleader, had used Jake Stillwell's money well. Her "casual" shorts outfit, in complementary tones of beige and olive, draped her body elegantly. Her jewelry had the soft expensive gleam of pure gold. Her perfectly lined eyes flashed at Michael. "You turned out nicely," she said. "Very nicely."

Annie was torn. Either she could retreat to the upstairs bathroom and attempt to reinvent herself as a high-fashion model, or she could march downstairs and make sure Candace kept her distance from Michael. Annie chose the latter.

Feeling self-conscious about her loose-fitting walking shorts and a tank top that showed off a farmer's tan—the kind that stopped at her elbows—she descended the staircase. "Candace, how nice of you to drop by."

"I'm glad to see you, Annie."

Her voice sounded sincere and friendly, without a hint of phoniness. Annie wondered if Candace had changed. Had motherhood transformed her?

When they hugged, the top of Candace's head grazed her chin. Annie felt huge and gangly compared to this petite attractive woman, but her feelings weren't because of anything Candace had done or said. It was her own insecurity.

Candace asked, "How's Lionel doing?"

"He's going to be fine."

As they chatted about Lionel's physical therapy, the beginning of a real smile touched Annie's lips. Life was very strange, indeed. Here she was, talking to the most popular girl from her high school, who actually seemed interested. Candace had graduated a year ahead of Annie, and they'd never really spoken, except for the occasional "hello" in the hallway. It would be strange if, after all these years, they became friends.

"We're all so proud of you," Candace said. "You're independent. You have a career in Salem. You're really doing something with your life."

"Thanks."

"You were smart not to waste your time getting married." She edged closer to Michael. "I wish I knew how to do something more than be a wife and a mother."

As she rambled on about her children, her tennis game and her endless struggle to make a good home for her family, Annie eased back into her familiar sense of estrangement. She'd never fit in with women like Candace. They were a different breed. The popular girls became wives and mothers, and taught their own daughters how to do the same.

She watched as Candace subtly wove her spell around Michael, alternately teasing him and building him up. He seemed to be enjoying her attention. Grinning sheepishly, he rubbed his sweaty hand across the white T-shirt he was wearing to work on the veranda. His black hair was a little bit mussed. He hadn't bothered to shave this morning and had a fashionable growth of stubble on his chin.

Candace turned away from Michael and beamed at Annie. "I can't believe it, Annie. You haven't changed a bit since high school."

When Annie reached up to smooth her hair, she discovered that the ponytail had fallen apart. Her hair must be going in all directions. Of course, she wasn't wearing any makeup whatsoever. "I was just going to tidy up."

"You look fine. Carefree. Somebody as pretty as you doesn't have to spend as much time as I do with my appearance."

Annie looked down at her feet, which seemed huge in her boatlike white sneakers. She slid backward in time to her high school years when she was the not-very-popular girl who won athletic trophies but never had many dates. Except for her brief interlude with Michael, which had ended so painfully and abruptly, Annie had never felt desirable.

She glanced toward Michael. He was probably embarrassed about their fake engagement. Why did she have to be such a dork?

He set down his water glass and came toward her. His

arm glided around her waist, and his body heat melded with hers.

"You caught us at a bad time," he said to Candace. His voice was low and sexy. "Annie didn't have time to comb her hair after we were, well, you know. I can't keep my hands off this woman."

Surprised, she looked up into his bedroom eyes. When he dropped a teasing kiss upon her forehead, confidence flooded through her. Though Candace had the sort of manner that most men appreciated, Michael wanted her—Annie Callahan, female cop and former all-star basketball player.

Rising slightly on the balls of her feet, she brushed his lips with a kiss. The pressure of his hand at her waist tightened. Unexpected shivers chased up and down her spine.

"Well," Candace said, "I guess I should offer my congratulations on your engagement."

"I'm very happy." His gaze on Annie's face was hot, devouring. "I should have married Annie a long time ago."

Inspired by his example, she rested her hand on his chest possessively and stared into his dark eyes. "I had to wait until you grew up. I wanted a man, not a boy."

"Are you satisfied with what you got?"

"Very satisfied," she purred.

He turned to Candace. "It's always good to see you, but we have a lot to do today. So, we'll have to say goodbye."

"I want to throw you a party," Candace said. "To celebrate your engagement."

Annie clearly read disappointment in the redhead's expression. Apparently Candace didn't enjoy being treated like a third wheel.

"Thanks for the thought," Michael said. "We'll be in town for a month."

"I'll get back to you." Candace headed for the door. "Bye now."

As soon as the door closed behind her, Annie gave Michael a bear hug. "Thanks."

"For what?"

"For making me feel like one of the popular girls." She grinned at him. "You're good at this fake-engagement stuff."

"I'm not faking."

He ran the back of his hand across her cheek and tucked her tumbled-down hair behind her ear. Slowly he caressed the line of her throat.

She knew he was going to kiss her. This time she was ready for him. Her eyes fluttered shut and she tilted her head.

His lips closed over hers, and she leaned against him, relishing the unusual pleasure of embracing a man who was a few inches taller.

He deepened the kiss and pulled her more tightly against his muscular body. Her breasts were crushed against his chest. She rubbed up against his thighs. He was hard and strong. He was the answer to every daydream, every yearning, every fantasy.

Sensations overwhelmed her. This felt good, so very right. Her heart sang with a clarion chord that resonated through her entire body.

When he leaned away from her, she didn't want to open her eyes. She wanted to live in this lovely mysterious harmony forever.

"You liked it," he said.

"Oh, yes."

Whatever else was untrue, their kisses were not.

Chapter Seven

Annie sighted down the barrel of her Glock automatic. Fully loaded with a fifteen-round clip, the gun—which was forty percent plastic—weighed only a little over two pounds. But it felt heavy. Her muscles quivered as she held it straight out with her injured right arm extended. The challenge was to hold steady and aim.

Bracing herself for the recoil, she squeezed the trigger.

The report echoed across the logging tract. The tin can she'd been aiming at didn't move. And her arm snapped upward a few inches. "Ouch!"

She glanced over at Michael, who was sitting on a tree stump. He'd insisted on accompanying her and had arranged for one of the neighbors to stay at the house in case Lionel needed help. Michael had also promised not to comment. Right now he was biting his lower lip to keep from saying anything.

"I'm usually a real good shot," she said.

"A broken arm might tend to mess up your aim."

"It's only a hairline fracture."

But the slight recoil on firing had hurt. Gritting her teeth, Annie took aim again. The logging tract where the trees had been cleared a few years ago made an excellent firing range. She'd set up six tin cans on tree stumps at varying distances. About twenty-five yards behind her targets was a clay embankment to stop her bullets.

Again she pulled the trigger. Again she missed.

"Ouch!" She lowered her arm. This wasn't going to work.

"Can I make a suggestion?" Michael asked.

"I'd rather you didn't," she said. Annie prided herself on her marksmanship. She always scored high at the firing range.

This time she braced her right wrist with her left arm. Standing square to the targets, she bent her knees. There was still a tremor in her arm, an instinctive hesitation. Though she sighted carefully, she missed again. This time it didn't hurt as much. She squeezed off three more shots. The tin cans didn't move.

Disappointed, she paced in a little circle, kicking at the dirt, twigs and wood chips. The acrid smell of cordite masked the earthy fragrance of the forest lands that stretched behind them, thick and verdant with more trees than anyone could count.

But Annie was utterly focused on the task at hand and hardly noticed her surroundings. She wouldn't give up until she had this licked. Confidence in her ability to aim and fire was essential. If Bateman attacked, she wouldn't have time for second thoughts. She needed to react automatically.

Once again she took up her firing position.

"Use your left hand," Michael said.

"I don't do anything lefty." But she lowered the gun. "Why do you think I'd be able to aim with my left hand?"

"Firing a gun has more to do with visual coordination than muscles. You're an athlete. I'll bet your reflexes are as good on your left side as your right."

She considered his suggestion. Though she'd used a rifle before, the very first time she'd held a pistol had been at

the police academy, and she'd been a fairly good shot from
the start. Maybe the same would hold true with her left
hand. It seemed like a ridiculously simple solution.

"I'll try it." She transferred the gun to her left hand.
The grip felt strange. When she squinted down the barrel,
it felt as if she was shooting in a mirror. She fired once,
then again. And the can leapt into the air.

"I did it!"

She finished off the fifteen-round clip, making direct hits
with half her shots. Annie felt incredibly pleased with herself. While she might never use her gun against Bateman
or anyone else, it was greatly reassuring to know she was
capable of protecting herself.

She pulled the clip and reloaded. "Oh, yeah, this feels
good."

"Told you," Michael said.

He rose to his feet and stretched. The white T-shirt pulled
tight across his muscular chest. Annie liked his roughed-up
appearance today, with the stubble and the uncombed black
hair. He looked like the bad boy everyone said he was.
"How did you learn to use firearms?"

"In the navy. We had all kinds of fun weapons to play
with. From pistols to grenade launchers. Cannons. Big
guns. You'd like those."

"Size doesn't matter." She tried to leer. "But I really
prefer the big guns."

"My, my, Annie. That was *almost* a dirty joke."

"I'm not really such a prude."

"Not when you're in my arms." He winked as if they
were sharing a special secret. "Not when we kiss."

And wasn't that the truth! When Michael held her, Annie's primal instincts came to the forefront. She felt wild
and wanton and sexy. It was impossible to stop thinking
about him, about how wonderful it felt when his mouth
claimed hers. She was greedy for more embraces, more

deep kisses. "It's funny. I always thought you had to be in love to enjoy sex."

"Maybe we are," he said. "We just don't know it yet."

"There's a disturbing thought." She'd never allow herself to fall in love with a man she didn't trust. Primal urges had to do with simple biology. Depth of emotion was something else entirely. "Love isn't so easy, Michael. There needs to be caring and sharing and commitment. Two people have to…mesh."

"Like this?" He snaked his arms around her and pulled her hips tight against his. "We fit together."

"Because we're both tall."

She pushed him away. On a spring day like this, beneath a full canopy of blue sky swirled with mist, it would be easy to imagine she was in love. Beyond the cleared tract, the lush green forest beckoned with the promise of secret glens and perfect stillness. Hidden by the towering oak and pine and spruce, it would be easy to make love in the woodland.

And that wasn't going to happen.

Michael fell into step beside her as she picked her way through the cleared land to set up her cans again. She needed to fire a couple more rounds to feel competent using her left hand.

"You used to love me," he said.

"And I used to be able to shoot ten free throws without a miss. I've changed."

"Could be you're out of practice."

"Don't be silly," she said. "Falling out of love isn't like falling off a bicycle. You can't climb back on and have it be the way it was before."

"It could be better. Eleven years ago we never made love."

And she hadn't had much experience since then. She'd had two serious boyfriends in college and a hint of what

real passion was all about. But she'd never been thrilled
with the outcome. Making love had been an experiment, an
exercise to satisfy her curiosity. With Michael, she knew it
would be different. And that was exactly why she needed
to resist him. Annie didn't want her world turned upside
down.

She returned to her position, several yards away from the
cans. With the first ten shots, she picked off all six. Then
she blasted away at distant leaves and rocks. The automatic
was beginning to feel comfortable in her grasp.

Proud of herself, she turned to Michael. "Not too
shabby, huh?"

"Sure," he said, "if you can convince your assailant to
stand still and wait while you sight down the barrel."

"What do you mean?" she called over her shoulder as
she went to set up her targets again.

"Can you shoot on the run? Can you draw and fire?"

"We'll see."

For the next round she played commando. She fired from
a crouch. She took three steps and pivoted. Laughing, she
dove behind a stump, leaped out and picked off another
can.

Michael set up the scenario. "Imagine you're surrounded. Those two cans are a couple of motorcycle thugs
coming at you. The big gray rock over there is the leader.
He's a big guy, a Hell's Angel, and it's going to take two
bullets to bring him down. That midsize stump, about ten
feet away from you, is somebody armed with a knife. Go."

Running away from the knife-wielding stump, she fired
twice at the rock, then whirled and took out the stump
before nailing the two cans. She paused and blew imaginary
smoke from the end of the barrel. "The name's Annie.
Annie Oakley."

"A pistol-packin' mama."

With the next round of ammunition, Michael threw quarters in the air, and she tried to plug them before they hit the ground. He made up another scenario, involving Al Capone. Then she pretended to be the long-lost sister of the Earp brothers at the OK Corral. Target practice had never been more fun, and it was productive, too. Annie was totally at ease using her left hand.

She hadn't realized how much she needed an afternoon like this one—a chance to laugh and be goofy. Her return to Bridgeport had been too intense.

As she walked back to the car with Michael, she felt the now familiar yearning toward him. She wanted another kiss, another embrace. She wanted to make love with him. But she dreaded the aftermath, the moment when she would turn around and find that he was gone. If her emotional judgment was half as accurate as her marksmanship, she'd be in good shape.

For the rest of the afternoon she tried to reconcile her desires with logic. There could never be anything lasting between them. For one thing he lived on a boat in Seattle, and she had an apartment in Salem. But that was only a matter of location. One or both of them could move.

A more complicated problem was their diverse standards. Michael had a criminal background, and she was a cop. She wanted to believe he'd reformed, that his military experience had changed him, but there was evidence to the contrary: his late-night phone call. His inside information about Bateman in prison. The fact that he carried a gun. His strange tactic of following her in Salem, then disappearing before the cops arrived.

She didn't trust him, and that was reason enough to avoid intimacy.

But late that night, as she lay in bed, she couldn't stop thinking about his kisses. What would happen if she went downstairs to the guest bedroom and slipped into bed with him? She groaned and kicked at the sheets.

There wasn't the slightest doubt in her mind that making love with Michael would be fantastic. He was a passionate man, a natural lover. His warm sensitive caresses drove her wild. And the taste of his kisses? Oh, my! Plus, he was incredibly handsome.

The reasons for making love mounted. Her grandpa approved of Michael. The whole town—with the possible exception of Candace—seemed delighted by their engagement. Everybody expected them to be sharing a bed.

When her bare feet touched the floor in her bedroom, her decision was made. Annie the Athlete was ready to run the one-hundred-yard dash in under nine-point-seven seconds, down the staircase and into Michael's bedroom. She'd dive onto his bed like a volleyball player going for a save.

Whoa! She gripped the edge of the mattress, anchoring herself in place. It was time for a reality check. They weren't really engaged. They weren't in love. And she still didn't trust him. Michael had already broken her heart once in this lifetime, and she wasn't about to go through that agony again.

However, if she made love to him with no expectation of more than only one night, she couldn't be disappointed. This didn't have to be a lifetime commitment.

Before she could change her mind, she flew down the staircase, rounded the banister and ran along the hallway. Her hair streamed behind her like a banner. Her feet were light as the wind. Breathing hard, she pushed open the door to the guest bedroom. It was time. Finally she would consummate the passion she'd felt for him so many years ago.

The forest-green comforter on his bed was smoothly tucked into place. "Michael?"

He was gone.

She turned on the overhead light. His shaving equipment was on the dresser. His clothes were still in the drawers and closet—a sure indication he was planning to come back. Apparently his absence was temporary. He'd slipped out for another late-night…what? Another mysterious phone call?

Sad and angry, she closed his door and meandered back through the kitchen, the hall and up the staircase to her lonely bedroom, where she tried to make peace with the overwrought anticipation churning through her body. Perhaps it was fortunate that he hadn't been there. Quite obviously Michael had some nefarious agenda that caused him to sneak out of the house.

Annie ought to be thanking her lucky stars she hadn't fallen into bed with him. She'd been spared a ton of heartache.

But only one thought centered in her brain, pounding as endlessly as the Pacific surf on the shore. She wanted him. She longed for his touch. And her desires would not be fulfilled tonight.

ON SUNDAY AFTERNOON, the tenth of June, Annie was surprised to find Police Chief Engstrom standing on her grandpa's doorstep. Though Annie had offered to come to the police station to officially file a restraining order against Bateman, the chief said he might as well drop by, and his Sundays were usually free. "I owe it to Lionel," he said. "After your grandpa's years of service to the community, coming over here is the least I can do."

She welcomed him inside, noting with some dismay that he wasn't carrying anything that looked like paperwork, such as the proper forms for filing a complaint. "I'm sure you have things to do on your day off, Chief. So let's get started. I want to file—"

"How's Lionel doing?" He craned his neck to look up the staircase. "Is he awake?"

"Yes, but—"

"Do you mind if I run up and say hello?"

"Be my guest."

Though she was anxious to set the legal wheels in motion, it was good for her grandpa to see old friends and acquaintances like Engstrom. Lionel was getting stronger every day and was able to move around for brief stints without using the walker. Since Michael had come to stay, her grandpa was more motivated. Not only did he follow his daily physical-therapy schedule, but he was careful about his nutrition, trying to eat the right foods.

When they entered the bedroom, he was sitting in the easy chair beside the bay window, talking to Michael. He greeted the chief with a wave of his hand. "Pull up a seat, Engstrom. I was just telling Mikey about the land I've got down by the river."

"By the old abandoned bridge," Engstrom said. "It's a pretty piece of acreage, Lionel. But you've got to worry about floods."

"The river would have to rise twenty-five feet," Lionel said. "My property is on a bluff."

"You never know. If I were you, I'd think twice before I started building there."

But Lionel had already considered his plans. He'd even applied for the necessary permits. While he outlined his ideas to Engstrom, Annie studied Michael's profile. She'd avoided talking to him this morning because she wasn't sure how to broach the subject of his absence last night. Explaining her presence in his room could be embarrassing.

"Annie," her grandpa said, "would you fetch me something to drink? I'd like some of that bottled water."

He'd been advised to cut down on his caffeine and was taking the instruction seriously. "I'll bring it right up," she said.

"Coffee for me, if you have some made," Engstrom said. "Black."

Michael offered, "I'll give you a hand."

"Not necessary," she said coolly.

"But I want to."

Engstrom chuckled. "Isn't that the way with young lovers? They don't want to be apart for even a minute."

Trapped by the lie of their engagement, she forced a smile at Michael as they left the room together.

In the kitchen he said, "Something's wrong."

"You know what it is." She pulled out a tray and began putting together the drinks and a fruit snack of grapes and sliced cantaloupe. "You went out again last night."

"I tried to be quiet. Sorry if I woke you."

"Where did you go?"

"The tavern."

"Again?" She whacked the cantaloupe with a sharp steel blade. "Michael, do you have a drinking problem?"

"Don't even joke about that. My father was an alcoholic. I never touch booze."

That was a wise decision, but she wasn't in the mood to pay him any compliments. Last night had been a big buildup without the payoff. She'd expected ecstasy, and she got…nothing.

"Did you make another phone call?" She confronted him with knife in hand. "Was it necessary to find a public phone to contact your first mate?"

"I was looking for answers, talking to the locals, trying to find out where Bateman is staying in town."

"He has an address. He needs one for his parole officer."

"But he doesn't live there," Michael said.

Annie dropped the knife on the counter with a clatter and proceeded to arrange the food and drinks on the tray. "Did you find out where Bateman was really living?"

"No."

"Why didn't you tell me where you were going?" It

sounded like a phony excuse to her. "I'd have come along."

"What's the real problem, Annie?"

"I don't appreciate your habit of sneaking around. It makes me think you have something to hide, some kind of secret."

"Get used to it, Annie. I'm not going to check in with you every minute."

With arms folded across his chest, he was the very portrait of muleheadedness. But if he thought he could match her stubbornness, he had another think coming. She imitated his posture mockingly. "So, you don't want to check in? Don't want to let me know where you're going?"

"I don't need a leash."

"Well, that's fine with me. I don't care where you are every minute or what you're doing or who you're talking to. I don't care if you're going into town to hook up with Candace or to plan a robbery. Matter of fact, I don't care about you at all."

She flipped her hand dismissively to illustrate exactly how much he meant to her. Then she turned away.

Irritation, disappointment and a whole lot of frustration filled her. Her stomach knotted with an insatiable hunger that wasn't about food. But how could she explain? Why should she? "Would you carry up the tray?"

She led the way back to Lionel's room, sat on the edge of his bed and listened while the men talked about land, the community and the batting averages of the Seattle Mariners.

Finally she cut in. "Excuse me, Chief Engstrom, but I'd like to know the results of your investigation."

"About the broken window?"

"Yes, sir."

"Well, now." He looked away from her and made eye contact with Lionel. "Sorry to say, we haven't got much to go on. There's no evidence except for the brick, and we couldn't get any prints off that.''

''What about witnesses?'' Annie asked.

''My boys checked with the neighbors. Nobody saw anything.'' He kept talking to her grandpa, pointedly ignoring Annie. ''Let me be frank with you, Lionel. If Bateman means to cause trouble, it's going to be near impossible for me to provide protection.''

''Why is that?'' Lionel asked.

''I don't have enough officers to spare an extra man.''

''Or woman,'' Annie muttered under her breath, even though she knew Engstrom's staff of five officers and a 911 dispatcher was entirely male.

''But I like your new security system.'' Now he was talking to Michael. Apparently he didn't intend to include her in this discussion at all. The police chief was a good old boy who preferred dealing with men, even though Annie was a law-enforcement professional.

''The alarm rings through to the police station,'' Michael said. ''Plus, it sets off a siren that should wake up everybody on Myrtlewood Lane.''

''Very good.'' Engstrom's chin bobbed. Annie could only see his profile because he'd literally turned his back to her. That was a mistake! She hadn't succeeded as a female officer by being coy.

She rose to her feet and tapped the face of her wristwatch. ''I'm so sorry, Chief Engstrom, but it's time for Lionel and Michael to get started with Lionel's afternoon exercises.''

''Hold your horses, Annie.'' Engstrom chuckled. ''Can't you see we're talking?''

''I see that quite clearly,'' she said. ''Would you please come downstairs? I think both Lionel and Michael would agree that it's far more appropriate for you to talk to me.''

''But we're discussing security matters,'' he said.

"As well we should be." She had his attention now. "And I want an update on further measures you intend to take in this investigation."

He frowned at Lionel. "Is this right? Do you want me to talk to Annie?"

Lionel gave her a broad smile as he nodded. "My little girl is pretty darn good at taking care of me."

Engstrom turned to Michael. "What about you?"

He silently shifted his gaze toward Annie.

A taut smile stretched Engstrom's mouth but didn't reach his eyes. "That must be how they operate in Salem, eh? The women give the orders."

"It's not really different from Bridgeport," she said. "The police handle security, and I am, as you well know, a cop."

She was a competent intelligent cop, and Engstrom needed to understand that he was dealing with her. She'd get him alone downstairs if she had to handcuff him and drag him down the stairs.

"All right, Annie. Let's go." He stood and cleared his throat. "I'll see you boys later."

He barely had a chance to seat himself at the kitchen table before she presented him with a sealed plastic bag containing the little Cinderella statuette. "I'd like you to test this for fingerprints. I found it in the house before we put in the security system."

"Okay." He leaned both elbows on the tabletop. "What exactly is bothering you, Missy?"

"The brick," she said. "There was a date written on it—six, thirteen. June thirteenth. Do you know what that date refers to?"

He shook his head. "Can't say that I do."

"How long have you been an officer in Bridgeport?"

"Nearly fifteen years," he said. "I've been the chief of police for five years come August. Why do you ask?"

"Eleven years ago on June thirteenth, there was an incident involving a gang of teenagers from Wayside. They were apprehended near the abandoned bridge."

"I remember," he said. "It's not far from where your grandpa has his property."

Annie nodded. She hadn't made that connection before. It was a rather chilling coincidence. "Tell me what you remember."

"I wasn't directly involved," he said. "The sting operation was run by the county sheriff in Wayside. Bateman wounded an officer. That's why he went to prison. And I seem to recollect that your boyfriend was involved."

"We've spoken about it," she said. "But I'd like to hear your perspective as an insider."

"Michael was only seventeen. I think he got off with nothing more than a slap on the wrist. All the boys did, except for Bateman and one other kid whose name I can't recall." He paused and she noticed a flicker of emotion across his face. His clean-shaven jaw tightened. "It was a damn shame."

"What was?"

"A girl got killed that night. Her name was Marie."

He glanced down at his hands, studying his fingertips and scowling ferociously. This unexpected display of emotion elevated him in Annie's opinion. He might not be much of a cop, but at least he cared about the victims. "What can you tell me about Marie Cartier?"

"She was pregnant at the time she was murdered."

Annie hadn't known about the pregnancy. It made Marie's death that much more tragic.

When Engstrom looked at her again, his face was once again impassive. "How is the date on the brick connected to this sorry incident?"

"The date has significance to Bateman," she said. "It's when we think he'll make his final move."

"And what do you expect this final move to be?"

She didn't know. Bateman's campaign of harassment and petty vandalism wasn't a good indicator. "It might be serious."

"Then you'd be smart to get yourselves out of town that day," he said. "Hole up someplace safe."

"Lionel won't want to run away," she said. "Neither will Michael."

"It doesn't seem to me that you have much trouble getting those two gentlemen to do exactly what you want. You've got them wrapped around your little finger, Annie."

Oh, how she wished that was true. More than anything, she wanted to keep her grandpa out of harm's way. That stubborn old buzzard was the only family she had left, and she wanted him to be safe and happy. And Michael? Even though she was irritated with him, she would never wish him ill.

"I might be able to help," Engstrom said.

"How?"

"On June thirteenth I could have Bateman arrested on some simple charge, like loitering or a traffic violation. I can keep him locked up for twenty-four hours."

"I don't think that would stop him." Bateman had been plotting his revenge for ten years. One night in jail would not deter him.

"I could cause some trouble with his parole officer. I might be able to get him confined for a couple of weeks."

"And then he'd be right back here."

A temporary solution wouldn't work. Besides, Annie didn't like the idea of trumped-up charges. Harassment was the worst sort of police work. If she started having Bateman arrested on fake charges, she'd be sinking to his level.

"Damn it, Annie. You're making this hard." His voice

sounded a harsh impatient note. "Let me take care of Bateman in my own way."

"We'll play by the rules," she said. "I want a legitimate restraining order, advising Bateman to stay one hundred feet away from me and Lionel."

"I'll put through the paperwork," Engstrom said. "But I don't need to tell you that restraining orders are near impossible to enforce. We don't have the manpower."

"I know," she said.

"From what I understand, he's already attacked you once. Isn't that how you got your arm busted?"

"I wasn't ready for him. Now I am."

"You better be damn sure you're ready." His eyes shone with suppressed hostility. He leaned forward, tapping on the table to emphasize his words. "You and Lionel and Michael could all be murdered in your beds. You understand me, Missy? And I don't want that to happen on my watch."

Why was he so angry at her? Because she was a woman? "If Bateman breaks a law and there's forensic evidence to convict him, I want him charged and arrested. Otherwise, no."

"Hell, Annie, you could get yourself hurt even worse this time. I heard he came after you with a club."

"A baseball bat."

Annie blinked. In the back of her mind, she remembered the pelting rain, the reflection of streetlights on slick asphalt and the helplessness. A chill slithered up her spine. She could feel the fear coming closer.

"Bateman's a rough customer," Engstrom said. "Don't you try to face him alone."

"I won't," she promised quickly. Her heart took a sudden lurch. A strange darkness shimmered around the edges of her peripheral vision. Was she going to faint? *No, not now.* Not in front of Engstrom. She wanted him to leave before she was overcome. ''Please keep me informed of any progress. I'll stop by tomorrow and sign that restraining order.''

''If that's the way you want it.''

''I do.'' She rose unsteadily to her feet. ''Thanks, Chief.''

Annie wasn't sure how she managed to walk down the hall behind him. She didn't hear herself saying goodbye. But Engstrom was gone, heading along the sidewalk toward his white police sedan. She closed the front door.

The sound of thrumming rain consumed her. And it was as dark as night. Her breath caught in her throat. She was gasping, choking on her own unreasoning panic. She felt herself sink helplessly to the floor in the foyer.

Strangely detached, she was aware of being unconscious. *This must be what blacking-out feels like.* Nothing to worry about. This was only a psychological reaction to being assaulted. She'd be all right in a minute. If only the world would stop twirling... If only she could catch her breath...

Chapter Eight

Slowly her eyelids lifted. Her vision was blurred in crazy overlapping images. Annie was seeing double as if her eyes were operating separately from each other.

She tried to focus on Michael's face, but there were two of him. They were on the floor with her. Two Michaels cradled her in their arms. How did she get here? What had happened to her? Annie remembered the rain and the baseball bat, but she was indoors now, in her grandpa's house.

She squeezed her eyes shut, concentrated hard and opened them again. But there were still two Michaels.

She felt strangely unalarmed, and her brain free-associated, meandering lightly through synapse and cerebellum. Though she knew it didn't make sense, Annie thought she might be seeing the truth. There really were two Michaels. One was a heroic upstanding citizen, former U.S. Navy, the respected captain of a charter vessel. The other was a bad boy, always getting into trouble, telling lies. Making her laugh.

Aloud she wondered, "Which one do I like best?"

"Which one of what, Annie?"

"You," she said. Her mouth felt dry and she licked her lips. "This probably isn't happening."

When she reached up to straighten the collar of his denim work shirt, the two Michaels blended into one solid handsome man. Much better! Just above the top button, she saw a hint of crisp, curling black chest hair. Her hand lightly massaged beneath his collarbone. His skin was warm and smooth but not soft.

Annie inhaled the scent of him. It was less a fragrance than a warmth. Like chocolate-chip cookies fresh from the oven with the gooey chocolate melting over brown-sugared dough.

"Annie?"

"What's up, cookie?"

His eyebrows lowered, and he looked much too serious and concerned. "Cookie?"

"Like the Pillsbury Doughboy."

"You think I'm a doughboy?"

How silly! She felt the corners of her mouth curving in a grin. "You're too hard to be a doughboy. You're Mister Hardbody. Nice body."

She relaxed into this strange limbo state between sleep and consciousness. Her responsibilities and worries seemed very faraway. All her barriers were down.

"What happened?" Michael asked.

She placed her index finger across his lips. "Hush."

"Annie, I'm worried about you." His voice was low and gentle. "I should get you to a hospital."

"Oh, dear. That won't do." She didn't want to go to a hospital. Struggling, she managed to sit up on her own. Though still encircled by his wonderful strong arms, she was sitting upright on the floor of the foyer. "You see? I'm okay."

Her double vision was replaced by sharp visual contrasts. Through the foyer archway, she saw the parlor and the brown clawfoot sofa and a red leather cover of a book on the table. Everything looked so clear, as if she was seeing it for the very first time.

Her gaze lingered on an enlargement of a sunlit photograph of her mother and father at the windswept rugged beach near Tillamook. They were smiling and gazing into each other's eyes. A handsome couple, they appeared very much in love. Behind them was the ocean, the Pacific, that had taken them away from Annie forever.

An old familiar ache rose up inside her. Oh, how she missed them! She missed hearing her mother's lyrical voice as she read poetry to Annie about exotic distant places, like big-shouldered Chicago and the canals of Venice. If her mother hadn't died when Annie was ten, she might have learned how to put on makeup and what to wear on a date. She might have been a whole different person—a woman who knew how to have a relationship, a husband, a child of her own.

"You're going to be all right," Michael said gently. "Do you think you can stand up now?"

He'd left her and joined the navy. In a way the sea had taken him, too. And now he was a captain. "You're careful, aren't you? On your charter boat?"

He cocked his head to one side, eyeing her curiously. "Don't worry about me."

"It's just that my mother and father were on a boat, their boat, and—"

The thunderstorm exploded in her mind, and she was deafened. Some words should never be spoken. Some thoughts should never be heard. "—there was bad weather, gale-force winds. They radioed for help, but no one could come."

They'd tried to return, tried to come back to her, but the wind and waves had been too much for their small vessel. Twenty-foot waves, the Coastguard had said.

"Almost made it to shore," she whispered. "The Coastguard thought they might have bottomed out on a rocky shoal. The boat shattered, and they were gone."

The only wreckage ever found was a piece of wood with

the brass plaque commemorating the date they'd launched their craft. "Six, twenty-five, seventy-six. That was all that was left. And we used it to mark their graves."

Annie closed her eyes and buried her face against Michael's chest. Hot tears squeezed between her lashes, but she wasn't really crying. Annie Callahan never wept.

She felt herself being lifted from the floor. Michael held her, cuddled against his chest. It was absurd to let him carry her like a child, but she offered no objection as he moved her to the brown velvet sofa and helped her stretch out on the tired old cushions. He placed a needlepoint pillow behind her head. Her grandmother had done the delicate needlework. Leaning against it was like resting on memories.

Enough of that! Annie closed the door on remembrance, sorrow and fear. She couldn't stand being in a place where thoughts popped up, unbidden. The only way she could navigate her life was to stay away from memories, to be in control. In the here and now. Being conscious was her refuge.

With a flick of her hand, she wiped the moisture from her eyes. Then she looked directly at him. Michael wasn't a cookie. He didn't have two heads. There was goodness inside him and mischief, too. "I'm all right now," she said.

He didn't believe her. She could see it in his eyes.

"Really," she said. For more than half her life, she'd been dismissing her memories. "Nothing to worry about. I'm fine."

"I'm sorry, Annie."

"So am I, but I won't dwell on it. Grandpa always says that you can't move forward if you're always looking back."

"Does he?" Michael felt a twinge of irritation at Lionel. He'd never allowed Annie to process her feelings about her parents' death. "It must have been hard for him, too."

"Yes," she said. "Could I have a glass of water?"

"I remember when your parents were killed. The whole town was in mourning." Everyone had attended a brief ceremony at the cemetery and had seen the plaque that marked two empty graves. The day was sunny. He remembered the light reflecting off Annie's long blond hair. "You didn't cry. You held your grandpa's hand and neither of you wept."

"Tears wouldn't bring them back," she said. "I really don't like talking about this, Michael."

"But you're reliving the tragedy every day of your life."

She shook her head, confused. "What do you mean?"

"Your parents were lost at sea. No one could help them. You said it yourself." Her expression lacked emotion, and he knew she would not allow herself to return to those memories. "And now? What do you do for a living?"

"I'm a cop."

"But you're not like Engstrom or Bobby Janowski. You didn't become a cop to exercise authority over people."

"Of course not. I became a cop so I could help people."

"To serve and protect," he said. For Annie the emphasis was on protection. It was her mission in life to take care of people who had nowhere else to turn. "By rescuing other people, you rescue your parents."

She folded her hands on her lap and went very still. Her feelings were encased in a concrete cocoon, and Michael knew he would have to break that shell with a jackhammer if he ever wanted to know the real Annie Callahan.

"May I please have a glass of water?"

Her tone told him that she would not speak of her sorrow anymore. He wished he could tell her that he understood, that he had also lost someone close to him. But the portrait of his tragedy was far different from hers, colored in shades of guilt.

Michael rose from the chair beside the sofa. "I'll be right back with your water. Are you going to be all right?"

She gave a terse nod.

"Are you comfortable on the sofa?"

"Not really. It's like stretching out on a sack of rocks."

"Would you like to move to—"

"I'm fine, Michael."

She watched him leave the room, then closed her eyes, trying to reclaim what was left of her sanity and waiting for the last quivers of panic to become still once more.

Though she'd never thought of her career as a way to rescue her parents, it made sense. As soon as Michael said the words, she knew he was right. She needed to protect— not only the people who were close to her, but the whole world.

Everyone must be safe from harm. No one should have to suffer loss and misery. And she wanted this so much that she needed a gun and a badge to fight the bad people, the bad things. But her heart told a different story. Solace was even more important than protection.

Tragedies happened, and Annie couldn't save the world. But she could help people, children who had lost their parents like she had. She could offer them comfort and empathy.

Michael returned with a glass of water which he placed on the coffee table. "Use a coaster," she said automatically.

"You must be feeling better. You're giving orders."

He pulled a chair close to the sofa and stared deeply into her eyes.

"Now what?" she demanded.

"Your eyes seem to be tracking now. You were unconscious there for a few minutes. You want to tell me about it?"

Her natural inclination was to keep her own counsel. She'd always been wary of revealing too much about herself. But the barrier she used to protect herself had a crack in it.

"I was scared." The words tumbled out. "All of a sudden, out of nowhere, I remembered the attack in the parking lot. The rain. It sounded so loud."

"Is this the first time?"

She shook her head. "I had the same sensation when I first encountered Bateman on the sidewalk outside the house."

"What happened that time?"

"You showed up, and I was so angry about the cavalier way you were treating me that the fear went away."

Though he hadn't intended to rescue her from that dark and scary place, his presence pulled her out of limbo and back to reality. And that was where she wanted to stay— in the real world where things made sense.

She took a sip of water and looked at the man who sat in a chair beside the sofa, regarding her steadily. He seemed very stable, and suddenly she was glad he'd come to stay with them. She needed his presence.

"I can understand how seeing Bateman might have affected you," he said. "But what happened this time? Was there a trigger?"

"An innocent comment from Engstrom. He mentioned the attack, and my heart started pounding." She rested her hand on her breast. "I couldn't breathe. It was like I flew straight out of my body. Then there was darkness all around."

She took another drink of water before continuing. "I've heard about things like this. Panic attacks. It's not uncommon for victims to have flashbacks after a traumatic event."

In her work Annie had spent a lot of time with victims' assistance counselors, and she admired their ability to help. Mostly they dealt with women who had been raped or beaten. "It's strange," she said. "I've never thought of myself as a victim before."

"We're all victims at one time or another."

Suddenly she remembered that Lionel was upstairs, and Michael was supposed to be putting him through his paces with the physical therapy. "What happened to your workout with Grandpa?"

"He was tired, Annie. And it really wasn't time for his exercises when you used that excuse to get Engstrom alone. He went back to the bed by himself without the walker. And now he's taking a nap."

"Please don't tell Grandpa about this. He'd be upset if he knew I collapsed. I can't believe I fainted like a..."

"A girl? Like a regular human being?" Michael rested a hand on her shoulder. "It's okay, Annie. You don't have to be the Rock of Gibraltar. You're entitled to have occasional weaknesses."

"But I hate being out of control. If I fall apart, who's going to take care of Grandpa?"

"You've always protected him, haven't you?"

"Of course not. It was the other way around," she said. "He took me in after my parents died. He watched over me."

"And you never told him when you were in pain. Or angry. Or hurt. Because you didn't want to upset him."

"Was that wrong?"

"I'll bet it was hard."

He was right. Physically Annie never had many problems. Emotionally she'd had to fight all the feelings that built up inside her and couldn't be shared. Years of disappointment and suppressed hurt churned relentlessly inside her like the hurricane-tossed sea.

"My parents," she said quietly. "I never really mourned them. Maybe I didn't know how."

"It's hard to lose someone you love," he said. "Someone who's a part of you."

His voice held an understanding that went beyond sensible comprehension. When she looked into Michael's dark eyes, she saw a reflection of her own endless abyss. "You lost someone, too. Who was it?"

He shook his head, and she knew he wouldn't tell her. He guarded his secrets jealously, carefully. He concealed his past and surrounded his present motivations in half-truths and mystery.

She asked the question that had plagued her since she'd seen him walk out of her grandpa's house and confront Bateman. "Who are you, Michael Slade?"

Was he still her ardent young suitor, the first man she ever really kissed? She wondered if he knew when he broke her heart, if he could hear her cries from a distance. He might be a young offender grown into a hardened criminal. Or he might be a brave sea captain. "Will you ever tell me? Will I ever really know who you are?"

"I'm just a man."

Complicated and simple, sullen and teasing, every time she thought she knew the answer, he showed another facet of himself.

But he couldn't hide himself forever. She intended to find out about his midnight walks, jailhouse contacts and phone calls from a public booth. Annie had connections, too. And she would use them to uncover Michael's secrets.

LATE THAT NIGHT, after Annie and her grandpa had gone to bed, Michael closed the door to the guest bedroom and took out his cell phone. Though he'd been instructed to make contact only on a public telephone line, today's events qualified as an emergency. There was no way in hell he'd leave Annie alone tonight.

Her collapse this afternoon worried him. For the rest of

the day he'd been watching her for physical symptoms—like dizziness or headache—something that indicated a delayed reaction to the concussion she sustained when attacked in the parking lot. But she hadn't complained. In fact, she'd been energetic, even chipper. Therefore, he didn't believe her collapse was the result of her injury.

Her panic attack had been exactly that—an attack of fear so intense that she'd blacked out. All her normal defenses had gone on the blink, and he'd glimpsed her naked vulnerability. He had seen the terrible sorrow she felt when her parents were lost at sea. It must have been hard for a ten-year-old girl to be brought up by a cranky football coach, hanging out with a bunch of dumb jocks.

To his chagrin, Michael had been blind to her tragedy. He was so involved with his own problems that he couldn't see Annie as anything other than a blond princess who lived in an orderly castle and wanted for nothing. She was good at hiding her pain.

Watching her this evening, while she picked out paint colors and tried to convince Lionel to replace the lumpy brown sofa in the parlor, he never would've guessed at all the turmoil inside her.

She'd been laughing, teasing, weirdly energized. And that worried him, too. What was Annie up to? The last time she'd taken off on her own, she'd gone running through town in her nightclothes and almost been caught by Bateman. Michael didn't want her going off half-cocked on an investigation that could put her at serious risk.

He punched in the number on his cell phone and waited. As soon as the call was picked up, he said, "This is Ahab. I'm talking on my unsecured cell phone."

"Why?"

"I can't leave this location,"

"Are you in danger, Ahab?"

"No, it's nothing like that. I'm concerned about—"

"Unsecured line," the disembodied voice interrupted. "Let's make it quick. New information— You might be exposed. An official source in Salem made inquiries about you."

That had to be somebody Annie knew from the Salem police department. Aha! She was looking into his background. Apparently that was her new game plan. "Anything else?"

"No further connections. We still don't have an address."

Michael had expected as much. They'd known from the start that tracing Bateman's movements and contacts would be difficult if he went to Bridgeport, where strangers were regarded with suspicion. That was one of the reasons Michael drew the assignment of keeping tabs on Bateman, who was known by the code name Minnow. He was one of the small fish—the bait—who would lead to a bigger catch.

Michael didn't know the identity of the big fish, referred to as Moby Dick. He assumed—because he was on loan to the FBI—that the big fish was involved in organized crime or the smuggling of illegal materials, such as drugs or firearms. But Michael really didn't care to know. His assignment was to keep an eye on Bateman and report all contacts, and his job was immeasurably easier because Bateman was following *him*.

Normally Michael worked with the federal marshals, but he wasn't really a cop. He was recruited through the bureaucracy of naval intelligence to be a captain. His charter boat was used as a safe house for protected witnesses.

"What's the current status on *Rosebud?*" he asked.

"No passengers until after the twentieth."

"Thanks and good night."

He disconnected the call, relieved that there were no new disasters looming on the horizon. At the same time he was disappointed that there were no new developments. Every night when he called in, he hoped to hear that his assignment was over and Bateman had been arrested again.

He wanted the threat to be over. And, in an unexpected way, he found himself dreading the discovery of information that might implicate other people in Bridgeport. Though he didn't give a damn about the town, Lionel loved this community and so did Annie. They'd be unhappy if this little bump in the road turned out to be a receiving port for illegal substances.

Michael stripped naked and crawled between the sheets. It felt good to get into bed, instead of hanging out at the local tavern, trying to read clues into a dart game and make dark connections from a casual conversation.

Last night Bateman had been at the tavern, and Michael had hoped to follow him home. The biggest question thus far in his investigation was Bateman's address. He'd given his parole officer the name of a motel in Wayside where he checked for messages, but he wasn't living there.

Michael had left the tavern early and positioned his Beamer to stake out Bateman's pickup, which was parked in the lot behind the tavern. The pickup hadn't moved. An hour later, when Michael went back inside, he learned that Bateman left shortly after he did. Either he was out roaming the streets and howling at the moon, or he had a place to stay in downtown Bridgeport, within walking distance of the bar.

Or maybe he was tailing Michael.

It was another long night of learning nothing. Nothing! Michael rolled over on the bed. There had to be a better way to make a living than chasing after scum like Bateman and reporting to somebody who sounded like a computer, only not as friendly. He was tired of working undercover.

There were benefits, for sure. He loved being captain of a seventy-foot sailing vessel, having a nice car and nice condo, provided by the secret service to suit his image as a wealthy playboy sailor. But he wearied of the tension, of never having anything—anyone—he could call his own.

The thrill of the chase was gone. He no longer enjoyed the game, the constant state of alert when protected passengers were on board. Most of these witnesses were criminals themselves, not admirable people. They whined about the food and the rocking of the boat. They knew nothing about sailing.

His life felt like a monotone, and he wanted a symphony.

He wanted to take Annie out on *Rosebud* and sail with her through the Mariannas. He wanted to see the Pacific winds whipping through her hair, and he wanted to make love to her in his cozy, wood-paneled cabin.

His gaze drifted to the ceiling. She was so close, only a staircase away. But he was fairly sure that if he popped into her bedroom naked, she'd shoot off his toe or another more central appendage.

He would wait, be patient.

Again he shifted in the bed, his solitary bed. So, Annie was investigating his background. He wondered what she hoped to find.

ON THE MORNING of Monday, June the eleventh, after Sam arrived, Michael and Annie prepared to leave the house. He had already set the alarm, and they were on their way out the door when the telephone rang.

"I'll get it," she said.

He closed the door so the alarm wouldn't go off. Annie had been particularly alert about phone calls since she'd started investigating him. But this time she uttered a series of *hellos* and slammed down the receiver. "Nobody there. That's the third or fourth call I've gotten like that."

Michael assumed the calls were for him. If he'd answered, there would have been a one-word message regarding his mission. "Probably a wrong number."

"Or Bateman," she said. "Should I try star-six-nine to see what number he was calling from?"

"Sure." If Michael was lucky today, the call *would* have been from Bateman and *might* have rung through, and he *might* have found out where Bateman was holed up.

She punched in the numbers, held the receiver to her ear and waited. "It's taking a long time," she said.

If the call was from the FBI, it would route through several electronically patched numbers, ultimately ending by being untraceable or by disconnecting.

"Hello?" she said into the receiver. "Did you call me?"

She frowned at Michael as she apologized for the ring and set down the phone.

"Who was it?" he asked.

"The 911 dispatcher at the police station." She shrugged. "The wires must have gotten crossed."

Or else somebody in FBI communications was enjoying a little joke. Michael plugged the code into the security alarm, and they whisked out the front door.

On Main Street, he opted for a parking space by the curb. "Okay, Annie. What all do we have to do?"

She consulted a written list. "Pharmacy. Hardware store. And police station."

Though they might have accomplished the tasks more quickly if they divided her list, Michael wasn't about to let Annie float around town by herself, especially not since he had reason to believe that Bateman was living down here. He held the door for her at the corner drugstore with the soda fountain at the front. Like the last time they'd been in this establishment, three customers occupied the stools. They might have even been the *same* customers.

"Soda?" he asked her.

"No, but that reminds me. I'm running low on choco-

late.'' In the candy aisle, she tossed an extra-large Ghira-
delli bar into her shopping basket. ''I need more when I'm
stressed.''

They left her grandpa's prescription at the pharmacy
counter and headed toward the police station, which was
housed in the three-story, white clapboard courthouse with
a bell tower on top. Formerly used as a meeting place, the
courthouse was perched on a hill. The lawn, like everything
else in the town, seemed overgrown and in need of tending.

''This is where your grandpa had his office,'' Michael
said.

''The municipal judge is still here. And the mayor and
the city councilmen. And the police station. With all those
supposedly responsible people, you'd think they could
manage to keep the place looking tidier,'' she said, stooping
to pick up a gum wrapper on the front stairs and toss it into
the trash can at the door. ''You'd think they were actually
busy.''

The police station was the first door on the right. Michael
took a seat on an oak pew by the door while Annie talked
to the dispatcher. When she came back over to him, she
was frowning. ''Engstrom isn't here, but he's expected
back in fifteen minutes.''

''We can wait.''

''I really wanted to get back to the house and talk with
Sam before she left.''

When she cocked an eyebrow at him, Michael could see
the next question coming. Before she even proposed that
he finish the errands, he answered, ''We're staying together.''

''I really appreciate your protection,'' she said. ''But I'm
in a police station. What could happen to me here?''

Though he was uncomfortable letting her out of his sight
even for a brief period, Michael had to admit she had a

point. "Promise to wait for me here. Don't go out on the street by yourself."

"It's a promise." She held out another list. "Here's what I need from the hardware store. Make sure the paint is the exact color."

Before he left her, Michael leaned over and brushed a light kiss over her cheek. "To keep up appearances," he whispered in her ear. "We are engaged, you know."

"Yes," she whispered back. "I know."

Out on the street, his thoughts turned again toward Bateman. Where the hell was the guy living? Michael glanced up at the second floors above the storefronts, some of which had obviously been converted to apartments, for curtains and shades covered the windows. A few of the big old houses at the edge of Main Street were listed as bed-and-breakfast inns, which was, in this instance, a quaint name for rooming houses with shared bathrooms.

There weren't any actual motels in Bridgeport. In the old days, when the logging companies were busy, the extra lumberjacks stayed in barracks out by the mills. Those structures were deserted now, but it was possible that Bateman had set up camp in one of these ramshackle dormitory-style buildings.

More likely Bateman had imposed himself on a local contact in town. When he'd been in prison, he'd received phone calls from public phones throughout Bridgeport and Wayside.

At the hardware store, Michael showed Annie's paint samples to the clerk, who hemmed and hawed and finally said, "Well, now, mixing up that paint is going to take me a while."

"I'll wait." Michael looked around. There was no one else in the store, and this guy was complaining about mixing paint. No wonder this town was going to hell. "Do you own this place?"

"My uncle." He picked up a can of matte white and stood there. "But we're not doing too well. Everybody goes out to the malls. If it wasn't for the gun sales—"

"You sell guns here?" Michael was suddenly alert.

"Mostly hunting rifles," he said. "But we've got handguns, too. Revolvers and automatics. Ammo."

Though an ex-con like Bateman could easily pick up an illegal weapon in a larger city, Michael hadn't thought the same was true in Bridgeport. Obviously he was wrong. The local hardware store was a dealer. "You get started with the paint. I'll find the other stuff."

"People like to have a handgun for protection," the clerk said. He waved toward the front door. "Hi, Candace. How's your mother?"

"She's fine."

Candace swooped into the hardware store. She fluttered a limp hand at the clerk and greeted Michael with a supposedly friendly hug that made him aware of all her assets.

"Where's Annie?" she asked.

"We split up to do errands." Not wanting Candace to get the idea that he was on his own or in any way interested in being with her, he added, "But she should be here any second."

"For example," the clerk announced, "Candace here bought a handgun just yesterday."

"I was so frightened," she said. "Did you know there was some crazy bag lady jumping out of bushes and scaring people?"

Michael nodded. "So I've heard."

"I don't have a man to protect me."

"You have children," Michael said. "I hope you keep your weapons in a safe place."

"Sure do." She patted her beige leather purse.

"Swell." For some reason, Michael hadn't considered the possibility that half the citizens of Bridgeport might be carrying concealed weapons. And one of them might be involved with Bateman. He wondered if Candace had a permit.

She flapped her eyelashes. "Maybe you can help me. It's so hard for a woman on her own to manage all the house repairs."

"What do you need?"

Digging into her purse, she produced a common three-hole hinge. "I have to replace this, and I just don't know where to find one exactly like it."

In less than a minute they'd found what she was looking for. But that wasn't the end of the conversation. First she complimented him on being so clever to find a hinge that was right under both their noses. Then she asked if it was wonderful to be a sea captain.

Michael decided to convince her, hopefully for the last time, that he wasn't potential husband material.

"On board, it's a hard life," he said. "Storms and gales and seasickness. It's always ice-cold in the North Pacific. Cold and wet. Sometimes we don't return to Seattle for weeks at a time. There are no amenities. A bathroom that's only two feet square. And no television."

She took a step back from him. "You make it sound terribly unpleasant."

"Most women couldn't take it," he said. "But Annie can handle the seafaring life."

"Well, she always was rugged," Candace said.

The door to the hardware store swung open and Annie burst through.

Michael was not amused. Not only had she disobeyed his instructions to wait for him at the police station, but she was obviously enraged about something.

About two inches away from him, she came to a screeching halt. "You've got some explaining to do, mister."

"About what?"

"This." She thrust the cheap little Cinderella statuette in his face. "Your fingerprints are all over it. *Only* your fingerprints."

Chapter Nine

Annie had drawn the obvious conclusion. When Engstrom returned the Cinderella figurine and told her about the fingerprints, she realized that Michael had to be the guilty party. He was the one who had harassed her in Salem, leaving odd figurines where she would find them. She shouldn't be surprised. Hadn't he already admitted that he was following her in Salem, practically stalking her?

"Why?" she demanded. "Why would you leave this Cinderella thing for me to find?"

"I don't know what you're talking about."

Annoyance flashed across his features. He was giving a fine performance of someone wrongly accused, but fingerprints didn't lie. "Oh, Michael. How could you?"

"I have to agree with Annie," Candace said. "It's not much of a gift."

Annie turned to face her. "I would appreciate if you stayed out of this, Candace. I'm talking to my...my..."

"Fiancé," Michael supplied.

"I don't blame you for being annoyed," Candace said. "That Cinderella looks like the kind of tacky little trinket you'd pick up at a garage sale. I mean, it's not only cheap, but it's old."

"How do you know?" Annie asked.

"It's cheap painted plaster and glazed paint," she said

with the expertise of a practiced shopper. "The action figures they sell nowadays are plastic. Safer for the kids, you know."

Annie turned back to Michael. "Where did you get it?"

"I didn't."

He seemed to be honestly insulted, and she wished she could believe him. Her initial inquiry into his background had failed to turn over any discrepancies in what he'd said about his current occupation and employment history. He appeared to be a former U.S. Navy man who was currently the captain and part-owner of a seventy-foot sailing vessel named *Rosebud*. He had no credit problems. No warrants or arrests.

But she was still digging. Today she'd contacted a friend in the court system who could get a transcript of Bateman's trial. Annie had the feeling that once she knew the details about Michael's involvement in that incident, she'd be able to better understand who he was and why he was back in Bridgeport.

The hardware-store door opened with sound of a tinkling bell, and a fourth customer walked inside. It was Jake Stillwell. He nodded to Michael, ignored his ex-wife and spoke to Annie. "I thought I saw you run down the street and come in here."

"What are you doing here?" Candace snapped.

Still refusing to acknowledge her presence, he said to Annie, "I'd like to invite you to the house on Wednesday."

"The thirteenth?"

"That's right. I'm having a reception for some Portland bankers, and they want more information about Bridgeport. You'd be a good representative for the town. Can you make it?"

"How dare you!" Candace transformed before their eyes. She went from spun sugar to sour lemon. "Don't you know Annie is engaged? She's not interested in you!"

With practiced coolness, Jake didn't respond to her. "What do you say, Annie? Six o'clock on Wednesday. It's for the good of the town."

Her instincts told her to accept and get Jake out of there as quickly as possible. "I'll be there. Your place."

"*His* place?" Candace snarled. "It should have been *mine*."

Jake whipped around to face her. "Excuse me?"

"You heard me, Jake. That mausoleum on the hill should have come to me in the divorce. I should have gotten everything."

"The house belongs to my mother. You weren't married to her, Candace."

"But I had to put up with all her artsy stuff. I had to pretend I was impressed by her stupid statuary and paintings. What do I get for that, huh?"

"Cultural enrichment?"

In spite of Jake's anger, his eyes softened when he looked at his ex-wife. Annie had been in enough domestic violence situations to guess at the probable scenario. Jake might have made some mistakes, but he was still in love with his former wife.

Candace, however, did not appear to feel the same about her ex. She raged at him with the unabated fury of a nor'wester. "Half the lumber mill should have been mine."

"You want half the debt? You're welcome to it."

"I need more money."

"You're doing okay," he said. "You got a house, a car and monthly support payments from me. I'm a damn good provider for my kids."

"You're a damn good tomcat. You've already gone after every other woman in town. Now Annie's fresh catnip." She reached into her purse and pulled out a gun, which she aimed at Jake's crotch. "I ought to blow them off."

Annie nodded to Michael. "You take her. I'll take him."

They went into action. While Michael spoke soothing words to Candace, Annie directed Jake away from the line of fire. In seconds Candace had turned over her weapon and was sobbing hysterically against Michael's chest.

Annie nudged Jake toward the rear of the store. "You should go now. Don't worry, we'll make sure she's taken care of."

His feet dragged. He was a beaten man. "Do you think she would've shot me?"

"Has she been violent before?"

"She used to break things when she got mad. But a gun? Why the hell does Candace have a gun?"

"She must feel threatened," Annie said.

"Not by me," he was quick to say.

"But someone you know?"

Jake had been part of the teenage gang. It made sense that Bateman would look him up when he returned to town. Plus, Bateman had been dressed like a logger. He might even be working for Stillwell Logging and Lumber Mill.

"Is that why Candace is nervous?" she pressed. "Could someone you know be bothering her?"

"Nobody threatens my wife and kids. Nobody."

He gazed toward the front of the store where Candace was loudly weeping. He took a step toward her, and Annie placed both hands on his chest, lightly restraining him. "Do you want to report her to the police, Jake?"

"No." Turning on his heel, he went out the back door of the store.

Of all the crime she encountered on her job, domestic violence was the most difficult. When passionate love turned to equally passionate hate, people became unpredictable and uncontrolled. In the aftermath they were often shocked by what they'd done or what their former partner had done to them.

Annie shuddered, thinking of the children caught in these

situations, swept away in an endless eddy of abuse and violence. The tension they felt must be unbearable. Even as an outsider, Annie felt it. Her skin crawled, and she found herself barely able to contain her overwrought emotions.

Carefully she arranged her face in a mask of calm before she returned to the front of the store. She needed to stay in control.

Michael had disarmed Candace and stuck her handgun into the back of his jeans. Her hysteria had calmed, but she was still clinging to his shoulder, mumbling incoherently.

"I know you didn't really mean to shoot him," he murmured as he looked over her head at Annie. "The gun wasn't even loaded."

Oblivious, the hardware-store clerk shuffled behind the counter and thunked down two paint cans. "Your order is ready."

AFTER EDNA came to pick up her distraught daughter, Annie and Michael gathered the supplies and returned to the house in time for a conference on the veranda with Sam. The cheerful physical therapist, with her positive report about Lionel, was an excellent antidote to Candace.

"Lionel is doing extremely well," she said. "He's following the proper regimen and can get around very well with his walker."

"How long will he have to use it?"

"We might graduate to a cane in a couple of weeks."

Annie was pleased. In spite of the apprehension that coiled tightly inside her chest, she was able to smile. "Is there anything else we should be doing?"

"Don't let him overexert himself," Sam advised. "His confidence needs to be nurtured, but don't let him sign up for a marathon."

"How much exercise is beneficial?"

"You might want to get him out of the house. Take a ride in the car and go for a short walk. More than half the reason for his marked improvement is his attitude. Lionel is extremely motivated to get back on his feet. Literally."

"Thanks for everything," Annie said. "We'll see you on Thursday."

"The fourteenth." Glancing toward the street, Sam frowned. "Who is that guy? I saw him before from the window of your grandpa's bedroom."

Without even looking, Annie knew the answer. Bateman. He shambled along the sidewalk in front of the house, hands in his pockets, taking his time.

Annie lost it. She stood on the edge of the top step and yelled, "I've got a restraining order, Bateman. You can't come any closer than within one hundred feet of me or my grandpa."

"That's fine!" he yelled back. "You can still hear my voice. You can still see my shadow."

She wanted to kill him. "Get any closer and you'll be back in prison."

"Prison?" Sam said. Her brown eyes opened wide. "He was in prison?"

"Nothing to worry about," Annie said. *Oh, sure, it was no problem at all.* Bateman was just a psychopathic stalker who wanted her dead. "He'll leave."

At the far edge of her grandpa's yard, he spun back toward them so quickly Annie almost jumped.

"You have yourself a real nice day," he snarled. He tossed something onto the lawn and kept on walking.

While Michael escorted Sam to her van, Annie cautiously approached the object Bateman had thrown. Expecting a hand grenade or a poisonous spider, she looked down and saw a tiny plastic bride and groom, the kind of thing that went on top of a wedding cake. Their heads had been snapped off.

Annie bent down and picked it up. This didn't make any sense. The figurines had come from Michael. His fingerprints were on Cinderella. Was he working with Bateman?

There was one good way to find out. As Sam's van pulled away from the curb, Annie headed directly toward him. "Would you care to explain this, Michael?"

"Bride. Groom. Decapitated." He started walking toward the house.

"Are you and Bateman working together?" She trotted along beside him. "What's the point of leaving these little statuettes?"

Not breaking stride, he went up the steps and into the house. As soon as Annie was inside, too, he closed the front door and set the alarm.

"Talk to me," she said.

"Are you ready to hear an explanation?"

If she didn't get some answers soon, she'd explode into a million little frustrated pieces. "Tell me you're not working with Bateman."

He glared. Beneath the anger, she sensed hurt. "You're not ready to believe me."

"If you'd tell me the truth…"

"Use your brain, Annie. I wouldn't hook up with a cheap crook like Bateman. I wouldn't go halves on a pizza with him."

"I know," she said. Michael wasn't one of the bad guys, and she knew it as sure as bees made honey. When he was a teenager, he'd made mistakes. But that was a long time ago. She sucked down a deep breath, fighting the tension. "I need for you to explain the fingerprints. I'm a cop, Michael. And this is evidence. I can't pretend it doesn't exist."

"Okay, I touched the Cinderella doll. I picked it up and I touched it. What's the big deal?"

He proceeded up the stairs to her grandpa's bedroom,

but Annie wasn't about to let him off the hook until she fully understood what was going on. She trailed him into Lionel's bedroom.

Her grandpa had returned to his bed, but he was sitting up against the pillows. He looked tired after his workout with Sam, but it was a healthy exhaustion. "What are you two bickering about?"

Annie held out the headless bride and groom. "This."

Then she dug into her jeans pocket and pulled out Cinderella in a blue ballgown. "Also this."

Aware she looked ridiculous while clutching the two figurines, she placed them on her grandpa's bedside table and backed away. She glared at the two men in turn, daring them to laugh. But there wasn't a grin in the room. Lionel opened the drawer in his bedside table and removed a small object, which he stood between the others. "I'll see your two and raise you one."

Made of cheap painted porcelain like the Cinderella, his figurine was a lion with a full mane and proud stance.

"Where did you find this?" she asked.

"It was on the floor in here. Sam found it when she was spreading out the mats." He shrugged. "I thought it was a present from you, Annie. A lion for Lionel."

But how did it get there? How was Bateman able to come so close? She turned to Michael. "Did you leave it here?"

"No."

She wanted to grab him and shake an explanation from him. "Why were your fingerprints on Cinderella?"

"I found the statue outside in the gazebo on the night we went looking for clues," he explained. "Like your grandpa, I thought it belonged to you, something left over from childhood. I thought it was sweet. You never seemed like the kind of little girl to play with dolls. Anyway, I left it in your room on the dresser next to your sports trophies."

"Why didn't you tell me?"

"Why is it important?" he countered.

Both men regarded her steadily, and Annie realized that the ball was in her court. Neither Michael nor her grandpa had any idea why the statuettes were significant.

"About a week and a half ago," she said, "just about the time Bateman got out on parole, some anonymous person started leaving these figurines where I'd find them."

"In Salem?" Michael asked.

"That's right. The first one was a skunk that somebody left on my desk at the station. I thought it was a joke. Then I found another one on my car. Another outside my apartment."

"Why didn't you mention this before?"

"They seemed so harmless. I didn't think these little trinkets were meant as a threat. Then I found the Cinderella in my bedroom." She remembered her revulsion, her sense of violation. "It upset me to think that Bateman might have put it there. That he might have been in the house, inside my bedroom."

"Why were you keeping this secret?"

Because she didn't trust him. The irony did not escape her. All this time she'd been on her high horse, demanding the whole truth from him, a full and honest partnership. At the same time she'd been withholding her own information. "I guess I should have mentioned something."

"I guess so," he said coolly.

"Now you know." Annie lined up the three figurines on Lionel's bedside table. "What does it mean?"

"They're clues," Michael said. "The first tangible clues we've gotten."

"We should check with the local shops, here and in Wayside. Find out who sells things like this. Then see if they remember Bateman coming in to buy them."

That was going to be a tedious job. Wayside was a beach town, very touristy, full of little shops that sold shells and trinkets. But it made Annie feel better to have an actual task. Finally there was something to do, instead of waiting helplessly.

"What else?" Michael said. "What can we figure out by looking at them?"

The first thing Annie noticed was that the bride-and-groom was different from the lion and Cinderella, in that it was plastic and generic. "Do you think Candace was right when she said the glass figurines were older?"

"Makes sense. I'm not an expert on kids' toys, but most of the stuff is plastic. These others are more like knick-knacks."

"A lion and a lady," Annie said. "The others were a skunk, a ballet dancer and a chipmunk. That makes it two dancers and three animals. And, of course, the bride and groom."

"I'd call that one a threat to you and me," Michael said. "The missing heads are fairly ominous. Still, I wouldn't want to report it to Engstrom."

"Why not?" Annie asked. "In a police investigation, every clue is taken seriously."

"If you were the investigating cop, I'd do it," Michael said. "But Engstrom is going to laugh if we say we've been threatened by figurines."

She wished she could defend the Bridgeport chief of police, but she hadn't been impressed by Engstrom's competence thus far. "We'd be more motivated to track down the source. If we can link the purchase of these statuettes to Bateman, they're evidence. Otherwise, they're just toys."

"Could be that's why Bateman used them," Lionel put in. "He's cagey. He doesn't want to get arrested. But he wants you to know he's around, watching. That's why he leaves this stuff behind."

"Like a dog marking his territory," Michael said.

"Thank so much, Michael, for that truly disgusting mental image."

He picked up the lion, studied it and returned it to the lineup. "How did he get this one upstairs into Lionel's room?"

"It might have been here for days," Annie said. "I'm not the world's greatest housekeeper."

"But Bateman was still taking a big risk to come into the house. That doesn't seem like part of his game plan."

Annie agreed. The brick through the window, she could understand. That gesture was crude, like Bateman himself. Likewise, deflating Michael's tires was the sort of vandalism she'd expect.

These figures had a different feeling about them. Though they couldn't be considered art, they didn't entirely lack charm. They were...touchable.

Lacking a logical explanation, Annie turned to her imagination. She tried to see the pretty little Cinderella dancing in her glass slippers to the music of a waltz. But she didn't hear an orchestra. Instead, she heard the simple sound of someone humming.

Her mind conjured a whole collection of pastel dancers and forest creatures, arrayed on a shelf. Once a week they were taken down and lovingly dusted. An ex-con would never keep sweet delicate figures like these.

"You're both missing the biggest clue of all," Lionel said.

"What's that, Grandpa?"

"As soon as Michael and I saw these things, we both jumped to the same conclusion. They came from Annie. And why did we make that assumption?"

Michael answered, "Because little boys play with G.I. Joe and little girls like Cinderella."

"Apart from the fact that you're being so totally sexist," Annie said, "you've got a point. The person who owned these statues was female. Do we know if Bateman had a mother or a sister in the area?''

"Even scum like Bateman had a mother," Michael said. "But his family is long gone. As far as I know, they moved back East somewhere, and he's not in touch with them."

"But Grandpa is right. When we find the woman who collected these things, we'll have some answers."

"In the meantime," Lionel said, "I'll be taking my afternoon nap."

Michael went downstairs to get started with the interior painting while Annie helped her grandpa get settled in the bed. She passed along Sam's assessment of his progress. "She said you're doing extremely well."

"Don't I know it. I stopped feeling sick and started to think of physical therapy as a workout, a way to get back into shape."

"Once a coach, always a coach," she said, smiling down at him. "Sam also mentioned that we could take you for an outing. A ride in the car."

"That would be real fine, Annie. I'd like to take you and Michael down by the old bridge to see my property."

"Maybe tomorrow." She still didn't want to encourage her grandpa's overly ambitious construction project. "Or you could come with us to Wayside to see if we can find out who sold these statues."

"I'll take a pass on that one. I never liked all those touristy shops." His eyelids closed. "Stay here and talk to me, honey. Tell me about your day."

"Well, there's never a dull moment in Bridgeport." She told him about the hardware store, about Jake and Candace, and Edna coming to pick up her daughter.

Just when she thought he was asleep, Lionel said, "Edna's a widow, isn't she?"

"I think so. Are you interested in her?"

"She's a chatterbox, but I like the noise, the sound of a

woman's voice. When you're not here, the house is too quiet." He rolled onto his side. "I need my nap, honey. See you in a couple of hours."

Downstairs she found Michael staring at the walls in the parlor with unopened paint cans at his feet. He'd changed into a white T-shirt and worn denim jeans with both knees split open. He looked sad, even a little bit lonely.

She never should have suspected him. In spite of the fingerprint evidence, she should have known that Michael would never do anything to hurt her or Lionel. She wanted to apologize and give him a hug, but it was too soon for him to forgive her suspicions.

Their relationship, past and present, was so complicated. With every new detail, she felt like she was peeling back petals on a tightly wrapped bud. And she was afraid of going too far, destroying the potential beauty of a rose in bloom.

He looked at her. "Ready to work?"

Usually Annie would've been right there with him, paint brush in hand, preferring action. She'd rather swim fast on the surface than dive into deep emotional undercurrents. But the panic attack had been a dramatic warning. She couldn't ignore her tension. If she suppressed her anger, her pain or her fears, they wouldn't simply evaporate. Instead, they would rise like the tide, mounting higher and higher until her barriers were washed away and she was left utterly without defenses.

"This might take two coats," Michael said. He removed a photograph from the wall, leaving a lighter rectangle against the old paint job. "We might get it in one if we wash the walls first."

She sank onto the lumpy brown sofa and propped her tennis shoes on the coffee table. "I'm worried about Grandpa."

"Why? He's doing great. You heard what Sam said."

"He's lonely, Michael." She hated to think of him, rattling around in this old house by himself after she returned to Salem. But she couldn't stay here. And she couldn't visit every single weekend. Her work was too demanding. She needed time for herself. "He was asking about Edna Grabow. As if he wanted her to spend some time with him."

"Edna the soup lady?"

"The woman who works at the mini-mart. Candace's mother. She's a widow."

Michael sat beside her. His long legs bent, exposing his knees, and she noted the difference in their bone structure. His was much larger, more masculine.

"Wow," he said. "Lionel must be desperately lonely."

"Edna's not so bad. She's got a cute little nose—"

"And a great big mouth," he said.

"Grandpa said he liked the chatter, but I don't think Edna's the solution. There has to be another way. Maybe I could arrange for him to come back to Salem with me."

"He won't go," Michael said. "Like it or not, Bridgeport is his home. Plus, he's got that property he wants to develop."

That was another reason he shouldn't stay in Bridgeport. Even if he was completely recovered from his stroke, an ambitious building project was too strenuous. "I can't leave him here alone. I should move back to Bridgeport. I could get a job with Engstrom and slap the local police into shape."

"Is that what you want to do with your life?"

"No."

Her answer came quickly and without a second thought. Though her life in Salem was far from perfect, Annie liked being on her own, having her own apartment and a responsible job.

Her gaze encompassed the parlor, the familiar surroundings where she'd grown up. This would always be her home, but she didn't want to settle down here. If she came back to Bridgeport, there were only two probable scenarios—becoming an old maid, or marrying one of the local guys and having kids and spending the rest of her life bored out of her mind. In Salem, at least, there was the possibility of something different.

"I don't want to end up like Candace," she said. "Divorced and so bitter I'd pull a gun on my ex-husband."

"You lost me," he said. "Were we talking about divorce?"

"It's what comes after marriage," she said with a cynicism she didn't really feel. "If I moved back here, I'd probably get married to avoid being a spinster."

"Give yourself a little credit, Annie. You're not the kind of woman who's given to compromise. You're way too stubborn."

He reached over and gave her hand a squeeze, and she felt the edge of her grandma's engagement ring pinching her finger. When she looked over at him, a fleeting thought crossed her mind. She would happily live in Bridgeport if Michael was with her. If their engagement was real...

"I know what you need," he said. "A sunset."

"What?"

"A perfect sunset over the Pacific." When he stood, he pulled her up with him. "We need to do some investigation in Wayside, anyway. Checking the tourist shops and looking for Cinderella's mate. Put on your glass slippers, Annie. And let's go."

THEIR DEPARTURE wasn't spontaneous. Not until hours later did Michael finally manage to sweep Annie away. They'd arranged for Edna to come over and feed Lionel dinner and sit with him until they got back.

Still, as Michael drove along the winding forested road

toward the coast, he felt as if he was escaping from under a dark cloud.

During the afternoon they'd done some solid investigative police work, splitting the telephone listing for shops in Wayside and making calls to inquire about the types of figurines sold in the shops. They had eliminated all but two.

At the first shop in Wayside they searched through bins of touristy statuettes made of plastic, rubber and glass. Nothing resembled their figurines.

In minutes they were outside again. The sun dipped low in the clear sky, and he reckoned that sunset was an hour away. He inhaled deeply. Though they were a couple of blocks from the beach, the air had the salty tang of freedom, which he always smelled in the moments before casting off and sailing away.

It felt good to be here with Annie. When he linked his hand with hers, she didn't object.

The town itself was pretty much the way he remembered. Though Wayside catered to the tourist trade with tacky commercial shops and foodstands, there were also upscale art galleries and restaurants, and a working dock where you could buy fresh catch right off the fishermen's boats.

At the second shop—Shells 'n' Stuff—they hit the jackpot. Though there were no ballerinas or Cinderellas, they found several woodland creatures and a lion similar to the one left in Lionel's room.

Annie took one of the lions to the clerk, a bearded young man in a Hawaiian shirt. She flashed her badge. "In the past two weeks have you sold any statuettes similar to this one?"

"I don't know," he said. "Probably."

"Do you record inventory items with each sale?"

"No, ma'am."

"We're looking for a white male, six feet tall, solid

build. He has longish blond hair and was probably wearing a flannel shirt.''

"Buying one of those? No way. I would've remembered that. Only little girls like those things.''

"How many other people work here?''

"There's six employees, including the part-timers.''

"I'll call tomorrow to talk to whoever's working,'' Annie said. "Thanks for your time.''

Once again Michael was impressed by her professionalism. Annie was a good cop, efficient and smart. If she stayed with the Salem police force, she'd probably be promoted to detective, then higher. If she went to work for the government, she'd probably wind up being his boss. "Where did you learn how to do this?''

"It's common sense,'' she said.

But he knew there was more involved. Annie had a unique ability to be an authority figure without being overbearing. "This must be the kind of policework you like. The detective stuff.''

"It's okay.''

"Not a very enthusiastic response, Annie.''

"I have a confession to make.'' Sheepishly she peeked up at him. "Some parts of my job don't really appeal to me. I don't get a big thrill out of tracking down and apprehending a criminal.''

"Then why be a cop?''

"Because I can help people. I can make their lives better by protecting them or taking them out of a bad situation.'' Her greatest satisfaction came from rescue work. "My captain says I identify too much with the victims, and he's probably right.''

"Why is that a problem?''

"I kind of get carried away,'' she admitted. She'd started keeping a stash of stuffed animals and coloring books in her desk to give to children who were stuck at the police station. "I can't stand to see the kids who get caught in the middle because their parents have gotten themselves arrested."

In the back of her mind she could hear her captain's voice. *It's not your job, Callahan. Let the social workers take care of them.* But sometimes the social workers couldn't show up for hours, and the poor kids were abandoned in a big scary police station.

"I wonder," she said, "if I'm really cut out to be a cop."

"You know how I feel about your career," he said. "I hate for you to be in danger."

She followed as Michael led the way to a busy little restaurant near the docks and ordered clam chowder to go. With their take-out containers in hand, they headed toward the boardwalk.

At the end of the block, they came into full view of the ocean. Transfixed by the sight of so much natural beauty, she stood for a moment and stared across the long sandy beach, tufted with long grass and dotted with driftwood. In the waning sunlight, the breakers whispered rhythmically as they kissed the shoreline. The light reflecting off the waves shimmered like miles of diamonds. Offshore jagged rock formations teased the imagination, making her think of tall ships, sea monsters and the mysteries of the deep.

When Michael draped an arm around her shoulders, she thought the world could not be more perfect.

"This was a wonderful idea," she said.

"No matter how bad I feel, this is the cure."

When she looked up at him, she saw serenity in his gaze. Finally, by the ocean, Michael seemed at peace with himself. "You must love your work."

"Some of it," he said. "Like you, there are things about the job I could do without. But you're right about one thing. I love the Pacific."

They walked on the sand, heading toward the northern

end of the long shorefront, where breakers crashed against a rugged outcropping of rocks.

"We stop here." Michael pointed to a piece of driftwood. "That's our dinner table, and I'm starving."

The chowder was fantastic, rich and creamy with large chunks of meat, and they both ate quickly. With her stomach full, Annie felt herself approaching a state of pure contentment.

There was only one niggling thought at the back of her mind. "I owe you an apology, Michael."

"For what?"

"In the hardware store I flew at you in a fury without giving you a chance to explain. I assumed the worst."

"That almost sounds like you're beginning to trust me."

She was. In spite of his past and her sense that he still wasn't telling her everything, she found herself believing that Michael was a good man—maybe not honest but good at heart.

"Take off your shoes, Annie."

"Why?"

"We'll go down to the water to watch the sunset."

She peeled off her shoes and socks and rolled up the legs of her jeans. Holding his hand, she walked across the warm coarse sand to the edge of the breaking surf.

Fresh breezes swirled through her hair. The icy water lapped her toes and feet, sending a pleasurable tingle through her entire body, and she laughed out loud. "I haven't gone wading in ages."

He gazed toward the horizon. "After I left Bridgeport, I used to write your name in the sand. Wherever I happened to be in the world, your name made it seem like home. When the incoming tide washed the letters away, it was like I'd sent you a message and I hoped you'd be thinking about me."

His baritone harmonized with the rolling waves, punctuated by the cries of gulls and terns.

"I thought about you, Michael. All the time."

As the sun touched the edge of the sea, he looked down at her. His eyes were warm.

Water swirled around their ankles, and Annie felt as if she was a part of the Pacific, a part of life itself. Her lips joined with his, and they kissed until the sun dipped below the waves, leaving them in a golden endless dusk.

Chapter Ten

Yesterday's sunset resonated in Michael's memory. The last shimmer of light still glowed in Annie's hair. When he'd looked into her eyes, he'd seen the ocean. They were closer now than ever before. The gulf between them had shrunk to the width of a drainage ditch, and they stood on opposite sides, eyeing each other suspiciously and wondering which of them would finally step across.

He was ready, more than ready, to move to the next phase of their relationship—the phase that included making love. With every embrace and every kiss, the possibility became more real.

Yesterday, she'd told him that she'd thought about him all the time after he left Bridgeport. He'd felt the same about her, carrying an idealized picture of the girl he'd left behind. But Annie was a woman now—strong, brave, complicated and fascinating. She was a good woman with a good heart who cared for Lionel without complaint and worried about the children affected by their parents' crimes. She fought to make everyone else happy, and Michael wanted to give some of that happiness and fulfillment to her. He wanted to hear her laughter and see a contented smile upon her lovely face.

Last night, after the romantic sunset, he'd thought the time for making love had finally come. But after they re-

turned to her grandpa's house, Annie had chatted with Edna
and tucked Lionel in, then patted Michael on the cheek and
sent him downstairs to the guest bedroom. It was like they
were an old married couple with none of the benefits.

Now she'd thrown a new obstacle in his path. Annie
wanted to take Lionel out for a picnic. And Lionel wanted
to show them his property by the old abandoned bridge.

Returning to the bridge was like taking a field trip to
hell. As Michael drove the familiar roads, his hands kept a
death grip on the steering wheel. His palms were sweating,
and there was a dirgelike throbbing in his head.

Beside him in the passenger seat, Lionel was in high
spirits, pointing out the new growth in the forest, delighted
to be out of the house. Annie was wedged into the backseat
with the folding lawn chairs. Occasionally he caught her
gaze in the rearview mirror and saw a hint of concern in
her eyes. She knew that coming back here was hard for
him, but she didn't know how hard. When he'd crossed this
bridge eleven years ago, his life had changed forever.

"A real fine spring day," Lionel said. "All these trees
and wildflowers. You never appreciate what you've got until you almost lose it."

The two-lane paved road leading through the forest had
not been maintained and was quite overgrown in parts. The
sheltering trees felt claustrophobic, like a trap.

"I'll have to get these roads repaired," Lionel said.

"Why?" Michael was praying for a fallen log that would
make the way impassable.

"Because I'm going to build here, Mikey. I've been doing a lot of thinking about what kind of structure I want to
put on this land. At first I thought it should be apartments.
That would bring more people to Bridgeport."

"If there aren't any jobs," Annie said, "why would people move here?"

"I've got another idea," he said, chuckling to himself.

They crested the final hill above the river, and Michael put the car in park. From this vantage point they had a clear view of the condemned bridge, which spanned a quarter of a mile. On either end was a long concrete ramp. In the center, above the Yaquina River, the single arch of rusted girders loomed like the skeleton of a dinosaur.

"That damn bridge should have been torn down," Lionel said. "Kids still come down here and hang out. It's only a matter of time before somebody gets drunk and falls into the water."

And that somebody would die, Michael thought. The plummet from the center, below the suspension wires, had to be sixty feet. "It should be demolished."

"It was built in the 1930s, you know, right about the same time as the Golden Gate in San Francisco."

"I know," Michael said. The Yaquina bridge was a dangerous artifact of man's ingenuity gone wrong. Built to be two-lane, it wasn't wide enough to handle the increased tourist traffic and the lumber trucks. When the state constructed a new bridge in Wayside, it was cheaper to make it four lanes and to close this one down, placing blockades and warnings at either end.

Destroy it. Michael would gladly punch the detonation cap himself. He'd cheer as the rusted bolts exploded sky-high, then splashed into the river. He hated this place. As he beheld the thing for the first time in eleven years, a knife twisted in his gut.

"My property starts after the next curve," Lionel said.

They descended to a graded road, where Michael turned right. The trees parted, and they came upon a clearing where they found the charred remains of a campfire and a couple of rusted beer cans. The leveled land was smaller than a football field and stretched from a rocky outcropping to the edge of a bluff.

Too well, Michael remembered this rugged terrain—the

gray rocks, the grasses, the flowers and the direct view of the bridge. The gang had met below this clearing at the foot of a clay bank. That damp rocky area beside the concrete pilings was where Marie Cartier had died.

When he stepped out of the car, he heard the chirping of birds and the hoarse cries of gulls. In his mind he heard echoes of gunfire, shouting and a single piercing scream.

It wasn't fair. Anger rose inside him like a futile demon, raging inside the bell jar of the past. He loathed this damned place. He hated what had happened here.

Annie came up beside him. "What's the matter?"

"We're close to where Marie died," he told her.

"We don't have to stay here," she said.

But Lionel had his car door open and had pulled himself to a standing position. "It's beautiful, isn't it? Twenty-four acres."

Michael cleared his throat. "Not much is usable."

"It's a great piece of land," Annie said with false enthusiasm.

She was torn between wanting to please her grandpa and her empathy for Michael. Yesterday at sunset she'd felt so connected to him. Now he was receding again, hiding behind his anger. Why couldn't he forget the past? Why wouldn't he let go?

This morning she'd had a phone call from her friend in the court system who informed her that the testimony of under-seventeen juveniles in Bateman's trial was sealed, and it would take a court order to open the files. It was also red-flagged as a sensitive document.

Annie couldn't help wondering why such a relatively simple case was being treated like a top-secret document. She assumed that since Jake Stillwell was involved, his father had pulled some strings to close the testimony and protect his son. Once again she was left knowing nothing more about what happened at the bridge than Michael chose to tell her.

The shop in Wayside had also led to a dead end. No one remembered selling any of the lions, and they kept no inventory. Annie feared she would never have answers. Time was running out. Tomorrow was the thirteenth.

While they unloaded their simple picnic lunch, set up the aluminum-frame lawn chairs and helped Lionel maneuver across the rocky ground using his walker, Michael's tension became more and more apparent. He didn't speak. His movements were brusque.

When she passed out the soda pop and sandwiches, he took one bite, then sat in dark silence, alternately glaring at the bridge and the sky.

Lionel was quite the opposite. Being with Edna yesterday had loosened his tongue, and he remarked on the feel of sunlight on his face. He talked about picnicking on this very spot with his late wife, Elizabeth. When he mentioned Bateman, Annie paid close attention.

"Eleven years ago," Lionel said, "this beautiful place saw a lot of pain."

"Let's not talk about it," Michael said tersely.

"I'd already bought the land," Lionel continued. "I was making payments. I had plans to build a house here, but Bateman changed my mind. How could I live so close to this tragedy? That's when I started thinking about an apartment building or town houses, something I could rent out to people who didn't know the history of the place."

"Better yet," Annie suggested, "you could sell the property to somebody else and let them develop it."

"Now I have a plan."

"Oh, good," she said.

"You're going to like this, Annie. It came to me yesterday after my nap while I was lying there listening to my heart thump and thinking about how my life was almost over and I hadn't left anything behind.''

"Grandpa, you're only seventy-two. That's not old. Sam says you're going to make a good recovery. You've got—''

"Hush, Annie. I know what I am, and I know where I'm headed." He gazed down at his hands. His withered skin stretched taut across veins, bones and gnarled knuckles. When he looked up, he was smiling. "Are you listening to me, Mikey?''

Michael's brooding silence lifted long enough for him to mutter, "I hope you're not talking about a monument. A fancy gravestone won't bring her back to life.''

"I want to help the living," Lionel said. "I want to use this land to build a halfway house for teenagers in trouble. I want to give them a safe place to stay. If they have good counseling and support, they might not have to go through the hell you did, Michael.''

Annie gasped. A halfway house? It was too much work for her grandpa. A halfway house would take all his time and effort.

It was also brilliant, a true culmination of his life's work. The whole time he was municipal judge, he'd reached out to the teenagers who had broken minor rules, like curfew, and set them on a straighter path. With the football team, he'd tried to instill values, teach sportsmanlike conduct, along with pass plays and blocking moves.

Though this was her heritage, she'd never really acknowledged it before. She'd been trained to care for others. She'd learned from her grandpa's example. No wonder she kept stuffed animals for the children in her desk drawer at the police station in Salem. Helping other people, especially juveniles, was a core tenet in her life. Finally she comprehended the real reason she'd become a cop.

"What do you think, Annie?" her grandpa asked.

"You're doing the right thing," she said.

Michael stood. He stretched his arms above his head. "I need to take a walk. I'll be back in a minute."

She watched as he strode along the graded road toward the overgrown two-lane. Though he still moved with the smooth athletic grace she'd never seen in another man, there was a hitch in his stride, a visible tension.

"Go with him," Lionel said.

"I think he wants to be alone."

"What he wants and what he needs are two different things. Michael's been alone too long with his memories. He needs to face them." He shooed her away. "Go ahead. I'll be fine."

Though her feet itched to follow Michael, she couldn't leave her grandpa sitting here, alone and defenseless. Even though Bateman hadn't shown himself, he could easily be hiding in the surrounding forests. "I'll clean up first. And get you tucked away in the car where you'll be comfortable."

"What you're trying to say is that you're worried about my safety."

"Yes."

"Give me your gun, Annie. I saw it in the picnic basket."

Stroke or not, he was a tough old coot. She turned over the automatic and gave him a hug. "I love you, Grandpa."

She sprinted after Michael. At the paved road she saw that he was going down toward the bridge. Running up beside him, she matched his pace but said nothing.

"Leave me alone, Annie."

"No."

"This isn't your problem."

"It most certainly is." She was stubborn. Annie wasn't going away without a fight. "Eleven years ago you left town because of something that happened at this bridge. My life turned upside down.''

He halted. ''What do you want from me? An apology?''

''An explanation. What happened here?''

''I already told you.'' He resumed walking. ''Go back and keep an eye on Lionel.''

But she wouldn't be dissuaded. ''You haven't told me everything, Michael. Through a friend of mine in the justice system, I learned that your court testimony is not only sealed but classified. Why?''

''You're spying on me,'' he said. ''You pay a lot of lip service to honesty. But when it comes to the real thing, you've got as many secrets as I do.''

''I doubt that.'' Her secrets were flimsy and on the surface. His were buried soul-deep.

At the edge of the bridge Michael froze.

Annie stood beside him. Even though she had no memories of anything that happened here, the bridge had an ominous appearance. The concrete footing above the pilings was thickly scrawled with graffiti and overgrown with vines. Heavy boards and a yellow sign that read Bridge Closed blocked the entrance ramp. In the center the rusted metal arch loomed above the dark waters of the Yaquina.

Michael followed a dirt path to the left of the pilings. At one time this area must have been cleared for construction, but the forest had begun to reclaim the land with slender young willows and hardy shrubs.

At the rocky bank, Michael stared across the river. ''This is where it happened. We gathered down here. There were six of us, and we were excited, planning to divide the take from the robbery. It wasn't as much as we thought. Our individual shares would have been less than a hundred apiece.''

''That's typical of amateur robberies,'' she said. ''Going to a lot of trouble and overestimating the take.''

"Thanks for pointing that out," he said bitterly. "We were a bunch of dumb kids, thinking we were super-criminals. We should have gotten a slap on the wrist and some time in juvenile facilities. But that's not what happened. Somebody died here."

She shouldn't have interrupted the flow of his memory. Michael still had deep feelings about the incident. It was almost as if he blamed himself for Marie Cartier's death.

Quietly Annie bent down and picked up a smooth rock. Using her right arm, which was feeling stronger every day, she tried to skip the stone across the water's surface and met with less-than-perfect results. Even more clumsily she repeated the exercise with her left arm. "I'm listening, Michael."

"There's something you need to know," he said, still gazing out over the water. "I've never told anyone else. I don't even think Lionel knows."

She looked up at him, waiting.

"Marie Cartier was my half sister."

SLOWLY, MICHAEL EXHALED the breath he'd been holding for eleven years. Now the words were spoken. Now, they would take on a life of their own.

Unable to face Annie and see her reaction, he kept his gaze on the river and continued his story where he'd left off. "We were down here, the gang. Everyone had flashlights, which we were waving around, and most were bickering about who got what. I didn't care—I just wanted it to be over. Then, it happened. The cops were hidden behind the pilings and up against the hillside. They had us surrounded."

In his mind he relived the moment in stark vivid strokes. Light beams had gone in all directions as they'd scrambled to escape. He'd seen the harsh glint of moonlight against the barrels of cops' pistols and rifles. "I stuck my hands in the air. I think I yelled something like, 'Don't shoot. We give up.' Then the gunfire started.''

And he'd seen Marie, running across the rocky shoreline toward him. "She came out of nowhere. She was wearing a white blouse that stood out in the darkness. And she called my name."

No! Marie, go back! he had cried. But she wasn't running anymore. It was already too late.

"She screamed once, then crumpled to the ground. I tried to reach her, but the cops had me in custody. My hands were cuffed behind my back. They were holding me. It took three of them. I never fought so hard in my life. But they had me on the ground. One of them might have kicked me, but I didn't feel it. I had to get to Marie. I had to protect her."

But he'd been too late. "I failed her in every way a man can fail. I couldn't comfort her before she died. I didn't hear her last words."

"Oh, God. Michael, I'm so sorry."

"So am I," he said softly.

Her senseless death had torn him apart inside. The shame and the guilt had overwhelmed him, and he'd wished with all his heart that he could have died in her place. "That's why I left Bridgeport. I couldn't stand to be here anymore."

"I understand." She lightly stroked his arm. "Michael, why didn't you tell me?"

His shame had been too great. His failure too devastating. "I wanted to do the right thing. I believed I could be something better than I was. Instead, I'd gotten my half sister killed."

He'd joined the navy hoping for redemption, and he volunteered for every dangerous assignment, trying to rescue Marie by saving others. In some ways he'd succeeded, earning citations for bravery and medals. Many would say he was a good man, and sometimes he believed he was worthy, even of Annie.

Ironically he couldn't yet tell her about his many assignments for naval intelligence and the FBI. He was stuck here in Bridgeport beside the bridge, confronting his boundless guilt.

"Tell me about her. About Marie."

Oh, God. He didn't want to talk about this. Now that Michael had opened this Pandora's box, he wanted to catch the escaped evils and lock them up again. "Maybe another day."

"We don't have much time, Michael. Tomorrow is the thirteenth."

"What are you saying?"

"We need answers. We need to figure out Bateman's scheme. That means I need to know *everything* about what happened here."

"In terms of evidence," he said, "the family relationship is all you need to know. Marie was my half sister. That's the only important fact."

"This so-called investigation isn't about evidence." Her clear voice lifted above the sounds of the river. "Bateman isn't harassing us out of any rational motive."

She was correct. Bateman was after them for revenge, to assuage an old hatred left to simmer for eleven years. No matter what the FBI or anybody else thought, their current situation was about old emotions. It was about anger. It was about guilt.

And Michael did not, by God, want to discuss his own culpability, his irresponsibility, which had resulted in Marie's death.

"Please, Michael."

Annie clasped his hand between both of hers, and the diamond winked up at him. He wished their engagement was real, that she had pledged herself to him. He needed that assurance before he exposed the darkest corner of his soul and opened the gateway to his personal hell. It wasn't a pretty place, and he wasn't sure how she'd react. She might hate him and think him a coward. Worse yet, she might pity him. Revealing himself was risky. Telling his secrets felt even more intimate than sex.

"I want to know you," she said. "I need to know everything about you."

He couldn't deny her the answers.

Gently he disengaged her grasp and turned again toward the river, imagining the rushing water could wash away his words and cleanse his guilt. "Marie was eight years older than me. She was the daughter of my father's first wife, a beautiful Mexican woman whose home was just outside Portland. We hardly ever saw each other because of the distance. I thought we'd get to spend more time together with Marie closer. But I only saw her three times after she moved to Wayside with her husband."

"How old were you then?" Annie asked.

"I was a freshman in high school, I think." He shook his head. "I don't remember exactly. I only went to her house once. It was pretty and delicate, like she was."

In his mind he clearly saw her heart-shaped face and thick black hair, like his own. The hair color was the beginning and end of their physical resemblance—but they shared the same pain. The curse of the Slades. His father.

He continued, "They say that women who've been abused as children tend to choose men who are abusive. Her husband fit the bill. Whenever we got together, Marie had fresh bruises. The last time we met by chance in Wayside, she had scars of cigarette burns on her inner arm."

He'd been enraged, ready to go directly to Marie's house and kill the bastard. But she'd stopped him. "She said she was going to leave her husband, that she'd met another man. She wouldn't tell me who he was, but said he was a good person.''

"Did you believe her?''

"I wanted to. I hoped she'd finally have a decent life.'' But the robbery had gotten in the way. "I should've gone home with her that very night. If I'd helped her pack and move away from him, she might still be alive.''

"You couldn't force her to leave him,'' Annie said. "It had to be her decision.''

"Yeah, that's the way it's supposed to work. That's what a shrink will tell you. Or a social worker. But that's not how I see it. Marie was like a wounded bird on the roadside—fragile and frightened and yearning to fly. She needed someone to pick her up and mend her wing. She needed me. Her brother.'' He would never stop blaming himself. "I should have protected her.''

"Why did she come to the bridge, Michael? Did you tell her what was happening?''

"God, no.'' At least he hadn't been that stupid. "But it was still my fault she was there. Somehow she learned about the robbery and the sting. She came to the bridge to warn me so I wouldn't be arrested with the others. And I let her die.''

The taut bonds of guilt constricted in his chest. His tethered heart wrenched. Even after all these years his shame hadn't loosened its grip. "Now you can understand, Annie. You can see why I blame myself for her death. If it wasn't for me, she wouldn't have been here.''

Finally he turned to her. He met her gaze, tried to read the emotions in her clear blue eyes. And he saw a plain simple acceptance of the facts. She said, "We can't change the past, Michael. No matter how much we want to.''

Her honesty pleased him. She hadn't tried to forgive the unforgivable, but he somehow felt absolved. His guilt was still there, but the tension eased. "But I had the chance to save her, Annie. When I saw her a few days before the robbery, I could've moved Marie to a safe place. She wouldn't have come here.''

''You'll never know.'' Annie shrugged. She didn't shower him with platitudes about how Marie's death wasn't his fault and how he should forgive himself. ''Life happens. I guess all we can do is learn from our mistakes.''

''You're right about that. Never again will I put the people I care about in danger.''

But that was exactly what was happening right now. A chill came over him as his gaze went from the river to the trees to the rocky shore where Marie had died.

History was repeating itself. Annie and her grandpa were in danger from Bateman. Annie had already been attacked once. He could feel the threat coming closer. ''Where's Lionel?''

''I left him where we had our picnic. Don't worry, Michael. He has my gun.''

But he was an old man who'd suffered a stroke. If Bateman came at him, Lionel couldn't protect himself. ''We should get back to him.''

''Wait, Michael.''

He halted midstride. ''What?''

''I'm glad you told me about Marie,'' she said. ''It helps me understand who you are.''

''Okay, fine.'' He was thinking about Lionel, about the danger that was all around them.

''Listen to me,'' she said. ''This is important. I'm trying as hard as I can to believe in you and to trust you.''

''Just accept me,'' he said.

''I can't. I know you too well.'' She cocked her head to one side and frankly stared at him. ''You might not remember this, Michael. But we were friends before we started dating.''

Impatiently he scanned the hillsides and the pilings of

the bridge, looking for danger. "You were one of the best friends I had. Even though you were a girl."

"Gosh, thanks for noticing."

"You know what I mean. It was weird to hang out with a girl, even if she could run faster and shoot baskets better than most of the guys. But when we were alone, just you and me, I probably talked more than I did to the guys."

"Even then, you were secretive. You never mentioned the abuse or the alcoholism. Never talked about your family."

"Neither did you," he remembered.

"I didn't talk much, but I listened. And I watched you. I knew when you were hiding something." She hesitated. "Like now, Michael. There's something else, something important you haven't told me."

He couldn't tell her. He wasn't at liberty to reveal his investigative role for the FBI. He hadn't denied his occupation; he simply hadn't mentioned it. "No lies, Annie. I haven't told lies about anything important."

"Except for this." She pointed to the sparkling diamond ring. "And a fake engagement is a whopper."

A gunshot rang out.

"Grandpa!"

She pivoted and flew across the rocky shore. Her feet barely touched the ground.

Michael was less graceful. He slipped twice on the uneven ground. By the time he got to the concrete pilings, she had already scrambled up to the road and was running full tilt.

He heard the rumble of heavy machinery before he saw the battered front grille and mud-splattered windshield of a huge truck, an eight-wheeler, capable of hauling tons of raw wood. It careered down the two-lane road, bearing down on Annie.

He would never reach her in time. "Jump, Annie!"

But there was nowhere she could go. The giant logging truck was capable of plowing through the underbrush, flattening shrubs and trees to chase her down.

In the shadow of this condemned bridge, the past was repeating. He wouldn't be able to save Annie, and she would die. Annie, his brave and beautiful Annie would be crushed under those giant tires. "For God's sake, Annie. Jump!"

But she stood stock-still on the edge of the road. The truck veered toward her.

Horrified, Michael could do nothing but watch. He was too faraway to reach her in time.

At the last possible second she dived into the high shrubbery and away from the path of the logging truck. The vehicle was too heavy to make the adjustment. The driver barely kept the truck on the road.

Now he was coming for Michael. The scarred grille was aimed directly at him, and he was glad. This was his chance for revenge. This was the moment when he would end the threat to Annie and her grandpa.

Michael positioned himself in front of the barriers to the bridge. The driver had to slow down. Otherwise he'd be on the bridge. Michael tried to see over the nose of the truck. Was that Bateman behind the wheel?

He wasn't slowing down. The son of a gun wasn't stopping.

Michael leaped onto a concrete piling as the truck crashed through the barrier, splintering the four-by-eight boards like matchsticks. Though Michael couldn't see inside the cab, he read the logo stenciled on the door: Stillwell Logging and Lumber Mill. Jake?

The truck roared onto the condemned bridge. The flatbed behind it was fully loaded. Tons of raw wood and metal raced onto a structure that hadn't been used in fifteen years.

The concrete ramp would hold, but the aging metal and rusted bolts were a risk.

The driver must have come to the same realization, because Michael could hear him accelerate, trying to get the huge truck to the other side.

"Annie?" he called up to her. "Are you all right?"

"I'm okay. Just a few bruises."

"Good." Because Michael wouldn't let this murderer get away. "I'm going after him."

"No!"

He stepped onto the bridge.

Chapter Eleven

Michael sprinted after the truck. He had no weapon. He had no plan. His pursuit was motivated by an instinctive rage that powered every cell of his body. His legs pumped hard. With each stride his arms reached out. He envisioned himself vaulting into the cab of the truck, pulling the driver out.

Huge tires roared onto the metal floor below the suspension arch. A sharp creaking split the air as rusted bolts tore against the web of girders, and Michael prayed the bridge would hold. He wanted this guy. Bateman? Stillwell? A hired assassin? It didn't matter. This time Michael was too damned close. He didn't want to lose him.

The eight-wheeler kept going. At the end of the opposite ramp, the truck's grille wiped out the barriers. The huge vehicle flashed its taillights and disappeared into the trees on the far side of the bridge.

Lost him again. Michael halted, his breath torn from his lungs. He bent double, then straightened. He was standing in the precise center of the metal arch.

To continue his pursuit was futile. The truck was long gone. The bridge had helped the guy escape. The rusted bolts and girders squeaked and wheezed as if laughing at Michael, taunting him. He'd failed again. A brisk wind whistled through the suspension cables, and he looked up at the metal ribs towering high above him, swallowing him alive.

On the bridge he could go forward or he could go back. Look toward the future or live in the past.

Michael stepped onto the narrow sidewalk on the edge of the two-lane bridge. He rested his hands on the guardrail and peered down sixty feet to the river, flowing smoothly, eternally, to the Pacific.

He stood in the middle of his life. His youth had been a nightmare with too many horror stories to count. He remembered the pain when he saw his mother cowering before his father's rage and the helpless sorrow when he tended to his little brother's black eye. Michael's own bruises never hurt as much as theirs. He remembered the constant yelling and the weeping that followed. He would never forget the stink of his father when he'd had too much to drink and passed out in a chair in front of the television. The last memory, the deepest scar, was the death of Marie, the sister he could have saved.

Why couldn't he let go? He wanted to hurl that part of his past into the river and turn his back as it washed away in a swirling eddy, but he couldn't change his heritage. It was as much a part of him as his arms, his legs, his heart. No matter what else happened in his life, he was still Michael Slade, a poor boy from a small town in Oregon who had lost every reason to hope—every reason except one. Annie.

He turned toward the Bridgeport side of the river and stared at the place Marie had fallen. Then his eyes lifted to the treetops and higher, to misted skies where a ray of light pierced the ragged-edged clouds. Bridgeport was also the source of his dreams, because Annie was here. She was his single ray of hope.

It wasn't too late. He had a chance with her now. They

could be together again, and he'd have a reason to believe
in the future.

He saw his BMW coming down the hill, Annie driving.
Michael let go of the railing and started back toward her.
He didn't want her driving onto this center section. It was
too perilous. He waved his arms and shouted, "I'm coming! Stay off the center."

At the edge of the concrete, she parked. But she didn't
stay put.

She left the car and ran toward him, charging fearlessly
onto the bridge. She flung herself into his arms and held
on tight. No words passed between them. None was necessary.

With all his strength, he clung to her. The feel of her
lean graceful body cured his rage. The fragrance of her
clean hair renewed his belief in the distant possibility of
happiness.

"It's over," he whispered. The FBI be damned. He
wasn't going to stick around here and spy on Bateman.
Michael needed to get Annie and her grandpa to safety. He
had to protect his future, his only hope for redemption.

"It's not over yet, Michael. Not until tomorrow."

"We won't wait for it. I'm putting through a call for my
boat. We'll be out at sea. We'll be safe there."

"It won't do any good," she said. "Bateman isn't going
away. He's still going to—"

"Hush, Annie. We'll let someone else worry about Bateman. I want us all to be safe."

As soon as he got back to the house, Michael intended
to contact his people and arrange for the charter boat to be
brought down the coast. Fortunately *Rosebud* was already
docked in Portland after delivering a witness. They
wouldn't have far to sail.

He slipped behind the steering wheel and glanced over

at Lionel. Michael was glad to see the old man scowling, glad to see him alive. "What happened?" he asked him.

"I was up on the hill minding my own business, and I heard the truck. When I twisted around, I could just see him up at the high point on the road, waiting. I wanted to warn you. So I fired a shot." His scowl deepened. "That was a mistake. My shot brought you to the road, right into the path of the truck."

"It worked out fine," Annie assured him. "If Michael and I had been together, he probably would've picked off one of us. By myself, I could lure him off to one side. I knew that if he committed to one direction, he couldn't change fast enough if I went the other way."

Michael swung the car around and drove off the ramp and back up the road. "How do you know so much about trucks?"

"For a couple of weeks one summer," she said, "I worked as a flagman. When those big rigs have to stop fast, they have to downshift like mad. It takes skill and muscle to drive a fully loaded truck. Do you think Bateman knows how?"

"The truck came from Stillwell's," Lionel said. "I saw the logo on the side."

Michael didn't want to encourage further investigation. The prudent course was to retreat, find shelter. "We'll report this to Engstrom and leave it at that. I'll have my boat brought close, and we'll drive up the coast to rendezvous with it."

"I won't run away," Lionel said. "This is my home."

"And you'll come back to it," Michael said. "After the thirteenth."

"One day won't make a difference," Annie said. "Today isn't the thirteenth, and look what happened."

"We can stay out at sea for a week. Maybe longer. Bateman is sure to make a mistake before then. He'll be back in prison."

"We have a truck-size clue here, Michael. If Bateman stole it, *somebody* must have seen him. We're not going anywhere until Engstrom has a chance to check this out. He might even be able to arrest Bateman today." She pointed at the glove compartment. "Grandpa, reach in there and hand me the cell phone."

Michael tried to intercept the phone as Lionel passed it into the backseat. "Annie, let me make the call."

"You're driving," she said. "You need to concentrate on the road. I'll put through the call to Engstrom."

He'd known it wouldn't be simple to convince her and Lionel to leave Bridgeport. Apparently it took more than someone with a lumber truck as a weapon to convince them their lives were in danger.

AFTER SHE REPORTED the incident to Engstrom, Annie put through a call to Stillwell Logging and Lumber, only to discover that Jake wasn't in his office. She spoke to his secretary. "Tell him Annie Callahan called."

"Good to hear your voice, Annie. It's me, Viv Appleton."

"Hi, Viv. How are you doing?"

"I'd be a lot better if the kids weren't out of school for the summer."

Occasionally Annie got together with Viv when she visited Lionel, and she'd always enjoyed the other woman's sense of humor, undiminished by the demands of caring for rambunctious six-year-old twins.

"I've got a question for you, Viv. Is one of the Stillwell lumber trucks missing?"

"Are you psychic? It was reported to me fifteen minutes ago. Stolen off the lot. I haven't even had a chance to call Chief Engstrom. Or tell Jake, for that matter."

"Jake hasn't been in?"

"He came in early, then left with a headache." In a quiet voice Viv added, "I think the name of the headache is Candace."

"Didn't you call him at home?"

"I left a message, but he didn't pick up. So what's this I hear about you and Michael Slade?"

"I'll call in a couple of days," Annie promised, "and I'll tell you all about it."

"He's been gone a long time, but I always thought you two were perfect for each other," Viv said. "Give Michael a big wet kiss for me."

Annie said goodbye and pressed the disconnect button. To Lionel and Michael she said, "Jake wasn't in his office."

It would be simple for Jake to fake stealing his own truck, and he probably knew how to drive the thing. Though she couldn't think of a motive, she wanted to follow up on the possibility.

If she had some answers, she wouldn't mind leaving town. A sea voyage with Captain Michael Slade would be lovely, but Annie would not turn tail and run from Bateman or anybody else. She didn't want to lose this war of intimidation.

The stakes were higher now. They'd gone from annoying harassment to a life-threatening assault. But wasn't that how they had started, in the parking lot outside her apartment? She'd known all along it would come to this.

"You'll love the *Rosebud,*" Michael said with forced enthusiasm. "She's a fine boat. And the sea air will do you good, Lionel."

Her grandpa peered through the windshield. "Looks like rain."

"A little squall," Michael said. "It'll pass."

They were almost back home to Myrtlewood Lane, and

Annie had pretty much decided on what she'd do next. She wanted to talk to Jake Stillwell. And she didn't want Michael's interference. Whenever those two men were together, they were too busy snarling at each other for her to have a straightforward conversation.

Quietly she transferred her gun from the picnic basket to her purse.

"Here's what we do," Michael said as he pulled into the driveway. "Throw a couple of things in a suitcase and we're out of here. Agreed?"

Lionel grumbled, "I've got a session with Sam scheduled for day after tomorrow."

"Sorry, Michael," Annie said as she climbed out of the backseat.

Before she could flit into the house, he confronted her. "This is no time to be stubborn. Somebody just tried to kill you. As a cop, you should understand the danger."

"Speaking as a police officer, the time to investigate is when the trail is hot. If Bateman is cruising around in a giant lumber truck, he's going to get caught."

"Let Engstrom take care of it."

But she wanted to talk to Jake Stillwell. If they were alone, she might be able to get him to open up.

"Please, Annie." He caught hold of her hands. "I swore to protect you. Let me do my job."

She met his gaze and saw the hint of anguish behind his eyes. For the first time she truly understood why it was so vitally important for him to be sure they were safe. After what had happened to Marie, Michael was obsessive about protection. He'd blamed himself, and he didn't want another death on his conscience. That was why he'd followed her in Salem, carried a pistol to Bridgeport and installed a high-tech security system at the house. He couldn't bear for anyone else to be hurt.

"I'll be careful," she assured him.

"That's not good enough."

"It has to be," she said. "Michael, you're going to have to trust me."

"Trust you?" He smiled. "I thought it was the other way around."

"Trust goes both ways."

She broke away from him to help Lionel out of the car. In spite of everything, her grandpa was making remarkable physical progress. Though he leaned heavily on her shoulder, he was able to climb the staircase with only three rest stops.

After she got him settled on the bed, Lionel caught hold of her arm. "You're up to something," he said.

"Don't worry. I'll be careful."

"I don't want you taking risks. Let Michael handle this."

"Why?" She searched his weathered face, looking for answers. "Why would you think Michael was better qualified to handle risk than I am?"

"His military training," Lionel said. "And..."

"What else?" There were secrets between her grandpa and Michael that she hadn't even begun to unearth. "What else does Michael do?"

"It's not my place to tell you."

Her grandpa had kept tabs on Michael and stayed in touch. "You knew about Marie Cartier, didn't you? That she was Michael's half sister."

He nodded. "I know that her death was the worst thing that ever happened to Michael Slade."

"We're going to have a nice long talk when I get back, Lionel." She patted his cheek. "But right now, you need rest."

Annie hurried down the stairs. She heard Michael on the phone and was glad he was preoccupied. In the kitchen, she wrote a note for him, promising to be back in half an hour. Snagging his car keys, she left the house. Annie was on her way to Jake's.

The beautiful old house on the hilltop was, as Candace had said, a mausoleum. There were pillars in the front, like a Southern antebellum mansion. When Annie pressed the doorbell, it echoed.

Jake answered on the third ring. He looked like a man who hadn't slept in days. Dark circles rimmed his eyes. His complexion was waxen, and the skin on his face seemed loose. Though he was dressed for work, his shirttail was untucked and his necktie loosened. "What are you doing here?" he asked.

"Can I come in, Jake?"

He stepped aside, allowing the heavy door to swing open on silent hinges. "Your timing sucks, Annie. I've been trying to get you alone all week, and now I'm in the middle of a crisis."

Why had he wanted to get her alone? She had a hard time reading Jake. From being a quarterback, he'd learned to look one way and throw in the opposite direction. "Your crisis wouldn't have anything to do with a missing lumber truck, would it?"

"What do you know about it?"

"I saw it being driven in an irresponsible manner."

"Where?"

"I'd rather not say." She glanced around the marble entryway. Though the soaring ceilings, sweeping staircase and crystal chandelier were impressive, the Stillwell home had seemed larger when she'd come here during high school. Back then she'd thought she was in a palace. Now it was just a big empty house, far too much space for one person.

"The truck doesn't matter. Besides, it's already been located." He ushered her into the formal living room. "Chief Engstrom found it parked by the side of the road not far from where it was stolen. The front grille is damaged and the headlights are both broken.''

"But it's otherwise intact?''

"With my lousy luck, the engine is probably wrecked.'' He poured amber liquid from a crystal decanter. "Drink?''

"No, thanks.''

The clean lines of modern furniture and glass-topped tables were designed not to compete with the art that covered the walls all the way to the ceiling. One entire wall was devoted to African masks. "I see your mother is still collecting.''

"She and Dad never come back here anymore. This house is nothing more to them than an expensive warehouse for them.'' He sipped at his drink. His eyes were already glassy. "Why did you come here, Annie?''

"You know what's been going on with Bateman,'' she said. "He's been harassing my grandpa and me.''

"Why come to me? Can't Mikey protect you?''

She ignored his sneer. "I want to know if you've heard anything. Have you talked to Bateman? I need your help, Jake.''

She could almost see his ego swelling in his chest. He liked to be the most important man around, the boss. With another few drinks he might be spilling information.

"As a matter of fact,'' he said, "Bateman came to me for a job.''

"Did you hire him?''

"If I didn't, he was going to blab about my involvement with his gang ten years ago. Right now I'm in the midst of complex negotiations with a bank in Portland, and I don't want them to know about the little problem I had in my youth.''

That was all it was to him. Marie Cartier's tragic death was just "a little problem.'' Annie compared Jake's superficiality to Michael's heartfelt sorrow and decided that Jake was a lightweight, a phony. What else was he faking? Was he dangerous?

Annie had kept her purse with her. Her gun was only a second away from her grasp. "Did you give Bateman a job?"

"I signed him up as a choker-setter, but he only lasted half a day. Then he figured that he could blackmail me so I'd give him a salary without doing any work."

"That's extortion," she said. And extortion was a crime. Bateman could be prosecuted and returned to jail. Her problems were over.

"Only if I choose to prosecute," Jake said. "And it would be hard to prove because I'm paying him out of the lumber-mill payroll as if he was actually on the job."

"I don't understand. Don't you want Bateman back in prison?"

"Frankly it's a lot cheaper to keep him on the payroll than to have this loan package fall through." He finished off his drink in one swig. "I'm real sorry that he's causing trouble for you and your grandpa. But I have to think of the lumber mill first. If I go out of business, this lousy town will vanish from the face of the earth."

She looked around at the big house and the expensive paintings. Jake Stillwell certainly didn't look like he was hurting for cash. "You're not making a profit?"

"It's not enough." He gave a short humorless laugh. "Supporting Candace is even costlier now that she doesn't live with me. You might pass that tidbit of information along to your supposed fiancé."

"You don't like Michael, do you?"

"No." He poured another drink. "He was always trying to be better than he was. It's best when people know their place, and I'm not saying that to be a snob."

She couldn't think of any other reason he might make

such a remark, but Annie kept her opinion to herself. She'd learn more if she allowed Jake to ramble.

"I met his father," Jake said. "Old Man Slade was pure evil, and the apple doesn't fall far from the tree."

"Do you blame Michael for getting you involved with Bateman?"

"I'd like to think it was Mikey's fault that I went so far. I probably would've backed out of the robbery before I got arrested."

His words were beginning to slur. She noticed that his shirttail was dirty. It was possible Jake had been driving the truck, dropped it off and raced back here. Hadn't Viv said that she'd tried to reach him earlier and he hadn't answered?

He lifted his tumbler in a toast. "Here's to that girl who got killed."

"Marie," Annie said quietly.

"That's right. She was pretty in a cheap sort of way. Like plastic beads and bangles."

Annie stiffened. If anybody had ever deserved a punch in the mouth, it was Jake Stillwell.

He drained his glass in one gulp. "My mother never forgave me for what happened that night. She liked that girl. Marie."

That was a surprise. Annie always thought that Mrs. Stillwell was prim and proper, at least as status conscious as her son.

"Marie worked for us. Cleaning the house." He sauntered through the archway into an adjoining room, which was devoted entirely to his mother's collections. One of the glass exhibit cases was filled with lovely Dresden figurines. "Mother took a shine to Marie because she'd sit and listen to her endless droning about art. I mean, look at this junk."

Annie couldn't tear her gaze away from the graceful china figures. Among the larger figures were a shepherdess, a cavalier and several courtiers. If Marie had admired this collection, she might have tried to duplicate it with her own, more humble figurines. It seemed so obvious. The statuettes must have belonged to Marie. But who had saved them? And why was he using them to harass Annie?

"...never forgave me," Jake was saying. "Mother said I was responsible for the death of a gentle soul. But I was *her son*. What about my soul, huh?"

He crumpled onto a Queen Anne chair, and Annie felt as if she was seeing the real Jake Stillwell for the first time. He was a dissolute snob.

Wanting to get away from him as soon as possible, she abandoned any attempt at subtlety. "Do you know how to drive a huge rig, Jake?"

"Why would I? I'm management. The trucks aren't my job."

"Is there anything else you've done for Bateman? Any other little jobs he's blackmailed you into doing?"

"I might have done him a favor, like putting him on the payroll. Bateman might have access to all the Stillwell equipment. The axes. The trucks. Dynamite. But I'm not working with him. What are you getting at?"

"I'm asking the questions," she said. And there was only one more. "Why did you want to get me alone?"

His tongue rolled out of the corner of his mouth. He waggled his finger at her. "I know what you're doing. This is an interrogation, huh? You're trying to work your cop tricks on me."

He wouldn't think that unless he had something to hide. "Did Bateman ask you to get me alone?"

"You're not so smart," Jake snarled. "You think you know everything, but you don't."

"Then why don't you tell me? Tell me what I've missed."

"You're a good-looking woman. You've got pretty legs,

long legs.'' He staggered to his feet. ''Maybe Bateman asked me to arrange for you to come up to the house tomorrow, but I wouldn't mind getting you alone.''

''There isn't a meeting tomorrow?''

''Nobody would've been here but you and me.''

And Bateman. Annie stalked toward the front door. ''Goodbye, Jake.''

WHEN SHE RETURNED to the house, Michael was waiting. He ripped open the door before she could insert her key in the lock. ''Where were you?''

It was such a pleasure to see him again. Michael was everything Jake was not. ''I missed you,'' she said.

''What?''

''You're a good man, Michael. Sensitive and strong. You're never intentionally cruel.''

''Thanks,'' he said suspiciously.

Feeling lighthearted, she breezed past him into the plain homey foyer. She glided her hand across the worn finish of the newel post at the base of the wooden staircase, which was gouged and marred from years of living. Overhead was a simple light fixture, and she thought it was a hundred times more beautiful than the chandelier in the Stillwell home. ''Is Grandpa okay?''

''Sleeping,'' Michael said. Arms folded across his chest, he regarded her sternly. ''Where the hell were you?''

''I think I have one piece of this puzzle solved.'' She patted his cheek, tweaked his nose and whisked down the hall to the kitchen. ''I went to see Jake Stillwell, and you're right about him. Jake is not a decent human being.''

Annie made herself a heaping bowl of chocolate-ripple ice cream while she told him how Jake had put Bateman on the payroll. ''But that's not the important part.''

''Gee, and I thought blackmail would be grounds to revoke his parole.''

"Listen to this." She described the Dresden china at the Stillwell house and her idea that Marie might have started a collection of her own. "What do you think?"

"You may be right. That's something she would do. I don't remember the figurines, but she had a lot of fluffy stuff in her house. Afghans and fancy pillows."

"What happened to her belongings?"

"I assume they stayed with her husband. His name was Ron."

"Here's a thought." Annie dug her spoon into the ice cream. "Could Ron Cartier, Marie's husband, be involved with Drew Bateman? They're both from Wayside, after all."

"It's possible." Michael had only met Ron Cartier once and hadn't liked him. Ron was too much like his father—tall and angry and always holding a beer. "He worked on the docks. I think he crewed on a fishing trawler."

Usually the trawlers went out every morning at dawn and returned every afternoon with their catch. There were also longer trips, putting in at different ports. If Marie's husband had turned to crime, he had a good occupation for smuggling and a possible connection to the FBI investigation. Had the anonymous phone calls from Wayside and Bridgeport originated with Marie's husband? Was he the link to Bateman? "Ron Cartier might be just the person we're looking for."

"We'll see." She bounced up from the table and grabbed the wall phone. "I'm calling information in Wayside."

Finally Michael had something new to report in his nightly phone call to the disembodied voice. But why wait? He had already contacted his immediate superiors and arranged for *Rosebud* to be brought down the coast. If anyone had been monitoring his calls, Michael's cover was pretty much blown.

She turned to him with a frown. "No listing for a Ron

or Ronald Cartier. But that's not a problem. I'll call one of my buddies at the Salem PD and track him down."

"Wait, Annie." The FBI wouldn't want the Salem cops blundering into their investigation. "I'll handle this."

If she asked why he thought his contacts were better than hers, Michael was prepared to tell her the absolute truth about the FBI and naval intelligence. Once she was on board *Rosebud,* she'd figure it out, anyway.

But Annie was concentrating on the last bite of her ice cream. "Fine with me, Michael. You take care of tracking down Marie's husband."

He could see the wheels turning in her head. Her agile mind had leaped to another line of investigation. "What are you thinking?"

"From what you told me, Marie and Ron were on the outs. She had a new boyfriend."

He nodded. The memory of his last conversation with his half sister was still painful.

"Maybe that's who we should be tracking down."

The mysterious lover. Marie's escape from her abusive husband to a man who was supposed to be a good person. It made for a complicated string of connections, but Michael had a hunch she was on to something.

LATE THAT NIGHT, Annie was stretched out on her bed. The scent of fresh-washed sheets and the slippery feel of a satin short-sleeved nightshirt were pure luxury. In spite of everything that had happened today, she felt a warm sense of contentment. Both the people she cared about—her grandpa and Michael—were going to be all right.

Her grandpa's plan for building a halfway house on his property by the bridge was the ultimate fulfillment of his destiny. She'd help Lionel in every way possible with this endeavor. Her contacts with the victims-assistance people in Salem, the state capital, would facilitate referrals and funding for his project.

Somehow she knew her grandpa would be all right. He wouldn't be lonely or sad. His life had a purpose.

She exhaled a sigh. Then there was Michael. After his painful confession at the bridge, she finally felt as if she knew Michael Slade. The *real* Michael. His reaction to the death of his half sister made sense to Annie, and the depth of his feelings touched her.

Finally she knew why he'd left her. Deep in her heart, she forgave him.

Her bedroom door creaked open. "Michael?"

"Were you expecting someone else?"

"No one else." Not a movie star or a handsome prince. Michael had always been the man of her fantasies.

"It's after midnight," he said.

"June thirteenth." The day was here.

"Annie, I need to talk to you."

Just talk? She was ready for more. She turned on the bedside lamp. "Come on in."

He sat beside the bed on a desk chair that seemed much too small for his large frame. Also incongruous was the gun he placed on her bedside table, a reminder that they were more than potential lovers in the night. He was her protector, whether she wanted protection or not.

Once again he was wearing a white shirt as if he'd just left his bed and thrown on the first thing he could grab. Once again the sleeves were rolled up to reveal darkly tanned forearms. Once again his shirt was unbuttoned and her gaze was drawn to his crisp curling chest hair.

"Here's the deal, Annie. I want you to convince Lionel to leave town. We'll leave at dawn. I want you both on my boat where we'll be safe."

"You're overreacting," she said. "We have the alarm system here at the house. Nobody can sneak inside and hurt us. Bateman isn't going to show his hand because he doesn't want to go back to prison. He's been careful."

Chief Engstrom had dusted the entire truck for prints and had found nothing to incriminate Bateman or Jake Stillwell or anybody else. The eight-wheeler was a ton of clue that led nowhere.

"Don't worry, Michael. We're going to be fine."

"What if you're wrong?" Concern etched his features, deepening the fine lines at the corners of his eyes. He reached over to the bedside table and picked up her grandma's engagement ring. "I swore to protect you, Annie. And that wasn't a lie."

"We have no more lies between us," she said.

"None." Rising from the chair, he sat on the bed beside her. Gently he lifted her hand and slid the ring onto her finger. "I won't let anything bad happen to you."

His nearness took her breath away. She couldn't quite believe he was here, in her bedroom. But when he held her hand, the warmth of his touch spread through her in a chain reaction. She couldn't deny the reality of this strong sensitive man.

"We...we'll be okay," she stammered. "Really."

"Let me take care of you. Trust me, Annie."

"I do." She knew everything about him, from his horrifying childhood to his criminal past. Everything!

"Believe me when I tell you the danger isn't over."

He leaned over her to stroke her cheek. His hand lingered, lightly tracing her ear, teasing her.

Looking up at him, she knew she'd never seen a more perfect face. His dark eyes shone in the lamplight. The line of his jaw was strong and firm. And his lips, though unmoving, spoke to her of longing and passion.

She arched her back, pulling herself toward him. Supporting herself on her good arm, she tasted his mouth. Sensation fluttered through her body, teasing her, making her hungry for more. Any thought of resistance was abandoned when his arms encircled her and supported her against him.

His hand glided over the satin nightshirt. When he cupped her breast, Annie moaned with pleasure.

Slowly he unbuttoned the nightshirt and touched her with light arousing strokes. His gaze lifted to hers. His eyes were hot. He kissed the tip of her nose, her forehead, her eyelids. His every touch was choreographed to heighten the soaring tension, rising like waves at high tide.

Inspired by his example, she pushed aside his shirt and ran her fingers through his chest hair, caressing his muscular form. The heat of his body fired her touch as she traced lower to the waistband of his jeans, and lower until she touched the evidence of his arousal, bulging against the seams. She fondled its length.

He shuddered, and she reveled in the power she had over him, the power to excite and to fulfill.

"I need to make love to you," he whispered.

"Yes, Michael." She couldn't stop now. She'd waited years for this moment. She needed him.

When he kissed her deeply, the entire house trembled on its foundations. There was an explosion.

Her ears rang with the continuous scream of sirens. The house really had shaken on its foundations. "What happened?"

Michael tore himself away from her. His gun was in his hand.

Chapter Twelve

Michael knew when he smelled smoke that the explosion was intended as more than a warning. The security-alarm sirens screeched hysterically as he raced down the stairs, gun at the ready.

The damage had been done to the rear of the house, in the guest bedroom. The back wall smoldered where it had been ripped apart. The casement window was shattered. Flames climbed the curtains and spread across the bedcovers.

"Oh, my God!" Annie stood beside him, clutching her nightshirt together with one hand and holding her pistol in the other. "It's a good thing you were with me."

"A very good thing."

They'd come so close to making love. He was still ready. The image of her stuck in his mind. His hands remembered the feel of her skin. If the house hadn't been on fire...

"I'll call 911!" she shouted over the noise of the sirens.

"And I'll get the hose." He went through the back door, headed for the coiled garden hose at the faucet. Lights came on in neighboring houses. Half the residents of Myrtlewood Lane were witnesses to this latest disaster.

Cranking the water pressure to high, Michael sprayed the back wall. An arson investigation was necessary, but he knew enough about high explosives from his SEAL training to guess what had happened. Somebody had taped a bomb to the side of the house, lit the fuse and run.

Though it was a big step up from throwing bricks through the window or deflating car tires, the explosion followed the same simple but effective pattern. It was likely the perpetrator had swiped TNT from the lumber mill, but Michael didn't plan to stick around for the detective work. He'd had enough threats, enough violence. His only goal was to bring Annie and her grandpa to a safe harbor.

As soon as the fire department arrived, he returned to the house and hiked up the stairs to Lionel's bedroom. The old man was already up and dressed, as was Annie.

"Both of you get packed," Michael said. "We're leaving Bridgeport. *Now!*"

Annie nodded. This time there would be no argument. "We'll be ready in fifteen minutes."

"How bad is the damage?" Lionel asked.

Michael didn't have the heart to indulge in I-told-you-so recriminations. Annie's grandpa had gone through enough. "It's fixable. But I won't lie to you, Lionel. It's going to take more than a roll of duct tape."

"It was the guest room?"

"That's right."

"If you had been there, Mikey, you could have been killed."

"But I wasn't."

"Why?"

Michael exchanged a look with Annie. Now was probably not the best time to tell Lionel that his relationship with Annie had become intimate. "I couldn't sleep. I was up looking for a book."

She smiled at him and squeezed his arm. "I'll get the suitcases. Grandpa, you finish dressing."

Unaided by his walker, Lionel managed the seven steps to his easy chair. He sank down heavily. "I never thought it would come to this. I figured Bateman would hang around for a few days, then get bored and leave us alone.''

"It's hard to gauge a man's need for revenge.''

"All this violence. The hatred.'' Lionel's eyelids drooped and his shoulders slumped. He was weighed down by a weariness that had nothing to do with his stroke. "I'm sorry, Mikey. When this all started so long ago, I never dreamed it would—''

"It's okay, Lionel.''

"Let me finish, son. I've been meaning to tell you this for a long time. It comes down to one thing. I was wrong.''

Downstairs Michael heard the pandemonium of firemen and cops and half the residents of Myrtlewood Lane trying to be helpful. Up here in the bedroom was a stillness. Lionel Callahan was a proud man. It took a lot for him to admit to a mistake, especially a mistake of this magnitude, a mistake that had led to the death of Marie Cartier.

Still, Michael tried to spare the old man's feelings. "It's all right.''

"Please,'' he said sharply. "I need to say this.''

When Annie came flying back into the room, she must have sensed the moment. Quietly she set down the luggage and closed the door. "What is it?''

"Eleven years ago,'' Lionel said, "you two started dating. I'd warned all my football players that my granddaughter was off limits, but Mikey Slade always followed his own rules. At first, I wasn't too happy about the arrangement.''

Lionel fixed Michael with an unwavering gaze. "You were a troubled teenager. I'd seen you more than once in municipal court.''

Michael accepted the older man's judgment without comment or complaint.

And Lionel sighed. "I wanted more for Annie. She was

my bright, beautiful granddaughter. I wanted the best for her.''

A crash from downstairs broke the mood, and Annie came toward him. ''Ancient history, grandpa. We all survived. Everything turned out okay.''

''But it didn't,'' he said. ''Mikey came to me with a problem. He told me about the robbery that Bateman and his gang were planning. He asked for my advice.''

Annie drew closer, seemingly mesmerized by her grandpa's words. And Michael wondered what her reaction would be. It was likely she'd be angry at him for not telling the exact truth about the incident at the bridge. God, he hoped not. Her trust was not easily won.

''I worked with the county sheriff in Wayside,'' Lionel said, ''to set up the sting operation. And we told Michael he had to be there or else the others would suspect him. We allowed the robbery to take place.''

''Entrapment,'' she said. ''You had foreknowledge of a crime and did nothing to stop it.''

''If they hadn't committed the robbery, we couldn't arrest them. Believe me, Annie, those boys needed help. They were a wild bunch and they weren't impressed by warnings. They scoffed at the local police. We needed the threat of jail time to get their attention.''

''It was a bad call,'' Annie said. ''You weren't dealing with hardened criminals. These were teenagers. You could have brought them in for juvenile detention, recommended counseling.''

''I knew better,'' Lionel said stiffly. Confession did not come easily to this proud man. ''Over the years, I've second guessed myself a hundred times. There were so many other alternatives. And I'm afraid I encouraged the sting operation for my own reasons.''

''What reasons?'' Annie demanded.

''I wanted Mikey to realize how dangerous a life of

crime could be. If he was going to be with my Annie, I
wanted him to be cleansed. I took a risk, and I was wrong.
The county sheriff was wrong. My god, Michael, I'm so
sorry. Marie paid the price for my bad judgment.''

"Wait a minute," Annie said. "Are you telling me that
Michael was never a criminal? That he informed the police
before the robbery?''

"Exactly right," Lionel said. "We arranged it so he
wouldn't have a criminal record.''

"You sealed the testimony at Bateman's trial," she said.
"You and the county sheriff made it impossible for anybody to know that Michael was part of your sting operation.''

"But it still wasn't right," Lionel said. "Mikey, I'm
sorry for everything that went wrong. And I'm sorry for
what's happening right now.''

"It's water under the bridge," Michael said. "I'm not
living in the past. Not anymore.''

Annie flipped open the suitcase on the bed. "Okay, it's
time for the future, boys. And if we plan to have one, it's
time to get packed.''

Tentatively Michael approached her. He didn't want to
lose the relationship that was building between them, and
he knew how much she valued honesty. He placed his
hands on her shoulders and turned her to face him. "This
doesn't really count as a lie, does it?''

She regarded him steadily, measuring his sincerity. Then
she winked. "I guess it doesn't.''

"Why not?" Immediately he backtracked. "Don't get
me wrong. I'm glad. But why—''

"Because I always knew in my heart that you couldn't
be one of the bad guys.''

HOURS LATER, Annie stared at the scarlet dawn that
stretched above the open seas. "Red sky at morning," she

whispered. "Sailor take warning."

They'd driven half the night to reach the dock near the coastal town of Seaside, where they would rendezvous with Michael's boat. Though Lionel had slept during the ride, he seemed exhausted as she helped him out of the car and positioned his walker on the docks.

"Where are we, Annie?"

"I can't say for sure, but Michael seems to know where he's going." He'd made a dozen calls on his cell phone to finalize arrangements. "We'll have to trust that he knows what he's doing."

"He won't disappoint us," Lionel said.

Though the streets and highways had been empty during their ride, the docks were busy at dawn with professional fishermen in trawlers and well-equipped powerboats.

A clean-cut young man appeared with a wheelchair. "Captain Slade said you could use this, ma'am."

"Thank you."

She helped Lionel sit while the young crewman unloaded the suitcases from the trunk. "Follow me," he said, easily lifting all three bags.

Annie didn't know what to expect. *Rosebud* was a charter boat, which meant it must be in fairly good condition or nobody would rent time on it. She knew it was a schooner with sails, and it was seventy feet long.

Nothing could have prepared her for the magnificent vessel at the end of the dock. The lower hull was shining ebony with a strip of wood trim just below the decks. At the fore was a long teakwood bowsprit, gleaming in the dawn. Towering above the deck were bare masts and rigging. Michael stood at the gangplank. He seemed even taller with the wind ruffling his hair, and he was clearly in control, calmly issuing orders to another young man who scurried around the deck.

Michael's dark-eyed gaze focused upon her, inviting her into another world, his world, his livelihood beyond Bridgeport. When he stepped onto the dock and held out his hand to her, Annie felt like the most special woman in the world, the mate of Captain Slade.

"She's beautiful, Michael."

He glowed with pride. "She was launched twenty-seven years ago, and every owner has treated *Rosebud* with the respect she deserves."

With his young deckhands helping, Lionel got onboard and down the companionway into the area belowdecks, where Michael gave the grand tour. "First we go through the galley. On the other side of the bar is the main salon."

There were plush bench seats against the wall and a table fastened to the floor. Two other captain's chairs made an attractive conversation area, and there were also a television and stereo speakers. Though the accommodations were tight, they were luxurious.

"Back here is your stateroom, Lionel."

Michael supported her grandpa as he maneuvered through the narrow hall and into the larger of three rooms— a tasteful masculine room with wood-paneled walls and a white ceiling. Lionel wasted no time lowering himself onto the forest-green comforter. "This is first class, Mikey."

"Annie, your room is across the hall," Michael said. "You probably want to get settled while I finish casting off."

She realized it wasn't a request but an order. This was Michael's domain and he was the master. Without waiting for her response, he left the stateroom.

Though Annie could have guessed that Michael would be strong and competent in whatever occupation he chose, she'd never really seen this side of his personality. And she was fascinated. Captain Slade? He was nearly as spectacular as his boat.

In moments she had her grandpa settled into the bed. In spite of thermostatically controlled heat, there was a slight chill belowdecks, but he had plenty of blankets and a down comforter. "What do you think, Grandpa? Are you going to be okay?"

"Better than that. We'll be safe." His eyelids closed. "I need to rest now, Annie."

She hurried through the salon and the galley, up the companionway and onto the teak deck where Michael was dismissing one of his crew, the young man who had toted their luggage. "Take my car back to Seattle. I'll be in touch."

"Aye, aye, Skipper."

When Michael turned and saw her, he introduced Peter, a husky seaman with a shock of pale blond hair. "Peter is first mate," Michael said. "He's in charge when I'm not around."

"Pleasure to meet you, ma'am."

"Likewise." She shook his hand, then turned to Michael. "And where do I fall in the chain of command?"

Michael grinned. "I wouldn't touch that question with a twelve-foot yardarm. Peter, prepare to cast off."

Michael led her to the cockpit at the stern, behind the raised boathouse on deck. A natural commander, he took a position behind the spoked wooden wheel set in front of a control panel. From this position they were looking down the length of the vessel.

"Is there anything I can do to help?" she asked.

"Not until we're away from the docks."

He fired up the engine and signaled to his crewman onshore, who loosened the guy ropes and stood watching as *Rosebud* eased away from the docks. He almost seemed to be standing at attention. "Is your crew former navy?"

"Former SEALS. Like me."

"You were a SEAL? I'm impressed."

He guided the vessel away from the busy dockside area. The tall schooner glided majestically, like a queen amid the humble fishing boats. The fresh seabreezes swirled around them, seeming to blow light into the skies as the dawn faded.

Annie perched on a cockpit locker and took this chance to study Michael while he was preoccupied with navigating safely past the offshore rocks. His strong legs braced against the slight rocking of the waves. He held the wheel with both hands, making constant adjustments as they left the noisy harbor behind and headed for the open sea.

Soon the only sound she heard was the hum of the engine and the lapping of water against the hull. Michael's gaze concentrated on possible hazards. His movements were confident.

Annie sighed as she watched him. Nothing in the world was sexier than a man doing his job with skill and competence. She was so turned on. She could hardly wait to get Michael into her stateroom and consummate the passion they had tested in her bedroom.

After they had put some distance between themselves and the shore, he beckoned to her. "Do you want to take the helm?"

"You bet." She bounced to her feet.

"Stand here." He positioned her right in front of him, maintaining his grasp on the wheel. "Grab the wooden pegs and hold a steady course."

"Where are we going?"

"Back up the coast to Seattle, but we have plenty of time for side trips because we don't have to be back until the twentieth."

"You know today is the thirteenth, don't you?"

"How could I forget? It started with an explosion at midnight."

Though it was only hours ago, the threats from Bateman

seemed faraway. Annie would've liked to believe that *Rosebud* existed in a different dimension, a special place where no one could touch it. But she knew better. ''What if there are new developments in the investigation?''

''I arranged to be in touch with Engstrom,'' he said. ''He'll keep us up-to-date.''

Though she didn't want to think about Bateman, the danger was never far from her mind. He'd come too close to be readily dismissed.

Tightening her fingers around two of the protruding wooden pegs on the steering wheel, she nestled against Michael's warm hard body. She was simultaneously excited by the power of handling the boat and the powerful man who was her captain. A former member of the elite navy SEALS and a captain. What other accomplishments had he neglected to mention?

Annie stared down the gleaming length of *Rosebud* to the sea beyond. ''How do we know which way we're going?''

He leaned close to her ear. ''On the Pacific, the horizon is generally to the west.''

''I know that.'' She glanced down at the myriad dials and compasses built into the helm. Navigating a boat of this size looked more complicated than flying an airplane. ''What happens when we can't see the shore?''

''I'll tell you where we're headed.''

He released his hands from the wheel and stepped back. She was alone at the helm. A thrill went through her. ''For a control freak like me, this is heaven.''

''You never really have control. The ocean is always stronger. The secret is to mate with the waves and to hope they won't turn angry.'' He leaned over her shoulder and kissed her cheek. ''It's like being with you.''

He left her holding the wheel while he and Peter moved purposefully around the boat, checking the rigging and removing the sail covers. Michael's cable-knit fisherman's sweater stretched tight when he moved, outlining his muscular shoulders. No wonder he was in such good physical condition. There seemed to be dozens of tasks, testing guy ropes and inspecting the sails.

He returned to the cockpit and turned off the engine. A beautiful quiet surrounded them. "Prepare to hoist sail."

"What should I do?" she asked.

"Stand right here and watch. It's an automated winch system." He returned to the captain's position behind the wheel and flicked a series of switches. "Get ready. This is the most beautiful sight in the world."

The glistening white mainsail unfurled above them like an angel's wing. Annie gasped in delight. Then the foresail flapped into place.

While Peter checked the rigging, she glanced back at Michael, whose concentration was split between the sails and the steering that balanced the rudder. He adjusted the set of the sails. They billowed, then caught the breeze. The wind propelled them across the dark waters.

"Can I go up to the front?"

He pointed toward the cockpit locker. "Put on a life vest and I'll come with you."

He motioned to Peter, who agilely dodged the boom to join them in the cockpit. "The course is set," Michael said. "Take the helm, Peter."

"Aye, Skipper."

Patiently Michael answered her every question about the winches, the stanchions, the sails and the rigging. Memories of her parents' boat rested gently on her mind as they traversed to the bowsprit at the peaked end of the foredeck. She pointed to the low triangular railing at the edge. "I want to go out there."

"It's my favorite place onboard," he said. "You've got

to sit at the very end with your legs dangling over the edge.''

Ducking under the foresail boom, she did as he said, straddling the railing at the very end of the boat. Michael sat behind her, cradling her hips between his thighs. Suspended above the water, she watched as the prow sliced through the dark blue Pacific waves. Ice-cold water sprayed her legs, and she shivered with pleasure.

She was flying, reveling in a sense of absolute freedom, soaring over the waves like a wayward gull. They had escaped the stalking, the harassment and the danger. And yet, in the corner of her mind, there was still a question, and she knew the threat was not resolved.

She leaned against Michael's chest. ''Are we safe?''

''At this moment, yes.''

''I want to stay here forever. Just like this.'' She lifted her gaze to the horizon and breathed in the fresh salty air. ''With no responsibilities. No worries.''

''You'd be bored in half a day,'' he said.

''Would not!'' She poked an elbow into his ribs. ''I'm as lighthearted as the next person.''

''You need to take care of people, Annie. It's your nature. Your eyes lit up when your grandpa mentioned a halfway house for teenagers.''

''Of course,'' she said. ''I'm happy for him. That's the perfect job for Lionel.''

''And for you.''

His arms wrapped lightly around her torso, and it felt good to be held. She didn't want to argue with him, but she couldn't let this pass. ''I have a job, thank you very much. I'm a cop.''

But was she a good cop? Of course, she did her job and followed orders. But her superior officers always told her that she worried too much about the victims. She lacked the motivation and drive to track down the criminals.

Working at the halfway house with Lionel might be good for her. But she said, "No. I could never move back to Bridgeport."

He nuzzled her ear. "Whatever you say, ma'am."

His nearness had an even more powerful effect than the awesome view of the sea. She melted against him, encouraging him to hold her more tightly. "About what happened last night," she said. "In my bedroom."

"What about it?"

She wriggled in his arms, enjoying the warm confinement of his embrace. "I'd like very much for it to happen again. This time without the explosion."

"I think that can be arranged." He kissed her neck and traced a path to her ear, where he nibbled gently. His voice was deep and husky. "Feel the waves, Annie. There's nothing better than making love on a boat."

He gave her one last squeeze, then rose to his feet. "I've got to do some captain things. Like checking the weather and the wind. Is Lionel okay?"

"He's resting." She tilted her head backward to look up at him. "Tonight, Captain."

"Count on it."

Annie spent the rest of the morning climbing all over the boat, admiring Michael's seamanship as he hoisted the jib and checking on Lionel, who finally woke around noon.

Peter showed her around the well-equipped galley, and together they made coffee and prepared a simple lunch. While the first mate and Lionel chowed down, she returned to the deck with a sandwich for Michael, who stood at the helm watching the skies.

"There's a rain coming in," he said.

"We'll be all right, won't we?"

"Sure, but we'll need to go closer to shore."

She followed his gaze. Directly in front of them, beyond the bowsprit, dark clouds dipped from the skies to meet the lip of the northern horizon. "Is it safe to bring Grandpa up here?"

"No problem."

With Peter and Annie supporting him, Lionel managed to climb the stairs from the companionway. His eyes brightened as he beheld the sea. He inhaled deeply, then sighed. "By God, this is living!"

"I never thought you were much of a sailor, Grandpa."

"There's two types of Oregonians—seagoing and inland. The sailors and the loggers. I've always been an inlander, but I do enjoy a sail now and again."

She got him settled on a deck chair near the main mast with a blanket over his legs. Annie could feel the change in the weather. The waves swelled more aggressively, and she saw white caps.

"I'm going to bring her around," Michael called out. "There's no point in riding straight into the storm. Annie, you stay put. Don't get yourself whacked in the head by the boom."

In a graceful swoop *Rosebud* bridged the waves, heeling slightly as they retreated in a southerly direction.

Michael turned over the helm to Peter and came forward to join them. "I'm going below to check on the weather. Lionel, are you enjoying yourself?"

"I'm fine," he said. "I wish my legs were better. I'd climb that mast like a logging pole and see for a hundred miles."

Michael patted his arm before he dodged down the companionway into the captain's cabin belowdecks. As Annie watched him, she wondered if now was a good time to join him in his cabin and decided against it. Tonight would have to be soon enough.

She curled into a chair beside her grandpa, tucking her legs beneath her. Changing into shorts hadn't been such a great idea. "What do you think I am, Lionel? A sailor or a logger?"

"A bit of both. You get your love of the sea from your father. He was out here every chance he got."

"And my love of the forests comes from you."

"Maybe so," he said.

When Michael returned from his cabin, he looked worried. "There's a squall up north, and it's headed our way. We can't outrun it, but we might miss the high winds if we continue south."

"Back toward Bridgeport," she said. A chill went through her. They hadn't escaped, after all. The danger was still there, beyond the bow.

"We'll stay out at sea," he said. "I don't want to take a chance on putting in to port."

"Neither do I." She didn't want to be close to shore. She wanted to be miles and miles out to sea where no one could find them.

"I also checked in with Engstrom," Michael said. "As far as he can tell, the explosion was caused by TNT—which could've come from Stillwell's."

"Jake Stillwell isn't after us," she said, "but he certainly is providing the equipment. The truck. Probably the TNT. And he's even put Bateman on the payroll."

"It's suspicious," Michael said. "But Jake would rather forget the thirteenth than hammer on it."

Annie agreed. She couldn't imagine Jake Stillwell getting involved in anything that didn't ultimately turn a profit. Harassment wasn't a well-paying job.

A few hours later, when there should have been a beautiful sunset, the edge of the squall overtook them, turning the skies to gunmetal gray. Rain splattered in heavy droplets, and she had to get Lionel belowdecks again. He settled in the salon and turned on the television to watch the Mariners.

Shortly thereafter, Michael and Peter came below, too, shaking moisture from their slickers.

"Here's the good news," Michael said. "I think we've missed the major portion of the storm."

"And the bad news?" she asked.

"We're even farther south than when we started this morning. Bridgeport is due east."

Surely there was nothing to worry about. Bateman didn't have a boat, and Jake didn't have one he could borrow. Nobody knew they were out here. But Annie felt uneasy as she listened to the whistling winds and the rain pelting the deck overhead. "What are we going to do?"

"We'll stay about six miles offshore, drop a sea anchor and wait until morning to head north."

Her sense of foreboding stayed with her through dinner and into the evening, but Annie said nothing. She told herself it was only the rain. Even when the storm passed and the seas were calmed, she had flashes of unreasoning panic.

This time she was determined not to succumb. She tried to listen to the men's conversation, tried to blank the rising fear from her mind. *Get a grip, Callahan.* It's only rain, moisture from the skies. Not every dark cloud hid an assassin with a baseball bat.

By nine-fifteen Lionel was tucked in bed and Peter was on deck. Annie tapped on the door to Michael's cabin.

Shirtless, he answered. His tanned skin glowed in the lamplight. His chest was so broad. His smile, so handsome.

She wanted to make love to him but not like this, not while fear echoed within her. "Michael, I'm scared."

Chapter Thirteen

All evening Michael had been aware of her tension. She'd spoken little. Her gaze had turned inward. Now she stood before him, trembling.

"I hate the rain," she whispered.

"The storm is almost over. Come on, Annie. We'll go up on deck and I'll show you."

He tossed a windbreaker over his shoulders and directed her up the companionway and into the night.

Though steering was unnecessary with the sea anchor dropped, Peter had taken a position in the cockpit. He and Michael would split the night watch.

"Evening, Skipper. Annie." He raised a coffee mug to salute them.

"Quiet night?" Michael asked.

"See for yourself."

The rain had ended, leaving behind a thick wet fog. The only illumination came from the running lights on the boat, reflecting off calm waters.

Michael led her around the housing, and they stood below the main mast. "The weather service predicts no more rain," he said. "We're safe."

"It's so dark," she said. "I can only see a few stars."

"A smuggler's moon." He pointed up past the masthead to the sky, where they could see just a glimpse of moon.

"It's the perfect night for sneaking ashore with plunder and treasure."

"You'd make a good pirate, Michael."

"I thought we were finally clear on that point. I'm one of the good guys." He held her arms and gazed down into her eyes. "You see? The storm is over."

"For now. But we can't stay six miles offshore forever. When we go back, Bateman will still be there."

He couldn't deny the possibility. His communications with the FBI had produced zero results. Bateman's contact was still unknown. "That's tomorrow. Or the next day. Or next week."

"What do you mean?"

"Here's the deal, Annie. I'll stop living in the past if you stop worrying about the future."

She blinked slowly, and he saw the confusion begin to fade from her eyes. "Keep talking, Michael."

The swirling mists enveloped them in a damp cocoon, but he could feel the weather beginning to clear as surely as he felt the difference in their relationship. They were no longer adversaries. Everything that happened before led to this moment. "Nobody can go back in time and change what happened. You can't change who you *were*. You can only change who you *are*."

"And who are you, Michael? Here and now. In this moment."

He kissed her gently. "A man who wants very much to make love to you."

"I want that, too."

When he looked at her, he saw no fear. She was his beautiful Annie, the only woman he had ever really cared about. He swept her back to his cabin and closed the door.

She stood in the lamplight, shivering. But when she looked at him, she grinned. "I guess I should get out of these damp clothes."

"I'll watch."

She unfastened the Velcro strips on her flexible cast. The swelling was gone. The bruises had faded. The only reason for her to continue wearing the cast was to protect her bones as they healed.

"Annie?"

"Yes, Michael?"

"Could you go a little faster?"

She quickly unbuttoned her cotton blouse and wriggled out of her jeans. Standing before him in a wispy lace bra and panties, she asked, "How's this?"

"Perfect," he said. "You're perfect."

Lightly he traced the firm line of her shoulders. He bent down to kiss her breast. She moaned with pleasure but pushed him away. "Now, Michael. It's your turn."

Annie wanted his clothing to vanish. She was too impatient to wait for him to unfasten the buttons and zippers. Her fear was completely vanquished. She wasn't thinking of anything but this moment, this shining moment, when they would finally fulfill eleven years of yearning.

While he unbuttoned his jeans, she pulled his windbreaker from his shoulders. "Hurry, Michael."

She tugged his arm, pulling him toward the double bed beside the paneled wall. In an instant she'd slipped between the cool sheets. In spite of the chill, she was hot all over. And when she saw his virile naked body, she burst into flames.

He was beside her under the covers, and she greedily caressed and stroked, wanting more of him—all of him. Passion overwhelmed her. Sensations exploded. She was aroused in every part of her body, from the soft skin of her inner thighs to the crook of her elbows.

Yet he controlled her feverish desire. With skillful touches and kisses, he prolonged her excitement until her need was unbearable. His thrusts were maddeningly slow, then faster. Together they soared beyond satisfaction to the realm of ecstasy.

In this moment she experienced true bliss.

She snuggled beside him, settling in for the night. Softly she murmured, "I always knew this would be wonderful."

"Even when we were twelve and playing basketball?"

"Even then." They were always meant to be together. They were soulmates. "I wonder why it took us so long."

"We had to grow up first."

"I guess so."

"And you had to decide that you'd trust me."

They lay together quietly, cradled in the gentle rocking of the sea. Her fingers combed possessively through the hair on his chest. "We have no more secrets," she said.

"Which reminds me, I have some information about Ron Cartier, Marie's husband."

"Yes?"

"He's long gone. Lives in San Diego."

Vaguely she wondered how he'd found that out. "So Ron Cartier couldn't have been the one who kept leaving Marie's figurines behind."

She didn't want to think about their troubles, except as they reflected on Michael and her true knowledge of him as her friend, her lover, her protector. "Poor Marie. When I think of her collecting those little figures in an attempt to be like Mrs. Stillwell, it breaks my heart."

"Her death came too soon," he said. "Almost before she had a chance to live."

"It must have been awful for you, Michael. Especially knowing she was pregnant."

Abruptly he sat up on the bed. "What did you say?"

"She was pregnant," Annie repeated.

"How did you know? Who told you?"

She cast back in her mind, trying to remember the conversation. "Why is this so important?"

"Because no one knew," he said. "Her autopsy was part of the sealed record. No one knew except the pathologist and the county sheriff, who told me."

"Engstrom," she said. "Chief Engstrom mentioned to me that Marie was pregnant. That explains it, Michael. He must have had access to—"

"No." He slung his legs over the side of the bed. "Right after the sting, the county sheriff knew he'd done something wrong by getting me involved in their sting operation. He promised me that Marie's remains would be treated with respect. Her name would be kept out of the reports as much as possible. Annie, she was only six weeks pregnant. No one knew."

Michael was pulling on his jeans. The dreamy mood had vanished behind a cloud.

"Engstrom," he said. "I should have guessed."

"Guessed what?"

"Engstrom was in Lionel's bedroom. He could have dropped that lion statue." Michael turned to her. "He's been in the middle of everything. He found the damn truck that tried to run us down. He could have been the driver."

She was beginning to grasp what he was saying. "Chief Engstrom is working with Drew Bateman?"

"When you got that phone call and it traced back to the 911 dispatcher at the police station, it wasn't a bad connection or a crossed telephone wire. Bateman was staying there."

"At the jail?"

"In that old courthouse. The building is mostly vacant. I'll bet half the rooms are closed up and locked." Michael threw on a shirt and fastened the buttons. "It's a perfect drop point, a perfect hideout."

Sitting on his bed with only a sheet to cover herself, Annie felt very vulnerable. "What do you mean? What's being hidden?"

"Moby Dick." His dark eyes flashed as he leaned down and kissed her. His energy was almost frightening. "Excuse me, Annie. I need to make a few phone calls."

His hand was on the doorknob to a room she hadn't seen in her grand tour of the boat. Annie shouted, "Freeze!"

He glanced over his shoulder at her.

"Michael, you can't just say 'Moby Dick' and run out of the room. I want an explanation."

"Okay, I guess a few minutes won't hurt."

"Give me a shirt," she demanded. "I don't think this is the kind of news I want to hear when I'm naked."

"But I like you naked."

She rose to her knees, using the sheet to cover herself. "In case you haven't noticed, Michael, I'm not the kind of woman who lies around waiting to be pleasured while you charge off and do the heroic manly thing. We're partners."

He went to the tiny closet in his cabin and pulled out another white shirt, which he tossed to her. "We agree that I'm a good guy, right?"

She wasn't so sure. "If you have some other secret you've been keeping from me, if you seduced me without being completely honest..."

"Hey, you were the one tearing off my clothes."

Oh, how she wanted to love him! But if he'd lied to her one more time, how could she ever believe him? "Talk."

"After I went through navy SEAL training, I was recruited into naval intelligence. And I still work for them. This boat, *Rosebud,* is provided for federal marshals to use as a safe house for protected witnesses."

"It's not a charter boat?"

"We take people who are witnesses out to sea and bring them back when they're needed to testify." He pushed open the door he'd been trying to enter before. "This room is where I figure my navigation charts, but it's also a communications center, complete with sonar, which I've turned off because it's so sensitive that it blips every time a large school of fish swim by.''

She followed him into a small room that was packed floor to ceiling with complicated-looking equipment and computer screens. How could he have kept this from her? "When you came to Bridgeport, you were working undercover."

"I'm on loan to the FBI because I'm familiar with the area. When Bateman was in jail, he had telephone contacts from Bridgeport and Wayside. I was supposed to keep an eye on him, find out where he was staying and determine the identity of his contact person."

Michael's behavior was beginning to make sense to her. "That was the reason for your late-night phone calls."

"Between you and me, the FBI is a little paranoid about wiretapping and cell phones. They wanted me to use phone booths."

"What does this have to do with Moby Dick?"

"Bateman and his contact are small fish, minnows. The FBI doesn't care about them. They want the big guy at the top of the food chain. The great white whale. Moby Dick."

"Why?"

"I don't really know," he said. "I'm a low-level undercover guy. My job is usually just to sail *Rosebud* and make sure the passengers get safely to where they're needed."

She studied the array of screens and dials and switches with growing dismay. From the very start she'd felt that Michael had a secret reason, a special purpose for being in Bridgeport. "You didn't come to my grandpa's house to take care of him. Or me."

"Does it matter?"

"It does," she said sadly. "I thought I knew you, Michael. But you're a whole different person. Naval intelligence. FBI. Undercover cop. You should have told me."

Keeping his identity a secret was the biggest lie of all.

When she thought of how many times she'd scolded him for not following proper detective procedures, she cringed. "You must think I'm a fool."

"Never."

"Michael, you let me strut around acting like the professional detective when you're a hundred times more qualified and more highly trained." She shuddered. "There I was, forgiving you for being a juvenile delinquent, suspecting you of all kinds of criminal things. And you're an undercover cop."

"It's not like that."

She gestured at the bed. "Was this a joke, too? You allowed me to make love to a man who doesn't even exist. I don't know who you are."

Annie twisted the diamond ring off her finger. "I'll be returning this to Lionel. We don't need the fake engagement anymore. It's another lie."

"I want to make our engagement real," he said. "Annie, I want you to marry me."

A dull pain seized her heart. She'd been waiting to hear those words for years. "Your timing stinks."

"No time like the present." His expression was solemn. "Will you marry me?"

"It's impossible, Michael. You've been lying to me all along. Besides, you have your work, your boat."

"*Rosebud* doesn't belong to me. She's the navy's vessel." He took a step toward her. In the small room there was no way she could avoid him. "Marry me, Annie."

"Be logical. A marriage between us would never work. You hate my job, Michael. If I decided to quit being a cop and work on the halfway house with my grandfather, you'd hate living in Bridgeport. We're too different. We can't even be good partners. How could we make a good husband and wife?"

"You're right." His shoulders stiffened. "We've always

been different, and that won't change. I'll always be a Slade. You'll always be a Callahan.''

"That doesn't matter to me. I admire you for overcoming your horrible background. Look at you, Michael. You've done incredibly well for yourself.''

"And it's still not good enough." He sat in a low-backed swivel chair in front of the equipment panel. "If you'll excuse me, I need to make some phone calls.''

But she didn't want to leave now. She didn't want him to think she was rejecting him because she thought he was somehow inferior. Rejecting him? Moments ago Michael had been the fulfillment of her every dream. How could this be happening?

Seeking a reason to stay, to somehow repair the unfixable mess they'd created, she pointed to a dial on the panel. "Is this the sonar?''

"Yes.''

"And it shows any approaching boats or airplanes?''

"I turned it off," he said. "I didn't think anyone would find us out here. A dot on the Pacific. However, that was before I knew about Engstrom.''

"You've been in touch with him," Annie said.

"He knows our location." Michael lifted a telephone receiver from the panel. "Please leave, Annie. I have to make a call. It's confidential.''

She had no choice but to go. Numbly she left his cabin, casting one last longing gaze at the rumpled bed. Now it was truly over. Michael had proposed three times, and she had turned him down. It didn't matter who they were in the past or the present. There would be no future for them.

A sob welled up in her throat, and she swallowed hard. The golden circle of her grandma's engagement ring burned in the palm of her hand.

When she stepped into the salon, a light came on. Chief

Engstrom sat in one of the captain's chairs. He had a gun leveled at her midsection.

"This is nothing personal, Annie."

His words struck like a slap in the face. He'd said the same thing in the parking lot before he assaulted her with the baseball bat. Hearing the words again, she thought that facing him again would have thrown her into a frenzy of fear. But she was drained, unable to feel anything at all.

"It was you in the parking lot."

"I almost thought you'd figured it out," he said. "When I mentioned it, you looked real nervous."

That had been right before her severe panic attack. The trigger had been Engstrom himself. Somehow, in her unconscious, she'd known.

She regarded him calmly. He was dressed all in black except for spotless white sneakers. "How did you get here?"

"Your boyfriend was kind enough to keep me informed about your location. The seas calmed, and I came out here in a motorboat. It wasn't hard to find *Rosebud* with all her running lights turned on."

"I never did anything to you," she said. "Why did you come after me?"

"Because I wanted your grandpa to know what it felt like to lose the one person he loved. He set up the sting. He was as much responsible for Marie's death as the cop who pulled the trigger."

From behind her back Annie heard Michael moving around. The sound of their voices had alerted him. She wanted to keep Engstrom talking, to distract him until Michael could get in position. "You must have loved Marie very much."

"She was everything to me." His usually impassive face distorted in an expression that was somewhere between sorrow and hatred. "Marie and I were going to be married. We couldn't tell anyone. Not until after her divorce."

"And she gave you her little figurines," Annie said.

"Her collection. She wanted me to take care of them because her husband used to break them. I should have killed him. I should have killed everyone who hurt her."

"Instead, you told her about the sting. You were the one responsible for her being there at the bridge. You caused her—"

"That's enough, Annie." He was out of the chair, but he didn't come any closer. He was still too far away for her to make a move on him, and his aim held steady.

"How did you get onboard?" she asked. "What happened to Peter?"

"The kid on the deck? He's unconscious, and I'll untie him when I leave. Somebody's going to have to pilot this fine vessel into port when I'm done with you and your grandfather, and of course, Michael."

Annie heard the gunshot and she ducked to give Michael a clear shot at Engstrom. But nothing happened.

She turned and stared at the open door to his cabin.

Michael walked through. He stumbled to his knees. His head was bleeding. Behind him, Bateman held a gun.

Without thinking of her own safety, she ran to help him. "Michael, are you hurt?"

"Better," Bateman said with a laugh. "I disabled his fancy equipment. He can't call for help."

He shoved Michael with the gun. "Get up! I'm going to show you what happens to guys who rat on their friends."

Michael stood. Though he seemed only half-conscious, his eyes were alert. And she knew he wasn't disabled. He was waiting, biding his time.

She had to trust him.

Bateman shoved again and Michael fell against her. "Stay out of the way," he whispered.

"Over there," Bateman said, indicating the bench. "Both of you."

Annie knew the bench against the bulkhead wall was a bad position. She and Michael would have no chance with both guns trained at them. "He can't make it that far," she said.

Michael collapsed on a stool at the bar between the galley and the salon.

"He needs some motivation," Bateman said. He got up close to Michael's face. "How about this? Do what I say, and I won't kill your girlfriend slow."

He grabbed her bare right arm and wrenched hard. Pain tore through her. Through clenched teeth, she ordered, "Let me go."

"Do it," Engstrom said.

Bateman released her. He was ugly and dirty. His jaw worked at a piece of gum.

The well-groomed Engstrom must be totally offended. He was so tidy even his leather shoulder holster gleamed. "How can you be partners with Bateman?"

"We have something in common. Revenge."

"You're a police officer, Engstrom. Your partner is nothing but prison scum. The kind of person you want to put away."

Engstrom almost smiled. "Very good, Annie. You're trying to turn us against each other. But that's not going to happen."

"We have a deal," Bateman said. The fruity smell of his gum sickened her.

"Come on, Bateman. Do you really think he'll let you get away?"

"That's enough," Engstrom said. "Now we only need one more person to make the party complete."

"There's no point in trying to wake Lionel," Annie said.

Her mind worked frantically. She had to find some way to stop this. "He's drugged at night."

"You're lying," Engstrom said. "He woke up just fine when I tossed the brick through his front window."

"He can't walk," she said. That was almost true. He'd only been able to manage a few steps without his walker. "You're going to have to carry him out here."

Engstrom frowned, displeased by the messiness of the situation. "Bateman, go get Lionel and bring him out here."

"Why? We can shoot these two right now. Then plug the old man in his bed."

"That's not how it should be," Engstrom said. "First she dies while they watch. They have to know how it feels. They have to know my pain."

He was obsessed by his plan. It had to go exactly right. Nothing else would do. And she hoped that would be his undoing. "It's not going to work, Chief."

"It has to work." He waved his gun impatiently. "You heard me, Bateman."

"I'm not your slave. I got what I wanted." He eyed Michael with sheer loathing. With his free hand he slapped Michael's shoulder. "Come on, Mikey, move it."

Michael tilted backward on the stool. His eyelids drooped, but Annie could see the tension building inside him. She could see his rage.

Bateman reached out and slapped him again.

This time Michael reacted. In three swift sharp moves, he took Bateman's gun, knocked him to the floor and went into a crouch, aiming the gun at Engstrom.

But Engstrom's pistol was aimed directly at Annie's heart. At this range he couldn't miss. "What's it going to be, Michael? If you kill me, you're killing her."

His eyes were crazy. His mouth drew into a feral sneer.

Annie never would have guessed at the ferocity, the insanity, beneath Engstrom's neat exterior.

"Marie was my half sister," Michael said. "She was gentle. She wouldn't want you to hurt Annie."

"You never really knew her. Not like I did." A shudder went through him. "She was carrying my child. She will be avenged."

Annie could see Engstrom's finger tighten on the trigger, and she braced herself. Her muscles tensed. If she could anticipate his move, she could get out of the way.

A gun fired.

She hit the floor. When she looked up, Engstrom was staring down at his chest in shock. Behind him, she saw her grandpa holding her Glock. He fired again and Engstrom fell.

Bateman had risen to a sitting position, and Michael had him covered. The muscles in his arm were taut. An aura of rage surrounded him.

"Michael, don't," she said. "Send him back to prison where he belongs."

With one vicious chop he knocked Bateman unconscious and they stepped away. His arms dropped to his sides and he turned to her. "Are you all right, Annie?"

"I knew you'd protect me." Instantly she knew it was true. She'd trusted Michael with her life. There could be no deeper bond.

He turned to her grandpa, who had haltingly made his way to a captain's chair. "Lionel?"

"I've never killed a man before. But I'm okay. He needed killing."

With the gun in his hand and his forehead bloodied, Michael turned to her. "I won't ask you again."

"Then I'll have to do it," she said. "Marry me, Michael Slade."

A half grin curled his lip, and he glanced at Lionel. "She's an awful lot of trouble."

"But worth it," her grandpa said.

Michael held out his arms, and she stepped into them. "Promise me one more thing," she said.

"Anything."

"When our grandchildren ask how you proposed, we won't tell them about this."

"It'll be enough to say that you were the one who asked me."

She kissed him gently, knowing there would be a lifetime of kisses. Michael was her only love, her true love.

Epilogue

Annie stood in the middle of the newly renovated and re-paired bridge across the Yaquina River. From here, they had a perfect view of the Callahan Halfway House.

A fifteen-year-old girl with long black hair, one of the residents, stood on the narrow sidewalk beside her. "So what's the story?" she asked. "How did you and Michael get together?"

"We were on his boat, *Rosebud*. It was a cloudless night. There was a full moon. When Michael unfurled the sail, a million roses fell at my feet."

"Wow!"

A deep voice behind Annie said, "Liar."

She turned and faced her husband of eighteen months. He was the director of the halfway house, and in his arms, he held their firstborn daughter, Elizabeth. Annie was already pregnant again but not showing. "Michael? How do you remember the night when you proposed?"

"She took me out in the forest," he said to the teenager. "She'd hung a banner printed in gold between two trees. It said, Marry Me, Michael."

"Wow!"

"Or maybe it was that time in Hawaii," Annie said. "When you hired fifty hula dancers to act out a proposal."

"Stop!" the teenager said. "I get the idea. What really

happened isn't a big deal. The important thing is that you two guys really love each other.''

Michael put his arm snugly around Annie. "And we trust each other."

"We're partners," Annie said, gazing up at him. "In every possible way."

"Okay, yuck. That's, like, too much information."

As the teenager sauntered across the bridge that was now only one-way, leading to Bridgeport, Annie said, "I guess the kids think of us as parents."

"And Lionel as their grandpa."

"And this is our home."

She turned up her face for a kiss. Michael was still the most exciting man she'd ever known. He always made her feel safe.

THE SECRET IS OUT!

HARLEQUIN®

I N T R I G U E®

presents

By day these agents are cowboys;
by night they are specialized
government operatives.
Men bound by love, loyalty and the law—
they've vowed to keep their missions
and identities confidential....

Harlequin Intrigue

September #581   THE BODYGUARD'S ASSIGNMENT
      by Amanda Stevens

October #585   THE AGENT'S SECRET CHILD
      by B.J. Daniels

November #589   THE SPECIALIST
      by Dani Sinclair

December #593   THE OUTSIDER'S REDEMPTION
      by Joanna Wayne

Harlequin American Romance
(a special tie-in story)

January 2001 #857   THE SECRETARY GETS HER MAN
      by Mindy Neff

HARLEQUIN®

Makes any time special™

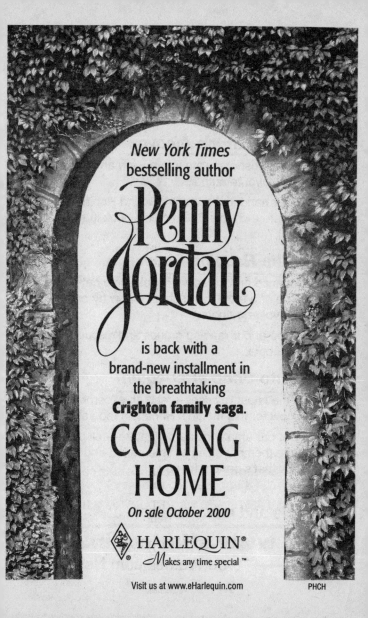

Daddy's little girl... **THAT'S MY BABY!** by

Vicki Lewis Thompson

Nat Grady is finally home—older and wiser. When the woman he'd loved had hinted at commitment, Nat had run far and fast. But now he knows he can't live without her. But Jessica's nowhere to be found.

Jessica Franklin is living a nightmare. She'd thought things were rough when the man she loved ran out on her, leaving her to give birth to their child alone. But when she realizes she has a stalker on her trail, she has to run—and the only man who can help her is Nat Grady.

THAT'S MY BABY!

On sale September 2000 at your favorite retail outlet.

HARLEQUIN®

Makes any time special ™

***Don't miss
an exciting opportunity
to save on the purchase of
Harlequin and Silhouette books!***

Buy any two Harlequin or
Silhouette books and save
$10.00 off future Harlequin
and Silhouette purchases

OR

buy any three
Harlequin or Silhouette books
and save **$20.00 off** future
Harlequin and Silhouette purchases.

***Watch for details
coming in October 2000!***

PHQ400

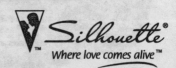